S T E P H A N I E   I Z Z A R D

THE
HOUSE
OF
TERMONN

THE HOUSE OF TERMONN TRILOGY
BOOK ONE

CONTENTS

PROLOGUE

JARN, EASTERN ENGLAND, 8TH
AUGUST 1977

The afternoon was sultry and oppressive as he steered his car towards the visitor parking for the airbase. Although the sky was blue over the baked countryside, clouds were on the horizon and moving fast. A storm was building to the west, and Jarn looked forward to the relief that would arrive with rain and fresher air.

He looked forward even more to returning to Termonn, already regretting this visit. The airbase commander, a Group Captain, had been frostily polite in his letters but it was plain that only pressure from his seniors had persuaded him to give Jarn the time of day.

It was understandable. Jarn's tale, that something very unpleasant was likely to soon hit the area and possibly the airbase itself, sounded preposterous. Jarn had been accurate with similar warnings in the past but that was information only a few in government were aware of and any historical records from previous decades were far too classified to be shared with a lowly airbase commander. Even fewer were aware that his contributions to national security dated back to the time of Queen Victoria. That was how it had to remain.

But an attempt at warning was necessary given the horror of what he and Issa had foreseen. Jarn hoped that this particular future was one of those that would be averted by other events. It did sometimes happen, but he struggled to feel optimistic.

Forty minutes later, he was staring at the rigid back of the commander, who gazed out the window of a utilitarian office at the comings and goings of his staff outside. Raindrops were now spattering on the window ledge and on the tarmac below. From the distance came rumbles of thunder. On the nearby runway, a Vulcan bomber was undergoing its weekly maintenance check, the crew working with more speed as the rain grew heavier.

The commander gritted his teeth and spoke.

'If I understand matters correctly, Lord Dechar, you are trying to put me on my guard against something of which you have no details. You can tell me nothing about the source of this information. And you can't tell me when it will happen, or even be sure that it will happen at all.'

He eyed Jarn with a glare that would have been withering for many men but had no impact on its intended victim, who had faced down emperors. 'Pray tell me, what precisely am I supposed to do with this so-called warning?'

'I realise it poses you something of a challenge, Group Captain.' Jarn found himself unable to suppress a note of wry humour, and the atmosphere grew even chillier.

'Challenge? It *should* pose me no challenge at all because I *should* simply ignore it and show you the way out, were it not for the highest ranks of Her Majesty's Air Force and the Ministry of Defence apparently having followed you in taking leave of their senses.'

The commander waved a letter with the embossed heading of a government department in Jarn's general direction and then threw it on his desk, where it was briefly illuminated by the first flash of lightning.

Taking control of the conversation seemed like a good idea. Jarn rose and moved to the window, where he took full advantage of the intimidating difference in their heights by gazing down at the airbase commander with an assurance that had been accrued over very many years. Had his dear friend, Victoria's Foreign Secretary George Clarendon, been present, he would find Jarn unchanged in both appearance and in his air of authority. Sadly, Clarendon himself had been dead for over a century.

'It is possible, Group Captain, that this potential threat relates to your duties with regard to *that* particular aircraft, and her sisters.' Jarn pointed towards the Vulcan bomber.

'And, before you have an apoplexy...', as the commander was indeed already opening his mouth to explode, '...I do have full military clearance, as you know. I am aware that at least one of those planes is constantly ready to be airborne within four minutes of an alert. I am aware of what they carry, that they are fully armed, and that the on-duty aircraft has already had its weapon ground-activated.'

Jarn had been briefed thoroughly in Whitehall prior to this trip, and now knew far more about nuclear weapons, and in particular the WE177 on board the Vulcan, than he had ever wished to know.

The commander, tried nearly beyond endurance, waggled an admonitory finger under Jarn's nose. Eyeballs bulging with anger, he again opened his mouth. But this time he was stopped by a vivid flash of lightning and just a second later came a booming clap of thunder. The wind had risen, the rain had become a downpour, and the standard on the roof of the mess opposite was whipping and snapping crazily. Both men turned to look out of the window and watched as the Vulcan's aircrew ran to take shelter, the ground crew and pilots racing to their aircraft to move her back into her hangar.

Before they could get to the cockpit steps, the air was torn apart by the shattering explosion of an enormous bolt. It flooded the airbase in a blinding brilliant white with a simultaneous ear-splitting crash.

'Oh my god,' the commander gasped, 'that hit the Vulcan.'

Showing a surprising turn of speed for a sedentary man, he ran out of the office, down the steps and across the tarmac. Jarn was close on his heels.

The crew around the Vulcan had been thrown to the ground by the force of the lightning but were already staggering to their feet and gazing with horror at their aircraft. Scorched and peeling, it was clear she had taken a direct hit from the lightning bolt. Aviation fuel was spilling out of a gash, splashing onto the tarmac. More men came running to attend to the stricken plane and the base's emergency sirens began to shriek, joined by the wail of fire engines.

Jarn had seen courage aplenty over his many years, and here it was again. Men racing towards a badly damaged aircraft spilling gallons of highly flammable fuel, damaged electrics still sparking, paint blistering, and an activated nuclear weapon on board. Sane men would surely be running in the opposite direction. He stood back with the commander to let the fire engines approach and the crews to direct their hoses.

Within minutes the plane and fuel were both doused with foam. The air hung heavy with the smell of burning metal, fuel and plastic, but it was now overlaid by the chemical fumes of fire retardants.

The fire-chief approached them, indicating it was now safe for the crew to tend to the aircraft. 'That was a bit like a firework which you've lit and it hasn't gone bang, sir. But I think we've got away with it.'

With a nod from the commander, the ground crew moved back towards the plane, and Jarn noticed that two of them went immediately to the weapon housing and started to carefully remove the casing.

He contemplated the scene thoughtfully. Was it possible that this was the event he and Issa had foreseen? But that some tiny alteration in the last days, some quirk in someone's actions, some change in meteorology, had led to a change in fate, minor in effect but profound in consequences? He wanted to believe it, but it didn't feel quite right.

He heard himself being addressed by the commander, who echoed his thoughts.

'Well, it may be that there was something in what you warned us of, after all. I'm glad it was no worse. Bad enough, though. I'm afraid I will have to ask you to take your leave now, I have reports to make to...'

The man was stopped yet again, this time by the crew who had removed the weapon casing. They were making rapid gestures to people to back away, *fast*. One of them ran to where Jarn and the commander were standing.

The man's voice shook.

'The bomb, sir, the WE177. It's badly damaged. The electricity from the bolt must have gone straight through to it. It's hanging by only one safety pin, the others have sheered. And the final arming process is at least part way through.'

The commander started to fire orders. *Evacuate all but*

essential personnel, set up a 100-metre cordon, alert the Ministry, get weapons specialists here, now!

Jarn well knew that a 100-metre cordon was wafting a tissue paper in the face of a tiger. A cordon of ten kilometres wouldn't be enough if that warhead detonated on the ground. But he didn't begrudge the commander his attempt to protect his staff, even if it was futile.

Taking advantage of the mayhem, he moved quickly and unobserved towards the weapon housing. Bending over it, he saw what the crewman had seen. All the arming lights were flashing red, only one was not red and that was flickering amber - the final arming sequence was almost complete.

He recalled his Whitehall briefing. WE177's had a series of safety measures that had to be activated in the correct sequence. After the initial ground activation, the rest of the sequence was automated. By some extraordinary quirk of fate, the arming lights showed that the lightning bolt had achieved, in the correct order, all but the last, an arming switch that connected power to fuses. Definitely a job for the weapons specialists.

Jarn backed off a little.

At least the storm was moving away and the rain was lessening. He brushed dark wet hair from his eyes. Time for a word with the wife. He reached out.

My love.

As always, their thoughts were immediately in tune despite the miles which separated him from Termonn. A sense of curiosity came back to him, tinged with concern.

This is more complex than we thought - the event has begun.

The response from his wife this time indicated alarm.

Do not be concerned, I will await the experts. I think the reality will not be as severe as the one we saw, something must have altered it. I will return tonight. I love you, Issa.'

A sense of warmth flooded him and Jarn revelled in the projection of his wife's love and need.

The comfort of their link was rudely shattered by the last lightning bolt of the storm. Not directly hitting the plane, it still electrified the air and the tiny charge was enough to trigger the final fragile link to the fuses. The last light changed from amber to red.

There was no time to think, only to fall back on reflexes perfected over the centuries. Arms raised, Jarn slowed time to the tiniest increment possible. He observed the start of the explosion, from its fledgling beginning with the weapon shell fracturing and a devilish chick breaking free. Then a wave of enormous energy moved outwards from the shattering casing. He grasped this tiny part of the world and shifted it to the empty space between realities, breaking away just before he released his control and time flowed on. The weapon exploded, but in that infinite icy black void there was nothing it could damage.

Except for himself. He shifted instantly, spinning through realities plausible and implausible, the force of the detonation destroying any attempt to control his travel. He hurtled through a thousand alternative worlds, seeing only glimpses of each – some with an airfield, some forested, some cities, some in ocean depths, some desolate lifeless planets. He sent his thoughts out to his wife as he tumbled helplessly into the grey world that rose before him.

Issa – I am sorry. I will try to find you.

He had no hope she would hear him, with so many worlds between.

CHAPTER 1
JARN, LONDON, 1ST AUGUST 1977

Jarn had seen many sights in his long life, but this location was in the top few for originality. He was in the wine cellar of Henry VIII, now hidden far below the streets of London and deep in the bowels of the Ministry of Defence in Whitehall.

On first entering the huge government building, Jarn had undergone unusually complex security procedures. His photograph had been taken repeatedly and he had signed document after document. Finally being rewarded with a visitor pass displaying his photograph and pinning it to his jacket, he had been ushered to a lift by a young civil servant.

Down and down they went, until the lift seemed to have reached its lowest level. Then they descended staircase after staircase, passing cavernous ill-lit storage vaults which seemed to go on for miles with no sign of any staff. Jarn wondered, irreverently, if the ark of the covenant was lost somewhere in those dim recesses.

Then, utterly unexpectedly, a sixteenth century arched stone door surround lay before them and his escort was placing an iron key into the lock of the ancient door. It swung open and they entered. The contrast between the utilitarian architecture of the government building outside the room and this last remaining part of Henry's glorious Palace of Westminster astonished Jarn. Perhaps seventy feet in length and half as wide, a magnificent Tudor brick vaulted roof dominated the space; long tables and wine barrels completed the picture. It seemed as if they had travelled back almost five centuries.

And today this wonderful and extremely secure location had been repurposed specifically for him, to complete a highly sensitive briefing. On the ancient table before him was an array of green files with very high security markings, and within them were papers describing the United Kingdom's strategic nuclear capability. Jarn had already been briefed verbally; these documents were simply back-ups to reinforce his memory.

As his escort nodded respectfully and withdrew, Jarn sighed and drew the first file towards him.

After an hour or so of hard reading, coffee and unexciting biscuits were brought down and laid on the table. Jarn thought he saw a glimmer of sympathy in the eyes of the young man and he felt it was deserved. There were still three more hefty files to wade through. He sipped the lukewarm coffee and grimaced. It was a perfect match for the biscuits.

Another hour later Jarn closed the last file with relief. He now knew enough details to help him cope with whatever awaited him and his visit to the airbase could finally be arranged. He stretched his head back to relieve the tension in his shoulders, and as he did so he spotted a cream file, tucked almost out of sight on the top of an old wine barrel.

Another file? But why not with the others? Was it part of his briefing?

It was an older file than the ones he had already viewed, and although the security marking was the highest Jarn had ever seen, it was the title that made him draw a deep breath.

The Dechar family, 1855 onwards

Jarn opened the file, with some trepidation. The first page was a covering note:

Correspondence from George, the 4th Earl of Clarendon, to his wife Katherine, Paris and London 1855. Letters removed from Volume 6 of the Clarendon archive in the Bodleian Library, Oxford, due to classification

Jarn was now certain he hadn't been intended to see this, it was not part of his briefing material. Perhaps the file had been brought down as part of the background to his mission, possibly to brief someone else, and had not yet been returned. Scanning the next page, he saw with emotion that the letter was in George Clarendon's handwriting, and his memories of George rushed back.

They had first met at the Russian court in St Petersburg in 1820, when Clarendon was appointed attaché to the British embassy. It was before he came into his title and so in St Petersburg he was simply young George Villiers. At the tender age of twenty, the attaché had been clever but inexperienced, feeling his way through the labyrinth of European relations. Jarn and his family had befriended George, sharing their knowledge of the Russian court and foreign diplomats. Jarn had thought it likely that the promising young man would go on to give many years of service at the highest levels of international diplomacy; any time he spent with him would likely be well worthwhile.

Clarendon had returned to England in 1823. Jarn himself, with his family, had left Russia just two years later, following the death of the Tsar. But their friendship had blossomed anew in Ireland in the late 1840's, during Clarendon's service as Lord Lieutenant of Ireland. He and Issa had lived at Termonn House near Dublin, where Clarendon and his wife Katherine were frequent guests. Their friendship had been close and Jarn still missed Clarendon. The loss of good friends over the long years of his life was always painful. Jarn and Issa had often wondered if George and Kat ever suspected there was something a little odd about the Dechar family; the families had known each other for decades, decades over which the Dechars' appearances had not altered. But not a word had ever been said, no questions had been asked.

He rapidly read the first letter.

Paris, 21st August 1855

My darling Kat

I hope all is well with your and the nestlings. You will know how much I miss all of you. But telling you of my progress here will fill the empty space until we meet again, which God willing will be soon.

Our Queen and the Prince Consort arrived safely three days ago and were conducted from Boulogne by the Emperor himself. On the advice of her doctors, the Empress was unable to undertake the journey to Boulogne, being in the delicate condition I have already told you of. The Queen looked well, and had taken considerable pains with her appearance, although I doubt her geranium embroidered dress was well received by the elegant ladies of France. English fashion is not appreciated in this sophisticated court.

As agreed, I took charge of Prince Albert Edward on the day after the arrival of the Royal Family. The Prince informed me he wishes to be known as Bertie. Although he is thirteen, he is nowhere near as studious as our own boys, or as accomplished as our girls. He is willing and polite, in fact his manners are beautiful, but he has no ability to concentrate for more than a few minutes. I can understand why he is the despair of his father and his tutors, and why there is concern as to his suitability for his likely high destiny.

But to my great relief our dear friend Jarn arrived yesterday, and with his charisma he actually seems able to influence the boy. We met in our Paris residence and partook of refreshments – the wine well-watered in the case of the young Prince, of course - and the lad hung onto Jarn's words and listened to the tales he tells so well, and which you and I have enjoyed so often in Ireland, of places and people in his travels. The tales of hunting in Russia and in the vast marshes further west seemed to be particularly well received by our young Prince. Tomorrow, we visit part of the Paris World Fair.

I cannot help but observe that in the decades I have known Jarn, he does not seem to have aged a day. It is a matter of some envy to me, that he does not suffer from thinning hair and an expanding waist as does your husband. But perhaps it is only my fading eyesight that gives this impression. I know you profess yourself uncaring about such cosmetic matters, my dear.

Ever your loving husband
George

So that answered one question. George had indeed

wondered about Jarn's unaltered looks. He had probably wondered the same about Issa's unchanging beauty as well.

But the earlier content of the letter took him back in memory to 1855 and to an evening when he had dined with George, by then the British Foreign Secretary. They had discussed the planned state visit of Queen Victoria and Prince Albert to Paris. The visit coincided with the Paris World Fair, the French response to Prince Albert's 1851 Great Exhibition in London. The elder Royal children would accompany their parents. Jarn remembered how George had shared with him the anxiety felt in the topmost circle of British government about the thirteen-year-old Prince of Wales. He was not thought fitted for his likely destiny, and the royal parents apparently had little hope that their eldest son would benefit from the display of the world's knowledge at the Fair.

Then, just a week before the State visit, Jarn had received an urgent letter from his friend. George had been informed he would have the highly unenviable task of being in charge of the young prince while his parents were under-taking state duties. In the letter to Jarn, Clarendon described how he had beamed diplomatically, said it would indeed be an honour and a very great pleasure, but was now writing in desperation to his old friend and begging him to share the burden. He suggested taking the Prince to the Fair's Palais de l'Industrie, an excellent and educational way of occu-pying one of the mornings with his young charge. And Jarn still recalled his words: 'Assuredly there will be so much to interest you, my dear friend, with your fascination for science.'

Jarn had sent a positive reply immediately and could envisage Clarendon's deep sigh of relief.

Jarn moved on quickly to the next of George's letters,

aware that time was passing and he was likely to be interrupted any moment.

Paris, 22nd August 1855

My beloved wife
I hope this finds you all in excellent health. I hope especially that this message, by diplomatic package, arrives before you hear of our events and become alarmed for my welfare. Rest assured, I am well, and so is the Prince and all we care for here. I take the liberty of an extensive description of today's strange adventure, knowing it will feed your curious mind. And I do not disguise that I would welcome your thoughts on these matters when we meet, my dear.

As I told you in my last letter, the plan of Jarn and myself was to visit the Paris World Fair with the Prince today. We duly set out this morning, in a carriage for the three of us and another carriage for his escort. Prince Bertie was not initially enthusiastic. I suspect he thought that even with our friend Jarn's charms he was still going to be subject to a series of tedious lectures. However, when we arrived at the Palais de l'Industrie, which, my dear, is between the Seine and the Champs-Élysées, its spectacular appearance seemed to excite him. He remarked on the difference between this building and the Crystal Palace back in 1851, and understandably he voiced the opinion that the English edifice was far superior. For myself, I had to agree with the Prince. The overall effect here is gloomy and ill-lit, very different to the sparkling brilliance of the Crystal Palace. Inside, the Palais is indeed spectacular in dimensions, but two additional buildings have still been required to house all the exhibits, the Galerie des Machines and the Palais des Beaux-Arts.

With Jarn's interests in mind – you will recall his fasci-

nation with science and engineering - we made our way to the Galerie des Machines, which runs parallel to the banks of the Seine. Inside, there is a true battle between English and French industry: locomotives, steam engines, rotary presses, sewing machines and many other wonderful inventions. It was of fascination even to me, your unscientific husband. The noise was immense, as many of the exhibits were fully functioning.

But it was there that we were nearly overcome with disaster, and a national calamity. We were studying the mechanism of Cockerill's steam engine and the attention of Jarn and myself was focused on the technical description on a nearby board.

Suddenly, without warning, Jarn turned in a flash towards the prince. Then, there was an ear-shattering explosion and a massive eruption of steam from the core of the engine. For a second, I saw that jets of scalding steam and fragments of metal were directed straight towards the prince and he was in the path of death. Prince Bertie was frozen, as I was myself.

I still recall the image with horror. Next to me, I felt Jarn raise his arms, but I knew he could not reach the boy in time to save him.

What then transpired, I am unable to explain. At one moment these huge jets of steam and metal were rushing towards our prince, and in the next instance there was, quite simply, nothing. All was calm and peaceable. But our friend had an expression on his face as he glanced at me which I cannot easily describe. It was questioning. I believe he was curious as to my view of the event. But he also appeared a little guilty, the look of a child discovered in mischief. He moved rapidly to scoop the Prince up and shift him some distance from the engine, where droplets of steam were already condensing on the iron surfaces.

I was not alone in my perception of the event, as a newspaper reporter was positioned close by and his reports have appeared in several Parisian papers, one headed 'English Prince in near fatal incident' and another 'Prince saved by miracle'. It is these reports which I hope you have not seen, and which may have led you to worry about my welfare, my dearest.

However, to be frank with you, my dear wife, I find myself unable to explain the sequence of events I know I witnessed. In one second, disaster seemed inevitable, but in the next second all threat had gone. I feel convinced that our friend was somehow instrumental in saving the life of the heir to the throne, but I have no concept as to how this was done. What I am certain of, beyond doubt, is that Jarn became aware of the threat a second before it occurred, impossible though that seems. I feel unequal to raising the matter with Jarn himself, as it is clear he would discourage discussion and would indeed prefer the event to be forgotten.

This, I do not think I can do. I will reflect over the coming days, but at present I am considering making a report to Palmerston, as there may be profound implications for our realm. The Prime Minister should be made aware.

Be assured of my safety, my dear, and I know I can rely on you to breathe no word of this to anyone.

Your loving husband, George

Jarn had long wondered what George had seen that day. He knew it had been noteworthy, as it had led to a secret agreement at the highest level of government regarding himself and his family which, even today, influenced all their lives. An agreement which had resulted in his many years of service to government, once those in power had realised what a priceless asset they possessed. But he and George had seldom touched upon the event of 1855 throughout the remaining years of Clarendon's life. Jarn had not wanted to encourage questions he would not be able to answer. What could have been said at the time that would have been either believable or wise?

The final letter, at last, spoke to him directly from more than a century before.

Westminster, 19th September 1855

My beloved Kat

By messenger, dearest, I send you this short note and hope it will arrive with you promptly and before your husband's carriage in a few hours.

I look forward to being in your arms this evening, my wife, and to seeing the dear children. I hope to leave Westminster before teatime and will be with you for dinner. We will discuss more tonight, in privacy, but for now I will simply say that my discussion with Palmerston on the Parisian event will lead to a memorandum regarding our friend being placed in a secure location in case of dire future need, and all future Secretaries to the Cabinet will be made aware of its contents.

You will appreciate that I had anticipated some scepticism from Palmerston, at the very least, as the matter I witnessed in Paris appeared so very incredible. I had thought to be accused of a ridiculous flight of fancy. But to my astonishment it appears that the event I witnessed was supported by an earlier report of some extraordinary happening regarding Jarn, and from a personage no less than the Iron Duke himself, shortly before his death three years ago. It is certain that no-one could accuse Wellington of possessing a fanciful imagination, and his tale, whatever it was, was consistent with mine and both Palmerston and Lord Derby believed it at the time. I have no details of Wellington's experience, and I doubt that more will ever be divulged to me. It may remain an intriguing mystery.

In the meantime, I have passed on your suggestion to Jarn of a possible suitable house for himself and Issa, as they have now definitely decided upon quitting their Irish estate and would wish to move to England and make a permanent home. The manor house in the Cotswolds attracted him greatly after he had viewed its location on the map in my rooms here and I believe they will view it shortly. I suspect it will become the new Termonn House and let us hope we will visit there in years to come. Although I imagine our friends will continue their extensive travels as before. One cannot envisage them nesting in one place, can one?

Your devoted husband, George

So that was the part of the story he had never seen before.

Jarn felt sad. He and George, Kat and Issa, had been truly close but the full tale had waited over a century to be told. And it had been his dear friends who had proposed their home, Termonn, in the Cotswolds. Jarn knew it had been Kat who had suggested it to Issa, but to see the origin of their beloved home, so clearly pointed...

Under the Clarendon letters was an index to the papers remaining in the file. Most were 'Notes for the Record', usually with a location and a date. Skimming, Jarn's eye fell on a few. Two groups contained lengthy subgroups: WW1 and WW2. Others included Washington, Dublin, Malaya, China, Kenya, Paris. There was a long list. All the locations meant something to him, sometimes happy but often sad recollections.

Jarn made to turn the page but at last heard footsteps approaching the old cellar. He hastily replaced the file on the barrel and reseated himself just as the door opened. The same civil servant entered.

'Lord Dechar, if you have finished here, the cabinet secretary would like a last word before you leave.'

CHAPTER 2
CLARE, OXFORDSHIRE, 3RD
JULY 2022

Our limousine travelled past Oxford on a congested dual carriageway. The driver struggled to make progress between lorries and holiday caravans.

I stretched my back against the leather and winced. My tailored grey dress and jacket wasn't the most comfortable outfit for a long car journey despite shrieking career professional to anyone bothering to pay attention. Sadly for me, that excluded my three travelling companions.

Apart from the driver, my fellow travellers and superiors were Sir Edward Manning and Dr Philip Reardon. Sir Edward was the previous Cabinet Secretary, the most senior position in the UK's Civil Service. He had retired four years previously amid a deluge of honours which included Knight Commander of the order of St Michael and St George - KCMG. The old joke that it stood for "Kindly Call Me God" was quite accurate despite his excellent manners and unfailing old-school courtesy. Sir Edward wielded just as much influence today as he had before his retirement: deference and respect were expected.

Philip Reardon, my other travelling companion, was, like me, attached to the Civil Contingencies Secretariat within the Cabinet Office, the group responsible for emergency planning for threats to the nation. His background in physics had led to promotion within the part of the Secretariat related to armaments and weaponry. He had an inflated sense of entitlement and a chilly demeanour I was finding increasingly irritating, and we also had some unfortunate history.

Earlier in our trip, we had broken the journey at a service station and Sir Edward had taken advantage of Philip Reardon's brief absence to raise a gently enquiring brow.

'If there is anything troubling you, Clare, about Philip's presence on this assignment, please let me know. I feel I have detected some slight awkwardness between you. I would not want to place either of you in a delicate position.'

I had winced. It seemed that I was transparent.

'No, Sir Edward, thank you. Philip and I are just acquaintances. We both attended one of the induction courses, that's all. Perhaps we are both a little – competitive.'

The truth was that several months earlier Philip had urged me to drop into a bar in Westminster after an induction course where he was one of the speakers. And that afterwards he had made a suggestion that was unwelcome. My relationship with Ian, a post-doctoral archaeology student who was now painstakingly wiping earth off pottery fragments in Turkey, was well and truly over, very amicably. It didn't mean I was so desperate for a man that I would agree to a proposal from someone I had only met eight hours previously, a proposal accompanied by an insinuation that he may be able to help my career advance. I suppressed a flinch when recalling the proprietorial hand on my back and the iciness in Philip's eyes when I rejected him. I suspected there was unfinished business as far as Philip was concerned.

Back in the car with at least a foot between me and Philip on the back seat, we branched towards Woodstock and then past Churchill's birthplace of Blenheim Palace. Several miles later we veered off onto quiet country lanes which took us deep into the rural Cotswolds, rolling green fields interspersed with buildings of golden stone. I wondered again why we were making this journey and what lay at the end of it. Coming from an academic background in classical history at Oxford, and only recently recruited into the Civil Service, it hadn't taken me long to conclude that the huge organisation sometimes seemed to exist solely for the purpose of preparing briefing papers and memoranda. The lack of any supporting documentation or even a pre-meeting briefing for this trip was unusual. The high-level security documentation I had been asked to sign yesterday was even more unusual.

Several miles later, Sir Edward turned to us from the front and spoke, calmly and quietly, 'Not too much longer now if I remember correctly. It is admittedly a few years since I was here last. But if memory serves ... ah, yes. Here are the old gates and the lodge house.'

The gates Sir Edward referred to appeared to be ancient and were gateposts rather than a full gate. We passed between them and took a sharp right turn next to the adjacent stone lodge house, with its ornate chimneys and mullioned windows. Then we were on a driveway leading up to a gentle summit, on either side pastureland dotted with majestic trees and sheep grazing. At the peak, our car slowed and allowed us to absorb the view.

Below us lay a glorious English moated manor house of

honeyed Cotswold stone. Of two storeys but with gable windows in the grey tiled roof, it nestled into its valley as if it had grown from it. From our elevation, we could see that the house was at the cross-section of four paths. One was ours. Beyond the house the path continued up a grassy slope to what looked like an old fire beacon. Another track crossed at right angles, the crossover centred on the house itself. On the left, a driveway led to an old tower on a hill. To the right, a path ran adjacent to a rill of water from the moat, leading towards woodland.

The sandstone walls of the house rose above the reflective water of the moat. On the side nearest to us, a bridge crossed the moat to a courtyard, and the huge stone and oak entrance to the house. It was idyllic, history palpable even from where we were. In the brilliant sunshine the driveway ahead of us shone dazzling, a golden path to the house. A glistening track continued on the opposite side of the house, up the grassy slope towards the beacon. What a strange trick of the light, I thought.

But suddenly, dizzyingly and sickeningly, I was hurled into *déjà vu* stronger than I had ever felt before. I knew this place, and I knew it well. Warmth, oak, tapestries and velvet, the scents of lavender and box, crackling fires, baking and old stone, all rushed past in an instant. In my mind I clearly saw the oaken front door opening, a golden-haired woman standing awaiting us. And a conviction, inexplicable but certain - this was my home. This was family.

And yet I had never been here before.

Fighting the overwhelming sensation and gasping, I could see Philip looking at me. Perhaps he thought I was about to embarrass him or destroy his Savile Row suit by being car sick. I turned away from him toward the car window, struggling to regain my composure. These attacks had happened over the years, and my mother, when I had confided in her as a child that I felt and saw people and places unrelated to the here and now, had said that it happened to some of us, and I needed to hide it. Others would not understand, she said. I must keep silent.

I hung onto her words now.

Meanwhile the car had continued its descent and had crossed the moat, moving off the bridge and crunching onto the gravelled courtyard. It slowed and stopped in front of the massive oak door. I calmed, my breathing slowly returning to normal as I gazed at the lovely house.

Sir Edward turned back towards us from the front seat.

'Philip, Clare. I am aware you have had next to no briefing for this meeting, and clearly this is not normal. But it is deliberate rather than an oversight.' He appeared his usual assured and calm self but there was an undertone of something I couldn't identify. It may have been trepidation, or perhaps a controlled excitement.

'The situation we are here to discuss is one of grave importance. It is classified at a very high level of consequence and at a high level of likelihood, which is why I had to ask you to sign the documents you were given yesterday.'

We were listening intently, and I was close enough to feel a tremor run through Philip's body. He may be a cold fish but he was as tantalised by this strange journey as I was.

'This is Termonn House. We are here to meet the owner of this house, Lady Issa Dechar, and request her assistance. Lady Issa and her family are known to the highest echelons of our government, and they have proved most helpful to us in the past. I ask simply that you observe, assist me where it seems appropriate, and be watchful. And if I make any suggestions, I would appreciate it if you would indicate your agreement.'

The great oak door opened, and a slender golden-haired woman stood on the threshold to her house. Just as I had foreseen, a few minutes before.

CHAPTER 3
TERMONN HOUSE, 3RD
JULY 2022

Sir Edward sat with a porcelain cup and saucer in his hands. Antique porcelain was one of his passions and he knew the cup was early Minton. He managed, but only after a titanic struggle, to resist the urge to turn it over and check the underneath marks for confirmation. Spilling tea dregs over the table was not likely to endear him to their hostess.

The hostess in question sat elegantly poised opposite him on a carved chair. Golden hair around her shoulders, she was impossible to age, perhaps somewhere between mid-twenties and early thirties. Her dress was perfect for an English summer afternoon, crisp linen in sea blue. She was petite and delicate, but there was something additional, the suggestion of an indomitable core. A small spaniel-type dog, in unusual shades of cream and white, lay close by in a basket near the hearth, watching her mistress closely.

They were seated in embroidery-covered chairs around a mahogany table. The afternoon sun cast long shards of light across a pale Aubusson carpet, and through the French doors and the open casement windows were glimpses of pasture. Sheep bleated in the distance and a breath of freshly mown grass scented the old room. No fire was alight in the carved stone fireplace on this warm summer's day, but an aroma of herbs and lavender came from the greenery arranged in the large grate.

Sir Edward took note, with interest, that Lady Issa was studying Clare more than her other guests. Her gaze on the young woman was intense whenever Clare was looking elsewhere around the elegant room. But when she spoke, Lady Issa's tone was neither warm nor questioning.

'So, Sir Edward, perhaps you can explain the reason for today's visit.'

It appeared that despite a veneer of politeness the lady of the manor wished to speed her guests on their way as soon as possible.

Sir Edward moved into the conversation with resolution.

'Lady Issa, I appreciate your welcome and hospitality. Thank you.' This was more in hope than expectation that there would actually be a genuine welcome at some point. Lady Issa regarded Sir Edward coolly and remained silent as Sir Edward fingered the rim of his saucer and continued.

'As you know, the government continues to rely on retired Cabinet Secretaries such as myself for assistance with particularly sensitive matters of national importance. Since my retirement, I have been privy to the most sensitive and secret matters threatening our country, and in this capacity I have been happy to continue to be the main link between your family and the most senior members of government. You are already aware, I hope, of my appreciation of the service your family has given.'

Lady Issa sipped her tea. Apart from a slight dip of the head she made no comment.

'In point of fact, we now have another ... issue we hope

you can assist us with. I'm afraid it is a very substantial matter.'

Sir Edward watched his hostess carefully, trying to assess how welcome any request for assistance, on the scale he had hinted, would be. He received no outward clues. She continued to regard him levelly. With no indication as to how to proceed, Sir Edward firmly set his shoulders and took the decision to plough on.

'You may recall, Lady Issa, that our government has received assistance over many years from a series of ladies. Ladies we have collectively termed our Cassandras.'

Issa's face took on an expression somewhere between humour and exasperation. When she spoke, her voice was low and held a hint of laughter.

'I am aware, Sir Edward, of a series of ladies who have received payment from your government for many years, for certain claimed services of a clairvoyant nature. A few, a very, very few, have not been charlatans.'

The use of the term 'your government' and a slight trace of indefinable accent were not lost on her guests. They hinted that Lady Issa might not share the full allegiance to government that was perhaps to be expected from a titled lady living in an English manorial house.

'Yes. Well, I will admit that not all of the ladies who have held the position over the years have actually ...', and here Sir Edward flinched slightly, '... actually performed as the government might have desired.'

'Jarn and I were always at a loss, Sir Edward, as to why a formal position was ever created. An informal arrangement with the occasional lady of some ability we could under-stand, but instead this sequence of ladies have occupied a status similar to that of Poet Laureate. They are expected to provide a regular and accurate foretelling service to the country, in return for the honour of the position, a permanent stipend, and grace-and-favour accommodation at Hampton Court. Why? When most of them can't even read tea leaves?'

Sir Edward was clearly unused to being asked to defend an established practice of the United Kingdom's government and winced slightly. Clare averted her gaze from her senior's discomfort but could see Philip staring blatantly. She had had no inkling of what awaited them at Termonn and Philip had presumably been equally ignorant, but he was making no attempt to hide his fascination at the exchange.

Sir Edward sighed but nodded slightly.

'Well, the formalisation of the position was only made under the reign of King Edward, back in the early nineteen hundreds. He appreciated the ... qualities of the Cassandra of the time very much. She was by all accounts a lovely young lady, and it was surmised that her skills were somewhat more wide-ranging than her formal position required.' The precise nature of the services provided by this servant of government drifted in the air of the Termonn drawing room.

Sir Edward coughed delicately. 'Of course, the appointment led to the Cassandra attending the Palace once a week, to inform the King in person of any visions she had received. And his late Majesty's regard for this Cassandra led to her receiving a substantial remuneration and the gift of accommodation, both of which were subsequently enjoyed by her successors.'

Lady Issa gave a delicate lady-like snort. 'And since then, you have been stuck with a series of ladies in formal positions of service to the government, but more suited to the circus tent than to the royal residences or to Whitehall.

Really, Sir Edward, I cannot find it in myself to sympathise with you.'

Sir Edward took on the expression of a public schoolboy mildly reprimanded by his head of house. He took a breath, a sip of tea, gazed longingly at the Minton cup and continued.

'It is true to say that none of the ladies over the last century have been especially informative to government. They have on occasion shown some foresight, but it has been more in the nature of the winner of sporting fixtures than in areas of more significance to government. Their visions have not entirely been what had been hoped for, from our Cassandras.'

'However,' Sir Edward continued, as his tone became more solemn, and he set down his cup, 'the current Cassandra is somewhat different. Her name is Mary. She came to us via a psychiatric assessment unit in Yorkshire, some years ago. Mary was diagnosed years before with savant syndrome and also with symptoms of severe autism. She had an especially brilliant understanding of times and dates; if she was posed any date over the last few centuries she could unerringly say, within seconds, which day of the week it was, and she was never wrong. But throughout the late 1990's there was a change in her behaviour. She disturbed the other patients in the unit by her constant talk about a plane hitting a high tower, and as several of her earlier dreams had actually seemed to precede events, the staff in the unit notified government, although no official notice was taken. In August and early September 2001 Mary became so distressed she had to be repeatedly sedated. And, of course, we know what happened in September 2001....'

Clare and Philip exchanged glances, and even Lady Issa raised a brow, but Sir Edward continued quietly. 'Our government did not feel responsible, of course. After all, there are many towers and skyscrapers in the world. How could we have known the actual target, even if the threat had been perceived to be real and not just the ramblings of an unsound mind?'

After a pause, he went on. 'After the terrible events of that day, our records show that Mary once again became quiet and calm, almost normal. Until there was a repeat, with the same agitation, and talk of water and huge waves, prior to what happened in December 2004. The Boxing Day tsunami.'

Sir Edward saw Clare look startled. Both she and Philip were playing close attention, neither had had any warning of what he was going to say and were rapt.

Lady Issa listened without expression, her head bent.

'At this point, of course, official notice was taken of her. The Cassandra of the time died in 2008, and with a regime of appropriate medication and a high level of care, Mary took on the role of Cassandra in 2010.'

Lady Issa leaned elegantly forward and refilled Sir Edward's cup, and also the cups of Philip and Clare, with more tea, asking 'and after she assumed this position, did the visions continue or did they stop?'

'They continued but at a mild level,' Sir Edward acknowledged. 'Nothing of huge significance, but neither was there much agitation from Mary. Her carers - she has two nurses in attendance on her day and night to assist her with life – have reported her utterings to us, and there has been no cause for alarm, although a few have led us to invoke certain actions – mostly overseas – which we may not otherwise have taken.'

It was clear from Sir Edward's tone that these actions were protected under secrecy laws and neither they nor the visions which led to them would ever be found in the recordings of governmental decisions.

'However, Mary's state altered about four months ago. Since then, she has become increasingly agitated and distressed. She is waking at night, talking of drownings, walls, trapped people screaming for help, and the setting for all of this seems from her statements to be a big city. We are concerned that it may be London. Her carers have again been forced to give her medication to calm her. In the morning, she remembers no useful details, although she has worked with an artist to recall some partial memory of images. The only thing she has said, again and again, is 'it is worse than before'.'

Sir Edward replaced his cup on the table, fingering the edge of the thin porcelain absent-mindedly now. He tapped the rim, paused and spoke.

'You will understand, Lady Issa, that if something is approaching us that is in any way similar to, or heaven help us, worse than the events which followed her previous visions, we would very much like to prevent it. That is why we are here with you today.'

He looked at his hostess with calm appeal. 'Any help you can give us would be deeply appreciated.'

Lady Issa was still for a few moments, gazing at Sir Edward. Then her hand reached out to a mahogany pie-crust table by her chair, and she fingered the silver picture frame standing on it. Her guests were too far away to see what picture was within. After a few moments, she turned back to her guests.

'I am not a psychic, Sir Edward. I am not able to share in Mary's visions. The abilities of myself and my family are different. And we have foreseen no event approaching.'

Sir Edward moved forward in his seat.

'Lady Issa, I know that the services of you and your family to our country have been in part based on a perception of events to come. I hoped that, perhaps, with this specific information you could undertake some search, some horizon scanning...'

Lady Issa regarded Sir Edward steadily and when she spoke it was with clipped precision.

'Perhaps you are unaware of the true nature of our abilities. We each have a view of alternative futures that is specific to ourselves. By itself it is limited and intermittent. It is only when it is paired with that of a true mate, with complementary skills, that our perceptions and abilities are fully realised. As you know, my husband was lost saving this country from a terrible catastrophe many years ago and we have been without him ever since.'

Lady Issa looked again to the silver frame.

'What I was capable of before the loss of my husband, I can no longer achieve. Nor do I have the desire to strive for it. He is no longer here, and my abilities have returned to the simple talents I had as a girl. Without Jarn I am powerless, and unable to assist you.'

She turned back to her guests, with an air of implacability.

'Sir Edward, any abilities I and my family have are devoted to our constant, never-ending search for my husband. I have been happy to assist you in small tasks over the last years, but this is beyond us.'

Sir Edward felt certain that Lady Issa was understating her abilities for the purposes of the conversation. There was something in her expression that suggested her talents were far removed from 'powerless'. And again, he noticed her thoughtful gaze flicker to Clare.

Nevertheless, he collected his papers together and reached for his case, somewhat wearily.

'Thank you, Lady Issa, for your time and for your hospitality. Our government will always be indebted to you and your family for your past services. We have the greatest sympathy for you in the loss of your husband through his duty to this realm and every support will continue to be given to you and your family.'

He reached into his case and took out a single sheet of paper.

'If these illustrations mean anything to you, or if you become aware of anything in connection with them,' and he handed the paper to his hostess, 'I would be most grateful if you could let me know. An artist worked with Mary to produce this, as she claimed to have seen these figures associated with her recent visions.'

Lady Issa took the sheet, and Sir Edward, keenly observing, saw a spasm of interest gleam in her eyes as she looked at it before her clear gaze moved back to himself. Clare, seated next to Sir Edward and closely watching, could see that the paper showed two sketches, one a drawing of flowers and birds and the other a badge of some sort. Neither meant anything to her. Sir Edward reached again into his case and quietly passed copies of the page to her and to Philip.

Lady Issa regarded Sir Edward and spoke slowly.

'Sir Edward, this may help, although I can make no promises. I would, however, need the services of a research assistant. Is it possible that I could borrow this young lady? I think it would be for no more than a few days.'

Sir Edward's face lit with hope and his tone was eager.

'Yes, of course, Lady Issa, if Clare is willing?' The quick

look he shot to Clare suggested that 'No' was not an acceptable answer and could be career limiting.

Clare responded immediately, mindful of the conversation in the car. 'Of course, Sir Edward, I would be very happy to stay and help. I have luggage for a few days.'

Sir Edward beamed his approval. 'If you need more, let us know and we will send a staff member with anything you require.' It was clear that absolutely nothing would be too much trouble, as long as Clare stayed at Termonn House.

Philip, leaning forward with body language clearly indicating irritation, murmured 'Would it be helpful to have more than one assistant, Lady Issa? I have also packed enough for several days.'

'One assistant is quite sufficient, I thank you.'

She stood and gently but deftly manoeuvred Sir Edward and Philip out of her drawing room and across the stone flagged hall towards the massive door and the courtyard beyond. Clare followed and the spaniel trotted after, committed to checking the strangers left the premises.

Philip tried to hang back, whispering to Clare. 'You must keep me informed. I can come over any time, day or night.' Clare managed a non-committal smile and saw them depart with mixed relief and trepidation.

As the heavy door closed, Lady Issa rang an embroidered bell pull which clanged in distant reaches of the old house. After only moments, a door opened and a kind-faced elderly lady wearing a dark dress came forward with a welcoming smile. Perhaps she had been behind the door, waiting for her mistress's call.

'Hettie will take you to your room. We will talk properly tomorrow. You are welcome here, Clare. Sleep well.'

In the limousine now heading back over the estate road towards the main Oxfordshire highway and London, Philip was unable to stop himself berating his superior.

'You shouldn't have left Clare alone, Sir Edward. She is too inexperienced, far too young. It would have been better if I'd stayed. I could have persuaded Lady Issa to trust me, to work with me, to share...'

Sir Edward cast a pained glance in the younger man's direction and made a mental note to append a critical comment to his annual report.

'Philip, perhaps you did not notice but Lady Issa made it clear she was interested very specifically in Clare. Her interest was obvious from the start of our meeting, and I am sure she would have engineered a way for Clare to stay behind somehow, regardless of how our conversation developed. What that family wants, it has over the years tended to get. It would take a braver man than I to stand in the lady's way, and I suspect that Clare will make the most of her opportunity.'

Sir Edward turned his gaze away from his disgruntled underling and watched the landscape of Oxfordshire pass the car windows. Silently, he reflected that his dinner a few weeks earlier with his good friend, the chair of classical history at Oxford, had indeed been beneficial.

CHAPTER 4
CLARE, TERMONN HOUSE,
4TH JULY 2022

I woke to the sound of sheep baa'ing in the distance, and the clip-clopping of horses nearby. I had slept like a log through the night, unaccustomed to absolute quiet and darkness. It took a few moments to recall the events of the previous day that had led to my installation in this beautiful large room, with its linenfold panelling, stone casements, leaded windows and fabulously comfortable bed.

Gorgeous crewel work hung at the windows and at the head of my huge dark oak tester. No specialist in antique furniture, I hazarded a guess that the bed was Restoration period, with its carved scenes from the Garden of Eden complete with naked, buxom and come-hither Eves and several distinctly lecherous looking snakes which faintly reminded me of Philip. The mattress was certainly not antique and would have been very acceptable in any luxury hotel, together with crisp linen sheets and starched pillowcases. It was only with difficulty that I extracted myself from the bed's embrace and put my feet to the faded carpet. The sun streamed in, casting patterns from the leaded windows across the floor.

Stepping across the carpet to polished floor timbers, I raised the window latch and opened it wide, letting in air scented with summer flowers and grass. Below me was a gravel path and beyond was a courtyard surrounded on four sides by an assortment of Cotswold stone buildings. In the side nearest me there was an archway leading into the courtyard.

The left side of the courtyard looked to be an old stable block, again bisected by an archway leading to an estate road. From my lofty window I could see fields and paddocks beyond, the estate land more extensive than I had appreciated on arrival yesterday. A truck loaded with hay was moving along the road leading to the pastures, basking in morning sunlight. As I watched, a groom led two horses across the courtyard and down towards the archway. One was dark and magnificent, prancing and clearly a temperamental handful. The other, a chestnut, was smaller and apparently more biddable, but as I watched she bent her head and snapped at the withers of the horse in front of her, exasperated at his antics and not remotely intimidated by him.

To the right side of the courtyard the rooms appeared to be accommodation and workrooms associated with the estate. The far side of the courtyard was two stories high rather than the single level of the other sides. It looked to have been converted into a residence, with arched stone windows and a large stable door now serving as an entrance. Above sat a clocktower, the time clearly showing I had slept in far longer than I did in London. There, by 7am, I would have been jogging down the streets and around the park near my flat. The thought reminded me to ask for my jogging gear to be sent over; the paths here looked infinitely more inviting than my usual routes.

Beyond the clocktower was the drive which led up the grassy slope I had spotted on our arrival yesterday. From the elevation of my window, I could clearly see the fire beacon at the top of the summit. Beacons such as these would have been used in centuries past to send alarms across the countryside, each being lit when the light from another beacon was seen. I wondered how old this one was.

Below, to my left, a golden sandstone wall intersected by an arch covered in white roses separated the courtyard from the gardens to the eastern front of the house. Straining out of the casement window and looking still further leftward, I glimpsed the drive leading to the tower. No moat could be seen from this angle, it was presumably only on the north and west sides of the house, but a ha-ha separating the gardens from the pastureland suggested where a moat may have existed in previous times.

As I gazed, getting my bearings, a door in one of the courtyard buildings opposite opened and the housekeeper Hettie, who had brought me to my room the previous day and who had supplied me with supper on a tray during the evening, emerged. In her arms was a laundry basket full of folded linens. A girl, in perhaps her early twenties and with long flaxen hair, emerged from below my window and crossed to the woman. Hettie met her with a smile and the girl took the basket, turning back to the main house. Was this a daughter of the house? But if Lady Issa's husband had been gone for the 'many years' she had mentioned yesterday that didn't seem possible. Also, she appeared too young to have a daughter of this age.

But then, as I had puzzled last night, surely she was also far too young to have a husband missing for 'many years'. It was perplexing, I thought, as I ran a shower in the elegant stone-panelled en-suite. Thankfully there was no Restoration period plumbing here. The side-jets pummelled my muscles and the tropical overhead shower deluged my hair and body, with a luxuriously scented range of shampoos and lotions near to hand.

Massaging suds through my hair and then rinsing off, I ran through in my mind what had happened the previous afternoon. What were the services Lady Issa and her husband had undertaken for the government? For how many years had Lord Dechar been missing? What was the significance of the drawings? What was the secret of this strange family with their apparent perception of the future? And why had the house seemed so familiar to me? Applying my old academic analysis skills, I reluctantly concluded that I had many questions but no answers.

At the end of my shower, I turned off the water jets and towelled my hair, still puzzling.

My wardrobe options were very limited until I received the additional items I had requested from Sir Edward in a late email to him last night. In any case, it was difficult to dress appropriately when the challenges of the day ahead were unknown. I picked out a green cotton t-shirt and cream linen skirt and slipped my feet into light trainers. My hairbrush struggled as it always did with my thick wavy hair, and I settled for pulling some of it back into a knot and leaving the rest curling over my shoulders. After a dab of make-up, my tummy was rumbling too much to remain in my room. I had to find food from somewhere.

I had my hand on the doorknob when there was a tap on the door. Opening the door revealed Hettie and as on the previous evening, she was balancing a tray. This time it contained a tantalising assortment of breakfast goodies. I could see fresh bread rolls from which delicious steam was still rising, honey, jam, butter, fruit, a jug of cream, and –

best of all – a large pot of something that smelt like strong filtered coffee. My tummy rumbled loudly.

'Good morning, madam!'

Hettie moved to the table by the window and pulled up a chair for me. I took my seat with alacrity.

'Thank you, Hettie!' I restrained myself with difficulty from ripping into the warm bread and I could see she was struggling not to laugh at my hunger. She poured steaming coffee into the cup.

'It is very good to have guests again,' she said. 'This house used to be full of visitors, and we never minded.' She moved towards the bed and started to straighten the bedding.

'This is a lovely room, Hettie. The bed, the furniture, the views...', I gestured around the room and towards the window, '...it is kind of Lady Issa to let me use it.' I had to stop as I already had a roll in one hand and a buttered knife in the other and was struggling to decide between honey and jam.

'This room was her son's, David's.' My hand stilled in its movement to my mouth, and I put the bread back on the plate.

'I'm so sorry, Hettie, I didn't know Lady Issa had lost a son.' The poor woman, I thought, chilled, to have lost both her husband and her son. 'When did he die?'

'Dead? Pray God, no. We hope he will return some day. It would kill the mistress to lose her son as well as the lord. We do not give up hope, for either of them.' Hettie bustled around, plumping pillows and fluffing the duvet, talking to me over her shoulder.

'Why is David missing then, Hettie? Where did he go?' I was intensely curious but didn't want to pry too much into painful memories.

'He set out to look for his father over four months ago. Of course, he has been away many times before over the years, searching, as has my lady. But he has always come back within weeks, two months at the outside.'

'But where is he looking? And how long has Lord Dechar been gone?'

'David follows the lines. But they are unpredictable, or at least that is what I've heard. I don't understand these things myself, best left to others who do. And Lord Dechar vanished in 1977, while visiting an airbase in the east of England.'

She gave the pillows a final twitch and shook the quilt straight as I gaped at her, shocked. Over forty years ago? And he was Issa's husband? How was that possible?

'But, madam, since we knew you were coming, I think my lady has been much happier. She asked yesterday morning for this room to be prepared for you, so we moved David's possessions to another room.'

I felt guilty that the room had been emptied just for me and she caught my worried expression.

'No, no,' she reassured gently, 'most of his belongings were already in the stable block anyway, my lady had arranged for them to be moved there in the spring. There were very few items left in this room. Lady Issa has always said that the stable block apartment was more appropriate for David, should he take a wife one day.'

She gestured towards the window from which the two-storey stable block could be seen. 'There is a lovely suite of rooms there, very comfortable for a couple.'

I felt somewhat happier, although completely perplexed by Hettie's revelations. My list of questions had expanded just from this short conversation.

Hettie topped up my cup with coffee as I popped warm

bread slathered with butter and jam into my mouth in as lady-like a manner as possible. Which wasn't very lady-like at all. I felt my long-dead grandmother's disapproval from on high, or perhaps it was from below. Remembering her character, I thought that location was rather more likely.

'Lady Issa asks if you would care to take a stroll with her in the garden. Ten o'clock would suit her well. If you come downstairs, I will take you to her. She will be in the break-fast room.'

'I do hope I can help her, Hettie. I'm not sure I can, though. I don't know much about old symbols or whatever it was that Lady Issa was interested in.'

'I'm sure you will be able to help our lady, madam.'

It was only after Hettie had closed the door, it dawned on me to wonder what she had meant by them knowing I was coming. After all, the decision had only been made during the meeting yesterday afternoon. Lady Issa couldn't have known to have this room emptied yesterday morning.

CHAPTER 5
DAVID, 'DORDONA', 4TH MAY 2022

Thyme and pine. For some reason, the scents in a new world always struck David before his other senses, closely followed by sound.

He was standing on stony ground. There was nothing around him but a valley in what appeared to be an arid Mediterranean landscape. Stunted olive trees and dried pasture, and in the far distance were mountains.

The place was familiar. Not exactly the same as in his world, of course, but that was to be expected. He found himself looking round for Melite but quickly realised it was futile; this wasn't her temple, or to be exact it wasn't the remnants of her temple. Half-buried ancient stones indicated what had been there before, millennia ago.

David had inherited patience from his mother. Most decidedly not from his father, who he adored but who couldn't be described as patient by any stretch of the imagination. David sank onto one of the more raised stones and waited. A light breeze drifted around, herb scented. The sun gradually lowered in the sky.

As sunset approached, he wondered if it was time to try

to return home. Time passed differently in other worlds, but he had been away for nearly three months and his mother would be worried. He stood and gathered himself to step. But just before the move, a figure clad in white robes emerged from the darkening, shifting landscape.

CHAPTER 6
CLARE, TERMONN HOUSE, 4TH JULY 2022

I headed down the huge, cantilevered staircase around which the whole house seemed to be structured. As far as I could see, it had no supports, it seemed to fly in the air. Hettie must have heard my steps tripping down the polished treads as she met me just after I reached the ground floor. She smiled and gestured for me to follow her.

I was shown into a panelled room in the northeast corner of the house. It had wide windows on two sides, on the east the windows overlooked the pastureland leading to the tower in the distance and on the north side there was a view of the estate road we had come down yesterday, towards the gates. To the east the morning sun streamed in, lighting up the panelling, the dark wooden chairs and sofa, and their crushed raspberry upholstery.

Lady Issa was seated at a table with silver coffee pots, cups and saucers. She stood as I approached and smiled, waving a hand towards a seat at the table near the beverages. I had already consumed more than enough coffee to last me the day but couldn't resist more. The Termonn

House brew was exquisite, strong and fragrant. I nodded happily and Lady Issa moved to the coffee pot, pouring the steaming liquid into a cup and moving the silver cream jug nearer to me.

'I hope you slept well, Clare? It is a pleasant room. Our son, David, has always liked it.'

I told her, truthfully, that the room was the loveliest I had ever slept in and the bed by far the most comfortable. I felt myself glowing as I couldn't stop myself from saying how ecstatic I was to be away from the incessant traffic noise of London, and in the heart of the countryside. Lady Issa must have seen my bubbling enthusiasm, and for the first time I saw her face light with a genuine and warm smile. I suddenly found myself liking her very much. Although she appeared not many years older than me there was something maternal about her.

After I had raised my cup and gratefully swallowed some of her delicious coffee, she reached over the table and brought forward the sheet of diagrams Sir Edward had given her yesterday.

'The sketches, Clare. What do you make of them?'

Two separate drawings were on the sheet. One resembled a starburst with a central design and the other showed what appeared to be five squat little birds, two flowerheads and a cross. I had studied the page Sir Edward had given me while eating my supper the previous evening and had then searched the internet until midnight, but I still had no inkling of what the figures meant, and admitted it, apologetically.

'Hettie?' Lady Issa called. 'Please bring the box with the lord's order.'

Once again, Hettie must have been just outside the door

awaiting instructions, because within seconds she entered the room carrying a large faded green velvet jewel box, which she handed to her mistress before returning to the hall.

Lady Issa opened the box and angled it so I could view the contents. Within was a large and beautiful starred cross with eight diamond-inlaid silver rays, and in the centre were three enamelled clover leaves, each containing a golden crown. The father of a friend of mine had once received insignia for an order of chivalry, and this seemed very similar.

'A badge of chivalry, Lady Issa?' I guessed and received a nod of confirmation.

'It is the Order of St Patrick, and it is my husband's. He was awarded it by the Queen for his service to the royal family.'

I felt Lady Issa's eyes on me and looked up from my perusal of the badge to meet it. She was watching me calmly but with the hint of a question in her gaze.

'You need to know, Clare, that we are a long-lived family. Time runs differently for us to most others. When I say the Queen, I mean Queen Victoria. She gave my husband the award in 1856, in gratitude for a great service he had given to her family. I was present at the ceremony, with our older children, and it was a very proud moment for us.'

I gazed into Lady Issa's clear blue eyes and moments passed as I absorbed what she had said. Then my brain sluggishly started working again and my heart speeded up.

I had lived all my life in a world where people lived and died after the usual range of years. All entirely normal and expected, for neighbours and family, for friends, for celebrities. A classmate hadn't lived beyond seventeen due to a hereditary illness, and it had had a big impact on my whole year group, face-to-face with the mortality of a contemporary for the first time. That time plodded on, writing history and taking lives with it, was never questioned.

But my own perception had always been different, in a way I couldn't explain. To me, time felt like a stream, rushing along or swirling in eddies. Sometimes still, in deep pools, when the world seemed to stand motionless, background noises fading. I would come back to find the world had moved on, without me. But occasionally time seemed to rush me ahead of everyone else, leaving me trying to catch up on things I had inexplicably seemed to miss.

It had made me feel abnormal. Wrong, even freakish. But now, without any warning, there were people surrounding me for whom time was also different. Suddenly I didn't feel so alone. Lady Issa's words, and the knowledge that this family had been alive in Queen Victoria's reign, should have been deeply shocking but it wasn't. It resonated with a world I had only had glimpses of. Perhaps there was truly something more, some explanation for the creature I was.

I found myself nodding at Lady Issa, hoping to show that I wasn't about to run screaming from her home and towards the office of the local newspaper. She treated me to another smile and something in her gentle gaze told me she knew at least part of my thoughts. She poured fresh coffee, giving me more time for reflection. I sipped my drink and gazed out of the window, my heart slowing to a more normal rate.

Eventually Lady Issa spoke.

'The order of St Patrick, Clare, has been dormant for many years and, apart from the present monarch, it is assumed there are no recipients left alive. That is not quite true, of course, but it is understandable that it is so thought.'

'It is lovely,' I said, with my hand hovering over the beautiful piece of jewellery, careful to keep my fingers from touching it. And it really was lovely, the centre piece encrusted with brilliant diamonds as well as gold and green enamel. But in what way did it help us with the mystery Sir Edward desperately needed us to solve?

Lady Issa had followed my thoughts.

'There are two aspects to the drawings of Mary's vision. The first sketch, the one showing the badge, shows something very much like this order. But there is also the other diagram, of a cross and five birds and the flowers. I sense that the solution is not just one of these sketches, but both joined together in some way.'

She fingered the drawings as I looked at her closely and wondered if the other sketch already meant more to her than she was revealing. Was I being tested?

'It would be very helpful, Clare, if you could consider these figures and see if you can extract any meaning from them,' Lady Issa said.

I nodded, unsure how to go about the task but fully prepared to try.

Then, seeing I had finished my coffee, she rose from her chair and moved towards the door, gesturing for me to follow her.

'But, enough of work. It is a beautiful morning. Would you care to take a tour around the grounds with me? Kimi?' She called for her little dog, the spaniel, who came running.

I put my empty cup down and followed her through the door, across the stone-flagged floor of the hall, across a passageway and down a step into a huge manorial kitchen.

A navy-blue range cooker covered the entirety of one

wall. I didn't know they came in such an enormous size. Hettie was supervising the preparation of dough by a girl I hadn't seen before, slim, dark haired and of Asian appearance. Hettie smiled at us as we passed her and headed towards a big stable door leading outside. Both the top and bottom of the stable door were open, and sunlight shone through, reflecting on the stone flags of the kitchen floor. I walked with Lady Issa through the door onto the path outside. We were underneath the room I had slept in, I realised, the stable block in front of us. Kimi trotted behind us but then darted ahead, aiming to be first at any delectable sniffs outside.

Lady Issa gestured for me to go to my left, along the gravelled path that ran under my bedroom window, and then to go through the archway in the old wall. She pinched off a few faded roses as she passed, delicious perfume wafting in the air. We turned round the corner to the left and the path led across the eastern front of the house. As we walked, the arched windows of what appeared to be a dining room were to our left. Away to the east a driveway on the other side of the ha-ha led through pasture towards the tower in the distance. The land was dotted with trees, casting shadows in the morning sun. Sheep were already clustered under them against the rising heat of the day.

'This house was built in the seventeenth century at the conjunction of four old paths, as you can see, Clare.'

Lady Issa gestured to her right.

'This east drive leads towards St Michael's tower. It is thought to be all that remains of a very old church, perhaps built on the site of an even older pagan temple. We have had its lower floors converted to quite comfortable apartments. Mordecai, our gardener and general help, lives on the ground floor and Hettie has the floor above.' I recalled the genial elderly man who had brought my luggage to my room the previous evening: it seemed that was Mordecai.

I followed her along the gravelled path, admiring the lovely herbaceous border with flowers of lavender and gold that ran between the path and the Cotswold stone house. Lady Issa nodded her thanks at my compliments and dead-headed some flowers as we walked past them.

Beyond the dining room were the stone casement windows and French doors of the drawing room we had sat in yesterday during Sir Edward's meeting, then the windows of the breakfast room we had just taken coffee in. From there, we moved to the corner of the house and turned left towards the moat on the north side. Here, box-hedged borders separated a narrow strip of lawn in front of the house from another lawn bordering the water of the moat. Ducks quacked and pigeons fluttered mindlessly.

I have never thought pigeons the Einsteins of the bird kingdom and these were certainly true to form, pecking and busying themselves in activity with little obvious purpose. Lady Issa paused and pulled from a bag some crumbs and seed for the birds, which she started to throw towards them. Happy quacking and a free-for-all ensued between ducks and pigeons. Kimi darted among the mayhem, scattering the birds in all directions as she approached, but they landed quickly again and after a few snaps from the ducks at the dog, they restarted gobbling. It was clearly a routine game understood by all, with no great harm meant on either side.

My hostess pointed up the northern drive, the way our car had driven yesterday. 'You may have noticed the old gates and the lodge house at the end of the drive, as you arrived yesterday?'

I nodded. 'The gates appear to be even older than this house, Lady Issa. Is there a history to them?'

Lady Issa nodded approvingly and gave me another sweet smile.

'Yes, indeed. They were the gates to the abbey that was on the site of this house, centuries ago. Those gates, or rather the supports of the gates, are all that are left above ground of that construction. The abbey was razed to its stone flagged floor in Henry's reformation. The stones from the abbey walls were gradually reused in houses in our estate village of Michaelcombe, just over the hill. Only the columns of the old gates remain. It is surprising that the gates survived, really. The lodge house is the home of our younger daughter, now.'

A son, and a younger daughter? So at least two daughters? I stored up the information, collecting every scrap about this extraordinary family.

We left the birds and their squabbling and walked across the gravelled driveway at the front of the house. An elegant, white-painted wooden footbridge led from the driveway across the moat to the path on the other side, which in turn ran adjacent to a rill of water leading to the west. I could see now that the rill was just an extension of the moat, although much narrower. It was almost jumpable.

As we walked along the rill, a few hopeful ducks waddling after us, I saw that the path continued to the west into the woodland, where it was bordered by sun-dappled grass amid the trees. Gold beams glinted in the woodland, a trick of the sunlight.

Lady Issa stopped where the rill met the wood. A statue of a Grecian robed woman poured water endlessly from an upturned pitcher. The spaniel lapped thirstily at the cascading water and took a half-hearted lunge at the nearest duck, which cackled contemptuously and strolled away.

'My husband designed the statue and the engineering for the flow of water. He is fascinated by science and mechanisms. This water originates from a lake higher in these western woods and flows down here underground, then rises to the pitcher under gravity because of the difference in height. In turn the water refreshes the moat, as there is a slight current which prevents it becoming stagnant. It is assisted by a bubbling well below this statue. We think water has always risen from this point.'

Lady Issa chuckled gently. She had a low melodic laugh.

'The whole family doubted Jarn's idea would work. But Jarn was right, yet again. Fortunately for all of us, he is occasionally very wrong, otherwise he would be completely insufferable.'

As we walked along the edge of the woodland she pointed in the direction of the beacon, rising in the distance above the stable block.

'There is another lake in the woods near the beacon, which is higher than the one on this side, and Jarn used the power from that to generate our electricity, back in Victorian times. He was one of the first to do that, and so Termonn was one of the earliest houses in the country to have electric lighting. It was amazing, at the time. The turbine has been replaced twice but it failed not long after Jarn vanished, and I do not like to replace it myself. He will know what to install when he returns.'

I smiled at her. Her invariable use of the present tense in relation to a husband she had not seen for over forty years was rather endearing. I was starting to hope very much that it was justified.

We made our way back towards the south side of the

house, the stable block and the laundry room I had observed earlier, from my room. The wide gravelled patio and path on this side was a homely area, the golden stone warm and welcoming, hanging baskets of summer flowers cascading over the walls in brilliant splashes of colour. A large wooden seat was set against the wall of the house outside the kitchen windows, to make the most of the south-facing aspect, and Lady Issa gestured for me to sit, sitting down next to me with her face turned up to the sun. Kimi flopped down and stretched out to grab a quick doze, tongue lolling.

'So, Clare, I am curious to know what you were thinking as you approached our house in the car yesterday. Do you remember how you felt?'

I knew, immediately, that this related somehow to the overwhelming sense of *déjà vu* I had experienced. I felt a deep desire to protect this quirk of mine, remembering my mother's urging that I should not reveal it to anyone.

'In what way, Lady Issa?'

'Anything unusual? Noteworthy?'

'Not really, I...' I was floundering and I knew she could see it.

'Very well, then. So, let us leave for a while what you felt. What did your eyes see? Tell me what you saw of the house and the grounds?'

I cast my mind back, not sure that it was wise to do so. Lady Issa's deep blue eyes seemed to see a long way below the surface.

'There was the house with the moat, in the valley, and the pastures and woodland beyond, and the driveways forming a cross. I could see the tower and the beacon, and the rill, although I didn't notice the statue as we arrived.'

'Yes?' An encouraging nod.

'And I felt that there was something behind me. Well, the old gates were, of course. They are on the same line as the drive we came down. On the path to the house.'

Another approving nod. 'What did the path you were driving down look like, Clare, can you remember?'

I contemplated saying it was just a gravelled driveway, unremarkable and normal. But I knew this was not going to satisfy Lady Issa. Somehow, she knew what I had seen. And I wanted answers to the mysteries surrounding the house and, I now suspected, myself.

I took the plunge.

'The driveway was a golden track leading from where the car was, where I was, through the house - it shone as well - and then up to the beacon hill on the other side. Although the path was more golden on my side of the house, it was a more muted gold on the other side, the beacon side.'

There was a spark in Issa's eyes now. 'And what, Clare, did you experience when you saw this golden road and my shining house?'

I felt the truth dragged out of me.

'I saw you, Lady Issa. And I saw the rooms and I knew them. The fabrics and the feel of the house, and its scents. They were all familiar. Even though I hadn't visited before.'

I stopped, but knew I had to go on. Golden beams were again glimmering around me, and there was a truth here that deeply mattered if I could just grasp it. Moments passed, while Lady Issa looked at me calmly.

'And I felt it was... home.'

My voice caught on the last word and tears threatened my eyes. I blinked to stop them falling, looking up to the cascading flowers in the hanging baskets. It had been such a long while since I had felt truly at home anywhere, for years burying myself in my studies to avoid my past. This mattered to me, more than I could understand.

Lady Issa transfixed me with her gaze. After what seemed years, she spoke, her expression compassionate and as golden as her house.

'Then welcome home, child.'

CHAPTER 7
CLARE, TERMONN HOUSE,
4TH – 5TH JULY 2022

I dined that night with Issa and the fair-haired girl I had seen collecting laundry that morning. She was introduced as Sylvie, and she was indeed Issa's daughter. With their blonde hair, they looked very similar, although Sylvie's was silver-blonde, and Issa's was golden. Someone called Fizz (had I heard this correctly?) should apparently have joined us but was working in the restaurant in the village of Michaelcombe this evening, having been begged to replace a waitress who had called in sick.

There were undercurrents, happy and loving ones, between mother and daughter, with conversation about renovations needed to the estate and farm buildings, the goings-on in the village of Michaelcombe, and Sylvie's planned return to college in Oxford in the autumn. Although they were careful to draw me into their conversation, I found my attention wandering. After the experiences of the day, including more internet searching to try to understand the sketches better, and my endless musings on my strange connection to this house, I was too tired to think. Instead, I found myself drifting away, wondering again and again about the missing David, what had happened to him and where he was. He was deep in my thoughts for reasons I could not understand.

Giving up, I made my excuses not long after dinner and retreated to my beautiful room which already felt like home. The unknown David's room. I looked out of my window and up to the beacon on the summit. In the moonlight it glowed gilded silver and I suddenly found myself very tempted to go for a late evening walk. I was about to head out when a gentle knock announced the arrival of a night-time drink.

I opened the door to a middle-aged woman I had seen in the distance during today's tour of the grounds. Hettie had told me later in the afternoon, in a foray I had made to her kitchen, that this lady was Maya, and she was voiceless. The dignified face that regarded me appeared to be of Australian aboriginal origin, with dark eyes and a broad nose and cheekbones. A scar slashed across from her brow down to her chin, and there were more tangled scars around her neck. She lowered the tray she carried to the carpet just inside the door and withdrew with a respectful nod.

I saw with glee but also some trepidation that it held a hot chocolate pot and a few delicious buttery biscuits. At this rate, I would have to start eating salad once I returned to my flat in London. The thought of going back to my cold flat was oddly dispiriting, and not just because of the prospect of an endless salad diet.

Putting it out of my mind I sent a quick update email to Sir Edward, saying I thought I was making some progress but was still working on the solution, and then snuggled between crisp linen sheets. I slept for a solid ten hours.

The following morning my breakfast tray was brought again by Hettie, this time accompanied by an invitation to a tour of the house with Sylvie. Stuffed with the usual rolls and jam and coffee, I duly appeared in the hall at 10.30, the suggested time.

Sylvie bounced in a few minutes late, dragging behind her the girl I had seen kneading dough in the kitchen the previous day.

'This is Fizzah,' Sylvie announced, with a gesture to the girl who was clearly her friend. 'She came here after the war, but we've both been away for some years studying in the USA. Hettie is trying to get Fizz back into cooking – she's forgotten *everything*. The only thing she can cook now is curries. And even those aren't great.'

They grinned at each other.

Which war, I thought? In this family, with a history back to Victoria and perhaps beyond, many wars were possible candidates.

Sylvie saw my unspoken question and smiled.

'World War Two, or two years after, actually, in 1947. My father was in Delhi with Lord Mountbatten when he was Viceroy of India, and the partition of India was being planned. Of course, he had been with Mountbatten earlier in the war, in something called Combined Operations. They were a combination of commandos and raiders. Suited Daddy perfectly!'

Just how old were the members of this extraordinary family? I desperately wanted to ask but held back. We had only just met. Hopefully they would tell me at some point.

We moved towards the kitchen, where Sylvie and Fizzah wheedled biscuits for us out of Maya, who was on duty today at the range. The scarred woman smiled silently and handed over three freshly baked chocolate chip cookies from a tray. We headed back towards the hall, munching, and Sylvie continued.

'There were massacres of all religions in India then, but in Delhi the atrocities were especially against Muslims, and Fizz's family were caught up in it. Father was on the streets one night and he was able to rescue quite a few people from the mobs, including Fizz. But then Fizz found herself with no home and no family left alive after that night, so she came back to England with him late in 1947, when we met for the first time. She's been here ever since. Except when we have been travelling, of course.'

A warm kiss was placed on Fizz's cheek, and in return Fizz glowed at Sylvie and put a gentle arm around her waist. This relationship was more than mere friendship. The personalities of the two were so distinct, the one fair, bouncing and effervescent, the other dark, quiet and demure, and it was transparent how much they complemented each other. I found myself grinning at the pair of them and they smiled happily back at me.

Our tour of the house started in the hall. There were paintings, ivory inlaid cabinets and the flying cantilevered staircase, which was apparently one of the wonders of English houses of this period, being supported only by the strength of the walls. We looked into the drawing room, where Sir Edward, Philip and myself had had our first meeting with Lady Issa just two days ago. Here there was a collection of Russian icons, two Chinese medicine dolls, eighteenth and nineteenth century English portraits and a Landseer of a Scottish landscape over the magnificent fireplace. Between the drawing room and the kitchen was the dining room, with its cabinets of early Minton and Worcester porcelain, mingled with some Sevres. There was the usual eclectic assortment of paintings on the walls but the room was dominated by a magnificent oriental mahogany dining table with a matching set of twelve beautifully carved chairs.

I was fascinated by every detail and was struggling to commit all I saw to memory, thinking how much my friends at Oxford's Ashmolean museum would love this and whether I could arrange for private viewings.

We finally arrived in the west-facing study, adjacent to the kitchen.

This spacious room had an enormous desk, club chairs, and huge floor-to-ceiling bookcases. It was clearly the operational centre for the management of the estate. The estate manager was in the room, poring over papers that looked like spreadsheets, consulting against his laptop. Greying-haired and genial, he was introduced to me as Adam Simpson, and he welcomed us cheerily but said he needed more coffee and some fresh air before he tackled any more finances as they were driving him to distraction. He headed for the kitchen, with his empty mug and the air of a man with caffeine needs unmet.

Once he had left, Sylvie and Fizz plonked themselves down on leather chairs – to be precise, Sylvie plonked and Fizz perched with graceful decorum – and gestured to me to also seat myself.

'Adam has been managing the estate for nearly thirty years,' Sylvie told me. 'We have tenant farms and also tenanted cottages in Michaelcombe. Adam grew up in one of the farms. I remember the night he was born, in a huge snowstorm, back in the 1960's.'

'And your father went out in a tractor to get the midwife,' Fizz reminisced.

Sylvie nodded. 'On the way, Father dropped Mother at Adam's parents' cottage and it was Mother who delivered

Adam. She's delivered lots of babies over the years. The midwife arrived at last, to find them all having a cup of tea and Adam in his cot. Anyway, Mother supported him through agricultural college in the eighties, and then he came back here and gradually took over the estate management. But it was awful in 2001 when his wife, Mary, had their twins and then died just two days later of a sudden haemorrhage. The whole village went to the funeral.'

Fizz added, 'the estate is like a family, Clare. All the houses in Michaelcombe are part of it, and very little has changed since the Dechar family arrived here. Many decades ago, far ahead of the time, the lord and lady set up the Termonn Foundation to provide funding and support for local people, so they can rent or buy properties on the estate and also locally, more easily. So, people tend not to leave, and often the children return here as well, to take over cottages that have become vacant. Some of the bigger properties have been split so there is more accommodation. With property prices so high now, the scheme has been really important and the whole community has benefitted. But the lady and Adam have recently developed new businesses and cottage industries. We have a pub with a restaurant, which is really successful. And a farm shop.'

'And,' Sylvie chipped in, 'there are Mother's ceramics. Her pottery is very sought after, and she's had exhibitions. Her shop in the village attracts tourists, and it is near the pub as well, so double the trade. We have a woodturner and a stonemason as well, and the village stores.'

'Don't they wonder about how long you all live?' I was surprised no-one had written a piece for a tabloid paper by now.

'No-one has said anything yet!' Sylvie said cheerfully. 'And the sense of community and also, I think, appreciation for the support the whole village receives from Termonn, means that anyone saying anything publicly would probably find themselves ostracised. They wouldn't be very popular.'

Sylvie gestured round the room.

'Anyway, this is the office from which Father would run the estate, and most of the rest of the country as well', she said, and I suspected she was only partly joking. 'I used to come in here when I was little, and he would lift me up to show me the maps,' she pointed to the huge, framed maps of the estate, the county, the country and several larger maps of different parts of the world that covered the walls of the office.

'He would show me where he had been, in the earlier days by himself and in the later years with Mother. And he would tell me tales of all those travels, the people, the sights, and most of all the adventures. He would often produce from his pocket an object he had acquired from somewhere; something that would be a focus for the day's story. It made me long to go myself.'

'He is a good man, a kind man', Fizz interjected quietly. 'He knew I was different, that I had a little of his nature, and that I had been tormented for it by my community, although my family tried to understand me. When they were murdered...,' Fizz looked to Sylvie as her voice trembled and Sylvie took her hand and squeezed it, 'and the mob came for me that night, he saved me. I owe him a debt I can never repay.'

Again, I noticed the use of the present tense.

Still holding Fizz's hand, Sylvie turned to me.

'Fizz is like us, you see, Clare. She can see other worlds. And we are matched, Fizz and me. We both have names which mean silver, because of our talents. Well...,' with a fond look at Fizz, '...her name means silver and mine just sounds like it. But since we have been together our abilities have grown so much, we can now see and do things we never envisaged before. We are a true pair, so very lucky to find each other.'

They exchanged loving glances. I couldn't help but grin back at them, reminded of what Lady Issa had said to Sir Edward, about the strengthening of bonds once true mates were paired. But my confusion remained. Other worlds?

So I asked the obvious question. 'Do you mean different planets? I know scientists have found planets like earth light years away, but...'

'No, when we say other worlds, we mean other versions of our own world,' Fizz had a gentle expression which suggested she knew this would be difficult for me to comprehend. And indeed, I was aware I was looking at her blankly.

Sylvie took up the story, with a light hand on my arm.

'It is hard to explain, Clare, but there are so many different versions of this world, our world. So many things, so many choices, can happen through history to alter the way a world develops. A different world is created from even a small change, like someone being split between the choice of going out one day or staying inside. Some are really minor, but each choice creates a new reality, or as we say, a new world. It is like a fork – perhaps the person went outside and met someone important, or they stayed inside and created a new book, or a different social system. Or perhaps they had an influence on someone who would be important to the future. Some choices, some decisions, are really tiny or unimportant and my father says the worlds they create almost always re-coalesce into a single world a bit later on. But all the really big changes create more worlds than it is possible to imagine, millions and millions. And each one leads to more millions. Eventually, most are far removed from ours, very different indeed. It is like an enormous tree with many branches, all leading to even more branches.'

'But you, your family, know they are there?' I was truly perplexed.

Sylvie nodded. 'Yes. And we can do more than that, Clare, we can visit them.'

'How is that even possible?' By now, I was tumbling down Alice's rabbit hole, my worldview wobbling.

'Well, in general, we travel to them via something we call the void. But it is perhaps best if Mother explains that to you.'

Yes, I would certainly ask Lady Issa. But I had one other question. No, to be frank I had many, but just one was burning.

'Sylvie,' I asked, tentatively, 'when you say 'like us', what do you mean? In what way am I like you? Like Fizz? I can see that you two are alike. But me?'

And, I thought, I had seen gold, but why was silver important to Sylvie and Fizz?

I could see Sylvie thinking before she responded.

'We are certain you are of the same race as Fizz and I, Clare. But perhaps again, it is best if Mother explains it?'

CHAPTER 8
CLARE, TERMONN HOUSE,
5TH JULY 2022

Issa met me in the hall after lunch and regarded me with her clear blue gaze. After my morning with Sylvie and Fizz, I suspected I still had the wide eyes of a gazelle caught in a hunter's' sight, but there was no avoiding the look that transfixed me and I knew I was about to learn even more. My desire to discover my own nature was now at war with a reluctance to learn how different the world was to the one I thought I knew.

And, sure enough, Issa went immediately to the key issue. Her gaze was unavoidable but also, somehow, caring.

'Clare, your description of yesterday, when you approached the house, suggests to me that you possess abilities like mine and my family's. These are rare, and it would be a shame not to develop them.'

She broke off to issue a reprimand to her dog, who was yipping at the retreating mail van, clearly desperate to chase it off the premises. The reproof had no effect whatsoever on Kimi, she simply returned to monitoring the grounds from a window seat with the occasional grumbling yap.

Issa sighed and returned her gaze to me.

'If you are willing, I would like to introduce you to some of the ways in which we make use of our unusual talents. They may help us with Sir Edward's problem, and perhaps with other things as well. But training is important, and I suspect you have received none so far. It may help you to understand your... heritage?'

A way to understanding my past? A door to the future? Could I face it?

After a few moments of wavering between eagerness and apprehension, I nodded gamely. My questions were bubbling, after the revelations of Sylvie and Fizz.

'Very good!' Issa beamed at me. 'I think the drawing room will do well for our first lesson.'

We entered the bright, peaceful room with its view of St Michael's tower. Kimi was not far behind and darted into the room just before Issa closed the door. She gave another gentle word of reproof to her dog, who again completely ignored her and curled up in her basket in the sunshine to watch proceedings.

Issa laughed.

'Kimi is a Tibetan spaniel. They are intelligent but fiercely independent. She only follows commands if she believes they were her idea in the first place, rather than ours. Having a Tibbie as a pet is a constant battle of wills. Every day, Kimi and I joust for supremacy. I am sorry to admit, she often wins.'

She then turned her gaze fully on me, as I swallowed my apprehension. I suspected the dog had more independence of will than I did when faced with this implacable woman.

'Now Clare, I need to ask you a few questions. I do know something of your ability, but more information is always useful.'

We sat down at the mahogany table, and she smiled at me encouragingly.

'Firstly, have you ever been aware of moving without intending to? For example, have you ever found yourself suddenly a few steps further on, or perhaps you have vanished for a second or two and then reappeared?'

I had actually experienced both. I didn't want to lie but struggled with the complete truth, my mother's warnings were too deeply imprinted. So, I hedged.

'I've sometimes felt my surroundings had changed, that they felt different somehow, as if I was in an unfamiliar place, even if everything looked exactly the same. It's difficult to explain.'

Impossible to explain. How could things be identical and yet different? But I knew what I had felt and it seemed Issa knew the sensation as well, as she nodded comfortingly.

'That is called *jamais vu*, Clare, and it is the opposite of *déjà vu* in some ways; the experience of feeling unfamiliar with something that is very familiar to you.'

I felt reassured, and able to continue.

'And I have had moments of *déjà vu*, which my mother said were a kind of dream and it was best to ignore them. Certainly, never to talk about them. She seemed quite frightened. I think she had experienced the same but was scared of it. I know she understood what I meant.'

'Yes, that is very likely. Talents run in families, typically from father to son and from mother to daughter. Your grandmother was probably the same.'

My recollections of my maternal grandmother were painful. Endless instructions and criticisms and arguments. She was impossible to please. No hint of *déjà vu* with her, I thought, casting my mind back over the years.

I said as much to Issa.

'That is sad, but it also explains some things, perhaps.' I felt Issa's gaze on me, curious but without any judgement.

'To not train one such as yourself is a serious dereliction of duty. But it is possible that your grandmother did not have the ability to train her own daughter, and then in turn your mother was unable to train you. I am sorry, Clare. It must have been very difficult for you.' I felt the warm waft of her sympathy and understanding.

Then she paused and said, reflectively, 'so it seems it is possible that your abilities came down in the male line, from your grandfather to your mother and then to you.'

'I have no idea who my grandfather was, my mother didn't know.' Then I added, with some reluctance, as it was so personal, 'I don't know anything about my father, either.'

Issa nodded understandingly. I thought it would take a lot to shock her, and she would not be one to easily pass any criticism either. But I cast my eyes downwards. There were other memories I couldn't bring myself to share and my connection to Termonn – the house I already thought of as home - was already far too important for me to risk. Silence was best.

There was a pause before Issa continued.

'But, in any case, what you have described is a short shift between realities, Clare. When your surroundings look identical but feel different, it happens because for a few seconds you are close to a nearby world. One almost like this but just slightly different, perhaps due to some recent alternative history. You would have maintained a physical body in this world, so no-one would have seen you disappear, fortunately. When a talent such as yours is completely uncontrolled it can lead to vanishings or rapid unexplained movements, and in the old days you would have been called a witch.'

Lady Issa's gaze was on the lovely view from the windows, but I sensed she was seeing a different scene and not a pleasant one. For a moment her golden hair obscured her face.

'Your *déjà vu* is similar,' Issa said, as she returned her attention to me. 'But that is more concerned with ripples in time and space. The threads of the universe are linked together, with... well, a mesh of fibres and strands is perhaps the best way to think of it. Every event in both space and time, even one as simple as us having coffee yesterday morning, is tied to a multitude of others, in a host of different versions of our world, and in different times as well.'

Different versions of this world, due to alternative decisions, rippling through the fabric of space and time? It triggered a memory of something I had read long ago, a new theory of physics, of a multitude of universes, which had seemed to me to border on fiction.

I thought quietly for moments and then ventured, 'Sylvie and Fizz told me yesterday that worlds are created from different choices. That people like us can go to these different worlds. That you travel by something called the void. And now, you say there is a fabric connecting everything. I've read something about this in science papers, but it's hard to understand it in real life.' And that, I thought, was an incredible understatement.

Lady Issa could see me struggling to understand. 'It is, Clare. And there is so much more. You are only at the beginning.'

She looked at my wrist as it lay on the table and put a gentle finger on my watch.

'This watch, for example. Let's say it was given to you on your eighteenth birthday. There are strands, created just because of that gift, linking every use you make of the watch back to the day you were given it. And you will use it tomorrow and next week and next year, so the strands continue into the future as well. Even this little watch will create a ripple across future times, probably small and affecting nothing of significance, but the effect will still be there. And that is one tiny example. The fibres of everything actually connect to everything else.'

Seeing me still bemused, she bit her lip thoughtfully and tried again.

'Perhaps, a different example.' Lady Issa reached to the table behind her and picked up a small object which she offered me on her palm. I took it up, at her nod, and examined it. It was a one Mil coin from Palestine, dated 1942.

'Think of this coin's story, Clare, if it could speak. It is made of metals, which all have their own history. Then they were smelted and this coin was made, perhaps as warfare raged around it. It found its way from pocket to pocket, and from merchant to merchant. Maybe it was in the hand of an old man with his own story, maybe it was given to a child by her mother to buy bread. At some point it was taken by my husband during his war service and so it found its way to this house where it has rested ever since. How many strands are interwoven, just in this little battered coin? And even today, the old strands rub against each other and against the new ones we have just created today. This little coin now has links with you, and your past. And your future.'

I produced what was probably a wobbly smile. It seemed to me that if I could truly understand this, insanity would likely follow quite quickly. Issa perceived my thought and laughed.

'It will become easier, Clare! But to return to your *déjà vu.* These fibres jostle and shift constantly through the fabric of creation and of course like all fibres and fabrics they criss-cross and brush against each other. You have a talent for feeling fibres when they touch and cross in your vicinity. It is why you knew this house without ever having been here before. Your future fibres entangled briefly with your present ones, and you were able to perceive the mixing of the threads and see along the different strands. Most people do not have such sensitivity.'

Lady Issa picked up a silver letter opener and fingered it absent-mindedly. I could see it was engraved but too faintly to make out the lettering.

'It is hard to explain but with training your senses will develop, and it will become more familiar to you. Eventually, if all goes well, you will see the fibres clearly and will be able to use them to your advantage.'

'Now, your talent, child, is rather different to mine when I was young. I have always been able to shift in space, although I could not control it for many years. But I did not know, until Jarn showed me what to do, that I could shift readily between worlds as well. I would like us to practice a little of both of those.'

She noticed my apprehension and put her hand gently on my arm.

'Do not be alarmed, I will move with you and help you, you will not get lost. This is only a very simple 'nursery' lesson. All my children did it when they were small.'

Issa was so maternal, it was impossible to do anything other than nod, trustingly. I also desperately wanted to know what I could do.

'So, there are two very tiny shifts that you will find can be very useful. The movements are quite similar. In the first, you do a little shift-step and by focussing on a different spot and pulling the fibres around you to that spot you will move instantly to the new location. Shall we try that?'

I was far from sure but nodded.

Issa stood and beckoned me to the window, from where we could see the tower in the distance. She stood in front of me and took both of my hands in hers. 'Just relax, Clare, and let your mind be empty. You need to do nothing, just be aware of the sensations.'

As she gazed into my eyes, the blue of them startlingly intense, I felt a new awareness creep across me, bringing glimpses of perceptions and knowledge I had only had inklings of before. There were indeed strands of gold shifting and rippling around me. A network, like a golden mesh. Mesmerised by the swirling glistening fibres, I felt the urge to reach out and touch them, to play with them.

Issa pressed my hands to bring my attention back to her. She was smiling.

'Be still, child, it is not playtime yet. We are going to move to the fireplace. Look at the golden lines shimmering around it. You see the lines? Yes? Now, use the fibres between you and those strands, can you see them as well? Good. Reach for them, gently. And now ... we move.'

I don't think it was a movement under my own control, the control was from Issa, but I felt the lines spinning past me as I grasped the fibres that lay in between. A fraction of a second later, lines and fibres vanished, the room was back to normal and Issa was watching me proudly.

'Well done, Clare, that was excellent for a first attempt.'

I was puzzled. What had I done to warrant praise? Then I realised that we were no longer in front of the window and that the fireplace was within reach of my arm. We had moved over ten feet without a single step. The room spun around me.

Issa pushed me gently into one of the fireside chairs, and chuckled. 'I should have warned you it can be a little disorienting until you get used to it. I apologise!'

'Lady Issa, was it you or me that did that?' I was looking round me in semi-disbelief.

'It was mostly me, this time, but you now understand the sensation of the move, and with practice you will be able to do it entirely by yourself. But I must warn you, Clare, to not attempt it without me being present. It is too easy to be swept too far, in both time and space, and you do not have control yet. I could feel you wanting to play with the strands, and it is a temptation you absolutely must resist. We have only just found you and we don't want you to wander off to Argentina or New Zealand unintentionally, lovely as those countries are.'

Issa let me rest for a few minutes, looking between me, the fireplace and Kimi.

My gaze fell on the silver framed picture she had touched the day I arrived at Termonn. A man and a woman, in clothing from the 1940's. The elegant woman was clearly Issa, the tall man with his arm around her shoulders and his face closer to hers than would be expected from a portrait of that time, must be her husband. Older than her and darkly handsome, with features strongly hewn. Jarn, surely.

Then Issa spoke, recalling me to our session.

'The second lesson is an equally tiny move but for this one you shift very slightly from this world into a transitional place between this world and a nearby world, one which is almost identical but just different in a very minor way. Such a world may have been created, perhaps, because someone nearby took a slightly differing decision the night before which influenced the future enough for the world to split into two.'

I was pretty much lost by this point but nodded.

'You will find it is possible to step into this place between worlds. You will have a presence in both of them but your physical body is in neither, but is instead in-between, next to something we call the void. This means that you will still be able to view the world you have just stepped out of, but the people in that world will not be able to see you, and anyone in the adjacent world will not see you either. It is a rather neat and useful trick. Jarn is especially adept at it, and over the centuries it has greatly assisted his, shall we say, information gathering. Being invisible is a very useful attribute for someone who wishes to spy. Of course, if you step a little too far you will shift into the other world completely and would then need to make your way back. I will come with you and, if that happens, I will bring you home. Shall we try it?'

NO, absolutely not, never, not ever, I thought. A meek 'yes' came out of my mouth.

'So, Jarn's little vanishing trick. I will do this for you, all you need to do is to try to sense what I am doing so you will be able to try it yourself at some point.'

Issa pulled the embroidered bellpull next to the fireplace and then stood in front of me, again holding my hands. Once again, fibres shone gold, weaving about me. This time I felt an awareness of multiple sets of fibres, interwoven between layer upon layer of strands. The layers were not flat but somehow, in a way I could not explain, they felt multidimensional. I was even more enraptured by the perception of this, somehow knowing that each layer led to a new world. It felt as if this was something I had always know was there but had never seen before. Now I felt us moving towards one set in particular and I reached for it, tantalised and itching to clutch it, but to my disappointment we stopped just short.

I found myself looking into two alternative drawing rooms, one apparently to the left and one to the right, although in my mind there was no longer any true sense of direction. Both rooms looked identical. Until I noticed the room to the right was darker, storm clouds approaching from the east.

To my left I could see, through the golden fibres surrounding us, that the door to the hall was opening. Hettie came in, responding to Issa's pull on the bell. She stopped in puzzlement and looked around her. After a few moments she shrugged and left the room. Issa's arm was reassuringly tight around me, one hand still on mine, gently suppressing my twitching fingers.

But as I watched, my perception of the universe suddenly and utterly unexpectedly exploded beyond the confines of anything I had previously felt. It was as if a world previously seen through a thick lens had suddenly burst into sharpness and colour, and in a million dimensions at once. I gasped, and Issa's hands tightened on mine, her arm gripping me close.

I felt us move back to the original set of fibres, and then slowly the golden glimmer of them faded from sight. I was left in the sunlit room, Issa still holding my hands, with not a fibre visible. I felt strangely bereft in their absence. And exhausted.

'Once again, Clare, you did well. It was me controlling our move, although I know what you saw and the control you were aware of. But most importantly, I could see your understanding blossom, which often happens when an inexperienced one such as yourself steps for the first time.'

Issa's hands gripped mine, warmly, and they felt a lifeline. 'You will become more adept, and eventually you will be able to move yourself, and also objects, from one reality to another, or into the void. But this is another trick you must only try when I am with you, do you understand?'

I nodded, as a child to their mother, feeling more tired than I had ever felt before but full to the brim with elation. I was increasingly a part of this house and family, with talents of my own that could now be developed. And my strange childhood and adolescence were slowly starting to make some sense. I no longer felt so alone. I had seen different worlds. My perception of time was not unique to me alone. And I *belonged* to this strange race. My understanding of reality had altered.

Forever.

'And now', Issa said, gently prising her hand from mine - I suddenly realised I had been clutching it probably quite painfully - 'I must go and make my apologies to Hettie for her wasted trip from the kitchen. I think that for you it is bedtime, child.'

She pushed me gently out of the room and towards the stairs, waiting at the foot until she saw I was safely back in my bedroom.

I walked across the floor to my bed in a daze and fell deeply asleep, in a hazy contentment.

After what seemed minutes but had actually been more than two hours, I stirred to gentle knocking on my door. Swinging my feet to the carpet, I suppressed a slight giddiness and moved to the door. Hettie was outside.

'I am sorry to disturb you, madam, but you have a visitor.'

Me, I thought, a visitor? Here? Who knows I'm here?

'Is it Sir Edward, Hettie?' I whirled to make myself presentable, grabbing the hairbrush.

'No, it is Dr Reardon, the one who was here with you when you first arrived. He says he needs to see you.'

Philip. My heart sank.

I followed Hettie out of my room and descended the stairs. It was indeed Philip standing in the hall. At his feet were bags, and I could see that on the top were a light coat from my wardrobe, summer sandals and my jogging trainers. I had requested just about my entire wardrobe from Sir Edward.

'Clare.'

Philip moved towards me with a smile. 'Sir Edward received your message and asked me to bring the things you needed.' I felt this was likely to be incomplete, as truths go. I suspected that Philip had bludgeoned his way into the role of delivery man.

'Also,' Philip moved closer and spoke low in my ear, his breath on my cheek, 'there are things I need to tell you. Is there somewhere we can walk, away from eavesdroppers?'

A wave of resentment washed over me at the thought of my new friends, my new family, being regarded as spies, but I swallowed it down. Perhaps Philip did indeed have useful information. I should listen.

I gestured towards the kitchen and Philip followed me. Hettie went past me as we walked through the hall. 'We will take your luggage to your room, madam.'

Philip raised an eyebrow as we walked through the kitchen to the stable door.

'Madam? Good grief, who on earth do they think you are?'

'It is just how they address guests, Philip, they are very polite,' I replied shortly and ignored his sniff of disdain.

I led him out the stable door and we turned left towards the archway, but instead of going left again to the path along the east front I led him to the right, past the outbuildings of the courtyard. For the first time I walked beyond them. The path led past a walled garden towards a gate, and once through that we were on the track up the slope towards the fire beacon.

'Clare, I have been investigating some of the history of this family, and there is something truly odd about them. I am finding it hard to believe. Perhaps there are generations with the same names, some aristocratic families seem to reuse names repeatedly, but if not, they would seem to be *extraordinarily* long-lived.'

Philip looked at me, inviting me to laugh with him, encouraging confidences. I gazed back, eyebrows raised disbelievingly, and said nothing.

'Do you know what happened to this family back in the 1970's?'

'Not really.'

Between what Issa had said to Sir Edward, and what Hettie had told me, I thought I had grasped the basic facts, but I wasn't telling Philip that.

I could tell he was pleased by my ignorance.

'Well, I have been looking at the event in 1977 that led to Lord Dechar's disappearance. I find it hard to believe he vanished so long ago, as his wife superficially appears quite young. But perhaps it is possible and maybe she is older than she seems or was very young when they were married. Anyway, the event was very odd. There's been a massive amount of research on the incident since. All *very* classified, of course.'

Now he looked smug, knowing he had seen material I was not privy to.

I looked hard at him but resisted the urge to ask. I knew he wouldn't be able to resist telling me anyway. And indeed, he carried on talking.

'There was a serious event involving a nuclear armed plane. A key part of our deterrent capability at that time. For some reason, Dechar was there, on that day, talking to the commander of the airbase. No idea why. He wasn't military. Not qualified in any way, as far I can tell, and he must have been a young man back then. Some parts of the records will remain classified for decades, but I can't imagine that anything in them could relate to someone as unimportant as Dechar.'

But shrugging his shoulders and dismissing the oddity, Philip carried on.

'Anyway, there was a lightning strike on the weapon plane itself, and of course all the ground crew were terrified the missile would explode if it was a direct hit. You won't understand, Clare, but these missiles are partially primed before the plane even takes off, so there is some vulnerability. But initially it seemed the bolt had just missed the central weapon housing with no apparent harm done.'

'When the commander went to the plane, with Dechar apparently tagging along behind him, the technicians were already there, and they could see that the lightning had actually done substantial damage to the weapon surround. Three of the four security switches had been triggered and the mechanism appeared close to detonating. So, the commander gave the order to evacuate the area. A detonation would destroy the base and contaminate the surrounding countryside to hundreds of kilometres. I know you won't be able to comprehend the potential, but it would have been catastrophic for the UK.'

I gritted my teeth.

'Anyway, everyone but Dechar obeyed. For some reason he stayed behind, not noticed in the general confusion. I presume he was simply unable to understand the danger or was too slow to move. But only a minute later there was another flash of lightning and, well, they say it never strikes twice in the same place but this one seemed to. Direct energisation of the air around the plane.'

'He died?' My heart missed beats.

'Who knows? When the technicians ran back, there was no more damage to the plane, but there was also no one anywhere nearby. Everything had gone.'

'Everything had gone? What do you mean?'

'Dechar wasn't there but even more astonishingly, neither was the weapon. Just some twisted metal.'

'How could that happen?'

After my lesson with Issa, and her mention of my eventually being able to move objects from one reality to another, or into the void, I actually had some idea. But I wanted to know what Philip thought.

'Well, to this day it is one of the most mysterious and most secret of the events of the last century. The weapon and its housing had vanished from the plane. There were the scorch marks, far more than would have been consistent with just a strike of lightning. There was some residual radiation of an odd signature which indicates the start of a nuclear detonation. But there was no weapon, and no Dechar.'

'And the key point is the weapons experts say that the control system of the WE177 bomb was designed to be as foolproof as possible. While it is plausible, apparently, that the last lightning bolt could have been enough to trip the final switch, it is almost unimaginable that the first bolt could have affected all three of the other switches, and - in addition to that - triggered them all in the right, the only possible, sequence. There were many fail-safes in the system.'

'What are you saying, Philip?'

'Just that whatever led to Dechar's disappearance doesn't appear to have been bad luck. The opinion of weapons experts is that it is virtually impossible. No, it looks to have been deliberate sabotage. As if the weapon was primed to explode by an electronic trip, like the first lightning strike, and would then actually explode if there was a further trip. In this case, the second bolt of lightning.'

I thought for a few moments as we approached the beacon. The grass here was less trimmed, although there were still some sheep grazing. It moved wavelike, rippling in the sun. Beyond the summit the land fell away, to a magnificent view of the pastoral landscape of the Cotswolds. Far below me were old golden stone buildings, as much a part of the landscape as Termonn was. It would have been beautiful if my mind had not been on what Philip had just said.

'Surely no country has the technology to prime a weapon's switches in that way, even now. Still less decades ago.'

'I don't know, Clare. I'm just warning you to be aware, and to keep your ears open. Anything on that matter could be very useful to m...' Philip stopped himself and then restarted '... could be of great interest to us. I would also like, or to be precise, Sir Edward would like, any more information you can find on Dechar. He seems to have been valued by UK government and I have no idea why. What expertise could an English lord and landowner possibly possess?'

Philip laughed dismissively. But I was thinking back to Sir Edward's words in the car and in the drawing room when we arrived at Termonn House two days previously. It seemed to me very likely that Sir Edward already knew a considerable amount about this family and far more than Philip. Philip was just frustrated he had not been more thoroughly briefed and his lack of knowledge was irritating him. He was hoping I would fill in the gaps behind Sir Edward's back.

My brow creased as I looked over the rolling land in front of us, and down to the far distant buildings glowing in the afternoon sun.

'We should tell Lady Issa about the accident being possible sabotage. That could be important in her search for her husband.'

'No! That would *not* be wise. You may have developed a certain attachment to the family, it is only to be expected now you are in the house and they are apparently being friendly, but we don't know what role they played in Dechar's disappearance. Best to say nothing. Remember how important this may be to our country, to its defence.'

But now, after just two short days, I knew without any doubt where my loyalties lay. I led Philip back down the track to his car, chattering inanely of anything that came into my mind. I even accepted a peck on the cheek as he got back into his car for the return drive to London and managed to be non-committal about my own return date, permitting a hint of possibility that we could meet up when I was home. My skin crawled as his car disappeared up the track towards the old gates.

Then I turned on my heels and went to find Issa.

CHAPTER 9
TERMONN 1979

'David has searched and searched. I have travelled myself, so very far. We have asked, everywhere. We have sent our message out, through gatekeepers and other *gerasi* in many worlds. There has been no sign of him.'

Issa was curled in an armchair in the drawing room, positioned to look over St Michael's tower. Her arms were wrapped tight around her slender body as she shuddered with fatigue and despair after this last voyage through endless worlds.

Hettie felt her own shoulders fall but she instantly raised them again. She would not let her mistress see how crushing the news was. Issa needed her support now.

'There must be hope, madam. Perhaps another search, after a rest?'

Issa's eyes were fixed on the path from St Michael's tower to Termonn, Jarn's own line of immense strength. Inviolable for so long. Useless now. She shivered, her face white, remembering how the path would glow a vibrant, brilliant gold in welcome whenever Jarn returned to the house from some travel or other. She had not seen the line aflame for over two years, not since the cursed mission for government from which Jarn had never returned.

Hettie could see it was taking her mistress an effort to remain in one position. She wanted, needed, to pace the floor, to beat against the walls of her house, and especially against the walls of the fate that had crashed down on Termonn two years ago.

The lady of Termonn turned and looked her house-keeper straight in the eye. 'Hettie, I cannot feel him, there is no sense of him. No trace, no ripples. Nothing.'

Hettie found herself desperately wanting to ask what that meant, whether Jarn Dechar was... dead. She could hardly think it, for a man so masterful, so vibrant and full of life. Lord of their estate, the head of the family. Husband, father. Commander of armies in centuries past. Adviser to emperors, kings and queens. Central not only to Termonn and to the estate village of Michaelcombe but respected by royalty and government alike.

But she couldn't bring herself to ask. Even if she had managed to get the words through her mouth, it would have been the ultimate cruelty to her mistress. All she could usefully do was go to the chair and, kneeling, take Issa's icy hands in hers, rubbing to bring a little warmth.

'I will bring you a little supper, madam, and perhaps a warm brandy?'

Hettie was not sure Issa had heard her.

After an hour of pacing, Issa could stand the confines of her home no longer. She needed to be outside. Without pausing to find a coat, she sped through the kitchen, leaving a concerned Hettie standing frozen by the range and Maya looking after her, uneasy. Issa's steps led her towards the beacon, and then left into the woodland. Now dusk, a chill wind whipped the treetops and a light drizzle was falling.

In a clearing, a giant oak loomed over her, planted by Jarn himself when it was still a sapling over a century before. Under its canopy the ground was still dry. Issa rested her forehead against the bark of his tree, pleading for knowledge but without hope. After minutes, she sank despairingly to the ground. The rain was heavier now, trickling through the canopy as if the huge tree was crying for its planter. Tears were running down Issa's face, echoes of the rain. She watched them fall and thought that clay teardrops would create a porcelain sculpture in her studio if she only had any creative spirit left. It seemed to have fled with Jarn, the man who had with all his strength given her everything.

The world swept on into darkness, realities now spinning around her as the evening mists swirled. Hope splintered, fragments shattering. Ice-cold now, Issa clung to what remained of her strength, searching, questioning.

More time passed, before two lantern lights came swinging through the trees. With gasps of relief, Sylvie and Fizz came running towards her. Wrapping her with rugs, they helped Issa rise unsteadily to her feet. She placed a hand on the bark of the tree, supporting herself as life flowed agonisingly back into her numb limbs. Her head was bent to Jarn's old tree and her thoughts ran on, as they had for hours. Through white lips and in a voice so low the girls had to strain to hear, she whispered: 'I think if he no longer existed anywhere, I would know. And we will search until there are no worlds left to travel to, which will take eternity.'

CHAPTER 10
JARN, 'WASHINGTON', 7TH APRIL 1982

He had stepped just hours ago from a completely different world of sunny beaches and blue skies, where dolphins and fish leapt in the waves. It had been very pleasant, for a week, and it had refreshed his fish spearing skills. But it was not home, and he was no longer sure how to reach home.

After centuries of pinpoint accuracy in his destinations, Jarn had finally been forced to acknowledge that he had no control at all. No matter how desperately he wanted to get back to Termonn, he had been trying for years and every attempt had resulted in a second in the void followed by a spin-off into heaven-knew-where. Despite the reality plainly confronting him, he was still finding it hard to accept. His abilities had always been part of who he was and a chunk of himself now seemed to be missing.

In the early months after the detonation, he had reasoned to himself that it was a consequence of the force behind the explosion, setting something in the void off-kilter. But that explanation had become less convincing over the years, as he had tried again and again to move to his home and had failed every time. Now, after another year of disastrous attempts where he had felt like a drunk in control of a car, knowing exactly where he was going but ending up somewhere completely different, he was growing increasingly wary of his attempts.

He had arrived in this strange world's version of Washington the previous night, finding himself on the edge of a city somewhat familiar to him from visits in earlier decades in his own world. Finding work quickly behind a bar, he listened out for indications of this world's issues. Less than a year before, he had found himself in a reality as close to his own as he had yet managed to get, and had seen that things were not too bad, either in the USA or in Europe. He had comforted himself with the knowledge that it was reasonable to think the same was true in his home world, that his precious family were still safe, before he had tried to move closer to home and had ricocheted far away.

But he knew, deep in his bones, there was something very wrong here. The change in this world was recent but also massive. If Jarn wasn't mistaken, and on such matters he rarely was, it was getting more catastrophic by the minute. He needed to know what was happening.

As he washed glasses, he listened to the conversation at the counter. A glum man was downing beers at a rate faster than advised by any health programme. His companion was equally low-spirited, although with a slightly slower intake.

'It all comes back to last year. Hal, if that lunatic hadn't shot Reagan, none of this would have happened.'

'True, pal. But then, if Bush hadn't been in that helicopter six months later... same outcome, we wouldn't be where we are now.'

'At least we're somewhere at the moment. But according to the TV and the papers, any day now we'll be nowhere –

blasted into particles. What are them in power doing about it? Nothing.'

'Yep. And I guess the papers are only telling us a bit. Scared if they tell us everything, they'll have mass panic on their hands.'

'Give me another beer, Ted. At least it might stop me panicking. Or make us so that we don't know when it all goes up in smoke.'

Yes, Jarn thought, something badly wrong.

He slept in the bar cellar that night, getting up early to head to the city centre. Curious as ever, Jarn wanted to know how things had gone so awry here. This reality had had a huge event, dramatically and recently. But why? When he managed to get home – and Jarn was determined to think it was when, and not if – there might be lessons to learn from this.

He was walking down Independence Avenue near the Capitol when he was staggered to hear his name called. No-one had done that since 1977.

'Dechar? Yes, it's you. For god's sake, stop.'

Jarn spun.

A tall, imposing man in US military uniform was walking up to him.

'Yes, it really is you. Have you been sent by the UK? Thank God. We need a miracle, you're the only person I've ever met on this earth who might be able to do it.'

With shock, Jarn suddenly recognised the man. Bryce Costello. With the military rank of a US colonel. Jarn had met Costello at the time of the Cuban missile crisis, when Jarn himself had been in Washington as an attachment to a UK delegation in 1962. As Jarn recalled, their delegation had been briefed in Washington on the developing Cuban crisis even before the Prime Minister, Macmillan, was aware of it.

So, a colonel. No. Jarn looked at the stars on his uniform and upgraded the man's rank. Four. Costello was now a general, in this world.

'It is good to see you again, General Costello.'

'Good? It's miraculous. Of all the people in the world, to find you, and today.'

The man seemed choked, his voice shaking. Jarn was immediately on edge. The situation must be truly serious to have brought this tough, battle-hardened soldier to the edge of panic.

'General, I'm afraid you will have to brief me. I've been out of circulation for a while. No idea what is going on here.'

'What?'

'Yes, it is still possible to be out of communication, it seems. Even these days.'

Costello moved up to Jarn until he was only inches away and spoke in low tones. 'I don't know where you have been hiding. But we are likely to be hit by a nuclear attack, any minute.'

Jarn swallowed. 'What has led to this?'

Costello looked away, in the general direction of the White House.

'As I may be about to die any second, it won't hurt if I tell you. Because that idiot in the White House believes that every threat should be escalated. Won't listen to people saying for god's sake talk with them, don't just prime the missiles, Mr President. But no-one has been able to get through to him. The fool thinks they'll back down.'

Costello continued, his voice shaking with urgency.

'Please, Lord Dechar. We had a brief on you before the meeting back in '62, saying you can do something with time. Highly classified. I didn't believe it then, of course, none of us did. A strange British quirk we thought... like UFOs, or people from space. Just hocus pocus. But now – *now* - we need decisions to be reversed. There's nothing else we can do here. Too much has happened.'

Lowering his eyes, the man continued.

'We - no, *he* - launched a strike on Volgograd yesterday, God forgive us. They are going to retaliate.' Costello face was grim. 'And I don't blame them. We have committed an inhuman crime.'

Jarn looked, and felt, bleak. 'I can't change things.'

'You mean you won't.'

'No. I mean I am unable to.'

'There are millions of lives at stake, Dechar. There must be something you can do. Think of all the children. Please. If there is anything, anything at all...'

Costello's shoulders still set firm, the stars on his shoulders glistening in the morning sun, but his head turned in despair.

'General, it is difficult to explain this in the short time we have,' and Jarn, stretching his perception, knew it was mere moments now, and that a full explanation was not just difficult but impossible.

'But you remember me from a different world. A world when yours and mine were the same. Things have diverged, suddenly, and for you, catastrophically. In this world, your president was assassinated last year, and then your new president died a few months later. I still belong to a world where I doubt any of this has happened. Presumably the man who is your president now is a different personality, more war-like, poorer judgement. But from those events, the gap between our worlds has grown wider and wider.'

'I don't understand. What talk is this? Different worlds? Are you mad?'

Jarn's words were just one step too many for Costello's

mind to take in at the moment, when he knew he was looking at losing his country and many of its citizens. Although... the soldier wasn't too sure. Recalling the briefing of years ago, classified at a level he had never seen before, he knew there was some mystery about Dechar. Beyond human, the briefing had said. None of the US side had believed it at the time, among themselves they had scoffed at the UK brief. But now, the man before him looked and sounded entirely sane, and also unaltered in two decades. Costello knew he would be prepared to suspend disbelief if it meant something, anything, could be done.

Jarn put his hand on the man's arm, reaching out to him with his strength and with compassion.

'General, I was surprised to see you here. Because in my world you died in Vietnam, in February 1965. The 7th of the month if I remember correctly. I recall telling my wife about it. I was... upset.'

The man whitened.

'I was shot that day. I damn near died, but I didn't.'

'But in my world, you did. And that difference may even have been the start of the split, the creation of this world. I cannot tell you how much I want to help. But it is beyond any power I have. Major decisions, actions, can't be changed retrospectively. It is beyond even us. We can influence things that are about to happen, but...' Jarn looked round, stretching out with all his senses and saw nothing but imminent disaster, it was unalterable, '...this is beyond that, it has progressed too far.'

Costello looked at Jarn with penetrating eyes, and with the perception of a leader he finally acknowledged that this extraordinary man was telling him the truth.

'My wife and children are in Baltimore, I sent them away. Will that be enough to save them?'

Jarn lied readily, his skills honed through centuries of deception.

'Yes, General, they will be fine.'

It was all he could give the man he knew was doomed. A little peace in his final minutes. And it was even possible that Costello's family would actually be safe, nuclear missiles had fairly small impact areas, it was just a question of how many hit and where. But now was not the time for science.

The sirens suddenly shrieked, wailing piercingly. Costello pulled Jarn away towards the nuclear shelter that Jarn foresaw was about to become a charnel house. In the ensuing panic and pressure of a running crowd, as hundreds converged towards the doors, Jarn found himself alone under a tree by the side of the road. He thought for less than a second. He could not avert this and he needed to leave. He stepped, as the world around him turned into a screaming hell.

CHAPTER 11
CLARE, TERMONN HOUSE,
6TH JULY 2022

The following morning, I was sitting with Sylvie and Fizz in the kitchen, shelling a huge bowl of peas. Hettie had instructed that when we had finished those, there were strawberries and raspberries to trim and wash, and then jams to make. An extensive array of empty jam jars stood ready near the range. It seemed our work was cut out for the next few days.

Hettie hadn't expected me to get involved, as a guest, but apart from fretting over the link between the drawings, and what Philip's visit had implied, and – foremost in my mind – what my abilities meant, I had little else to do. I also liked Sylvie and Fizz and was more than content to spend time with them. In my late-night email correspondence with Sir Edward, he had suggested I spend as much time with the family as possible, so I felt quite justified in giving my assistance to kitchen duties during what for me were still working hours.

A pea shell plopped into the compost bag as Sylvie asked 'so, when were you born, Clare?'

'In 1993,' I responded, running my thumb under the bright little green spheres and dropping them into the big dish.

'So young!' Sylvie said, with a chuckle towards Fizz, who nodded politely and smiled at me.

'But,' I puzzled, 'you both look as young as me, younger really. So, when were *you* born?' At last, the opportunity to ask the question.

Fizz was trying to prise open a reluctant peapod and said 'June 1921' absent-mindedly. I goggled at her.

'July 1916 for me...' Sylvie added, '...in France. Mother was with Father, trying to help in World War One, and she was doing some nursing while Father was fighting in Italy and, let's be honest, he was probably also meddling with the strands of the world and shifting whole regiments to places they had never intended to go to and were amazed to find themselves in when they got there. But that is why I have a French name. I was born in a field hospital just behind the trenches of the Somme, a few weeks early. I think it was quite hair-raising for Mother. She shifted me three times when I was only a few hours old, to avoid artillery shells. Father was horrified and apparently felt very guilty when he returned later that day – after all, he had been away having a wonderful time himself – and he whisked us both to Paris and put Mother and me in a lovely hotel. Well, Mother says it was lovely, once she had got the fleas out of her clothing. I can't remember myself, of course.'

'But I don't really understand.' I confessed, 'why do I look older than you?'

'You don't look ancient, Clare!' Sylvie laughed. 'But I think there will be an effect due to you not having been brought up to your true nature as Fizz and I were. Mother and Father took me world-walking from when I was very young.'

'And my grandmother did the same for me,' said Fizz, 'although not so much as Sylvie. My mother died when I was small and my father did not approve of such things, so my grandmother could only take me when he was not there. Did your mother or grandmother not do the same for you, at all?'

I reflected. 'No. I think my mother was similar to me – to us. But we seldom discussed it. It frightened her and she told me to keep it all quiet. My grandmother, well, she may have been the same as us, or more probably not, but she was a bad-tempered person, very strict and embittered. I can't envisage her skipping around between worlds at all, and she probably beat it out of my mother as well. I never knew either my father or my grandfather. So, I had no training at all until this week, with Lady Issa.'

'What a shame,' Sylvie sympathised, 'I can't imagine how it must have been for you. But never mind...,' with a warm hand on my arm, which was immediately joined by Fizz's hand on my other arm, '...you have us now. So, nothing to worry about!'

I gave them an uncertain smile, not too sure that this extraordinary family was entirely good news.

'But also, Clare, more seriously,' Sylvie added, 'you have not yet fully come into your powers. The teaching my mother is giving you will have already triggered your real nature....,' and as Sylvie spoke, I recalled the sudden sharpening of my perception into brilliant colour and clarity, Issa's hands on mine, '...and you will hardly age now, if at all, but to become fully as Fizz and me are will only happen when you meet a true mate, and that hasn't happened for you yet.'

A true mate sounded wonderful, but who, and where? Regardless of my drifting thoughts I pressed on with another question.

'Sylvie, when you said I was of the same race as you, what does that mean?'

Sylvie had grown bored with the peas and had now pulled the bowl of strawberries towards her, starting to pull out the cores, putting hulled fruit into a bowl and the cores into the compost bag. The scent of ripe strawberry was delicious. We all dipped into the bowl and popped the sweet fruit into our mouths.

'Mother and Father say that there is a name for us, for our race. We are *gerasi*. I think it means old or honoured.'

'Are we unusual?' I ventured, trying to understand this strange world I was now apparently part of. 'Are there many people like us?'

'There are very few of us in this world, as far as I know,' Sylvie looked to Fizz, who nodded gently. 'Talent runs in families, you see, and it tends to fade with generations. Fizz was the last in her family, her mother and grandmother had abilities but neither her brother or sister did. And *gerasi* with the strengths of my parents are really rare. I don't know why they are so strong, or where their abilities came from. Perhaps it is some sort of a mutation, just cropping up from time to time.'

'Like a new star!' Fizz chuckled.

'Can I ask you something else?' I ventured. 'You mentioned 'the void' to me. And Lady Issa mentioned it as well, yesterday, but she didn't explain what it was, she said I'd done enough for one lesson. What is it?'

Sylvie looked thoughtful.

'Well, I've only passed through it with Mother or Father or both, and I have only ever stayed there a few seconds, so it is difficult for me to describe it. It is the empty space between alternative worlds. But if worlds are very close, only slightly different permutations of our own, we can get to them much more easily just by shifting a few steps, and we don't need to go to the void. Mother stepped with you, didn't she?'

I nodded, glad that I had understood something.

'But to travel further, to more distant worlds – different realities, for you, Clare! – you have to travel via the void.'

Fizz added, thoughtfully, 'Lord Dechar told me once, while we were still in Delhi, that the void is like a nothing-ness. Dark, icy and empty. Like a black train station but other locations are visible from it to those who know how to see and reach them. Travelling away is one thing but returning is something else again. The idea frightened me so much that I have never wanted to go anywhere through the void. I only take tiny steps, as I used to do with my grandmother, and I don't go alone. Sylvie and I go together, or I sometimes step with the lady. But never to the void, I am too scared.'

I saw a haunted expression pass over Sylvie's expressive face.

She said, apprehensively, 'I have a fear, though, that Father may have been thrown into the void by the force of the weapon he took with him, and what if.... what if he is trapped there, Fizz? I overheard him say once to Mother that the void would drive you insane if you were there for long. And I know they have wondered if it is the only place where our kind age. What if we were to find him at last and he was old and mad? What if he has died of old age already, stuck in the cold void. Desperate and lonely. Away from us all.'

Fizz moved to sit next to Sylvie and put her arm round her, hugging her mate close.

'Your father is brilliant, and so resourceful, Sylvie, he is the strongest and bravest person I have ever met. He wouldn't let himself be trapped. He'll be working his way back to us, even now. It is just taking him a while.'

Sylvie smiled though tears were now on her cheeks, and she put her head on Fizz's shoulder.

'I only wish,' Fizz said, looking at me, 'that we could help more in the search for the lord. But our lines are quite minor and are separate from the lady's and also from David's. There are limits to what we can achieve.'

I looked from one to the other in complete perplexity.

'What are the lines? Lady Issa mentioned them and so did Hettie. She said David was following them to try to find his father.'

Sylvie lifted her head and said, 'perhaps it is time we showed you the Undercroft.'

The Undercroft was below the main house. We approached it by a stone staircase which led downwards from the passageway next to the kitchen. The staircase was brightly lit with electric lanterns and was well maintained and dry. I thought the scent of herbs and lavender seemed stronger here, and it became stronger still as we descended further and further below the house. The walls of the staircase seemed to become older as we moved down, with stone more reminiscent of the ancient stones in the old gates.

It reminded me that Lady Issa had said that nothing remained of the abbey *above ground* apart from the gates. Was this a remnant of the old abbey that had survived against the odds underground, covered by old stone floor-ing? Was it the chapel of the house?

We arrived at the bottom of the staircase and I saw a dimly lit space before me, which I sensed was cavernous. Sylvie clicked a switch and lights shone brilliantly. I stood at the threshold and gawped.

This was not, in any way, a religious chapel designed for the purpose of normal worship. This was a huge room built of stone-hewn blocks and dark wood panelling, and above the panelling the higher walls were whitewashed, with traces of ancient frescos still visible. We had descended some way downstairs and the height of the room reflected how far underground we had come. A vaulted roof, presum-ably below the floor of the hall, was a long way above us.

The room was octagonal. One step above the stone floor we were standing on were dark wooden stalls set around the panelled walls, with a carved chair at each quarter. Dark wooden staircases led up from this level to the upper tier perhaps six feet higher, where there were also four chairs, each chair set in between the ones in the lower row. So each side of the octagon had a chair, on either the lower or the upper level.

In the centre of the floor was an ancient pedestal. It looked like a font but was much larger, nearly four feet high and surmounted with an octagonal stone the size of a small tabletop. Was it really an old baptismal font? It looked more like a stone used for offerings in a pagan temple, covered with ancient carvings.

My attention was immediately drawn to eight slim chan-nels crossing the floor. They appeared to be of glimmering bronze. Each channel ran from the pedestal to a place on the floor below one of the eight chairs.

'It is beautiful, isn't it Clare?'

I heard Sylvie's voice behind me, but it was faint as I drew nearer to the pedestal. My feet were moving without me being conscious of directing them. Partly for support but also because I was unable to resist its call, I placed my hands on the stone surface of the pedestal and touched my fingers to the carved stone. The carvings started to shine, glowing more and more intensely until they were brilliantly, mesmerizingly aflame with pure liquid gold.

The room around me shifted as the eight bronze channels lit with brilliant golden fire, running from the stone edges of the ancient room towards the pedestal and me. The pedestal itself caught fire, not only the glowing carvings but the entire surface was now burning with blazing heatless flames. From a great distance I heard a gasp, from Sylvie or Fizz, or perhaps both, as a white gold shimmering shape arose above the surface of the stone in front of me. Pulsating and swirling, it assumed patterns and dimensions I couldn't comprehend but which seemed somehow familiar. Stars flickered and worlds shifted and coalesced around a slim black core. The huge shining structure grew taller, swirling faster and faster.

Unable to look away, my vision filled with gold flashing beams. In the far, far distance I felt one of the stars shimmer. Something was there, something important, something familiar. I struggled to focus through the golden clouds, and then there was a figure turning around. A man, dark haired. A connection grew, as if a chain was connecting us. I tried to see his face as he turned towards me but my view was dimming. I felt my hands sliding from the stone as I fell into blackness.

I opened my eyes to find myself lying on the cold stone floor. Lady Issa's face was above me, her hand on my wrist, feeling my pulse, her golden hair hanging down. Sylvie, with Fizz close behind, was running into the room from the staircase, looking scared. One was clutching a glass and the other a towel. Hettie was just behind them.

Issa put the towel, which was damp and deliciously cool, on my forehead, and stroked my hair back from my face. Her other hand was still on my wrist. Her gentle touch and caring gaze were indescribably comforting, and I relaxed.

'Girls, I am not sure it was wise bringing Clare here without any warning.' There was gentle reproof in Issa's low voice. Both girls nodded and looked abashed.

'She asked about the lines, Mama, and we thought we could explain better here.' Sylvie said apologetically.

'How do you feel, Clare?' Fizz asked, her hand on my arm. 'We are so sorry, we didn't expect you to have such a strong connection. When I first came, I saw the lines here and it helped me to understand, but you must have seen much more.'

Issa shushed her gently. 'Let us help you to your feet, Clare, and then we will settle you in your room. We can answer your questions, but it will wait until tomorrow. You have had enough for one day. Girls, please...'

Three pairs of arms helped me to stand. Feeling as if I had run a marathon, I drank some of the chilled water gratefully, leaning on Issa's arm, while casting a wary glance behind me at the pedestal. It was just stone, no hint of fire or the towering white brilliance above the carved surface. It was tempting to think I had imagined it, but I would have been lying to myself, I knew what I had seen was real. We made our slow way up the stairs.

Once back in my room, Issa, Sylvie and Fizz left, closing

the door quietly, but Hettie remained, bustling about me like a mother hen. I was soon between the sheets, with the lights dimmed and the heavy curtains drawn to shut out the daylight. Hettie drew a chair up to my bedside and chatted in a low voice of this and that until my eyelids drooped and sleep took me.

CHAPTER 12
CLARE, TERMONN HOUSE,
7TH JULY 2022

I woke the following morning, refreshed. The previous day's experience still clung to me but had only added to my curiosity about the house and family, and I found myself eager to get back downstairs to find more answers. Answers about this house, but also about me.

Hettie's knock on my door revealed the usual tray but today it only held orange juice, coffee and a cup. Instead, she delivered an invitation for breakfast with Sylvie and Fizz in the kitchen. They were looking forward to seeing me.

Yes, I thought wryly, after my performance in the Undercroft yesterday they probably had as many questions for me as I had for them.

Downstairs, in fresh jeans and a t-shirt, I sought out the kitchen, and found Sylvie and Fizz part way through scrambled eggs and toast. A plate with a large portion was placed in front of me by Maya with a gentle nod and I started in on it with a suddenly sharp appetite, ravenous after sleeping through dinnertime yesterday.

As we ate, Fizz repeated her apology, seconded by Sylvie. They were clearly genuinely sorry, but also intensely curious about what had led to my faint in the Undercroft. There was no reason to hold back, so I described what I had seen although without mentioning the dark-haired figure. I didn't think he had been in my imagination but it seemed too soon to talk about it. And also, intensely personal.

Sliding another slice of toast onto my plate, Sylvie was thoughtful.

'The shape you saw above the pedestal was the vortex, Clare. It shows the void, and other worlds. I've never been able to raise it by myself, neither has Fizz. It has a character, you know, a personality, and it doesn't seem keen on people who aren't sure what they're doing. Once, I was there when Mother raised it, and it gave me the impression it would be decades before it would do anything for me, it was really grumpy. And yet,' - another thoughtful glance at me - 'it seems it rose for you the first time it saw you.'

Fizz patted Sylvie's arm and gestured to the coffee pot, which Sylvie took up, readily. She sipped at her freshened drink.

'But it gets really irritable with my father. Father thinks it is related to the gatekeepers in some way, and he's never had a good relationship with them. I'm not sure why. So, the vortex is quite tetchy with him, and Father retaliates. But they love each other really.' This with a big grin at Fizz, who smiled back.

Gatekeeper – yet another thing I knew nothing about. I raised a questioning eyebrow, being temporarily unable to speak through a mouthful of egg.

'Oh, sorry. Well, as we understand it, many worlds have a gatekeeper and they regulate movements between worlds, or at least they stop too much transfer between different worlds. As it is only our kind that can do that, they act as policemen for us, which is probably one reason why

Father isn't keen on them. He likes to be independent. Gatekeepers are seers as well; they have some idea what may be coming and how worlds divide and reform. In this world the gatekeeper is in Dodona in Greece. Her name is Melite.'

It triggered a memory, and I swallowed my egg and chipped in.

'I remember my ex-boyfriend talking about Dodona and Delphi, he's an archaeologist. But I don't think he thought there was much left at Dodona apart from the amphitheatre. '

'Not to normal human eyes, Clare, but if you are as we are, there is a lot more to see. Mother and Father took me once.'

Sylvie looked at Fizz. 'I saw Melite and the atmosphere was a bit frosty between her and Father. I think he has history with her, and not in a good way. I decided not to ask! Of course, Father is the most powerful *gerasi* in our world, with lots of abilities, so Melite probably finds him a bit of a challenge.'

Sylvie's revelation about her father fascinated me.

'What sort of abilities, Sylvie? I know Lady Issa talked to Sir Edward about seeing alternative futures and she said that mated pairs have stronger perceptions. And she talked about us seeing the fibres of the universe and using them. She showed me how to shift to a nearby world, and how to move instantly in this one. Do we have more abilities?'

Sylvie smiled and nodded.

'Yes, there are more, although what you have described is about as much as Fizz and I can do. Some *gerasi* talents develop over centuries. Father is by far the oldest of us, so he can do much more. He is quite empathetic, especially with others of our nature. And he can also speak into the minds of other *gerasi*. I know he does that with Mother and David, but Fizz and I are too young to do it yet.'

'And he can hold time, just for moments,' Fizz contributed. 'He did it when he rescued me. A man had a knife against my throat, and I remember it was raining heavily on the tin roof of the shed I was hiding in, where the man had caught me. I was terrified, knowing I was about to die. But then the drumming of the rain ceased, as Lord Dechar came through the door, and all the noise and screams from outside stopped as well. Time no longer passed, for a few moments. It was all it took for Lord Dechar to take me from the man's grip and to take the knife as well. Once I was tucked safely behind him, the noise of rain and the screams all started again, as time moved on. It is an astonishing talent. The lady can do it as well, but no-one else in the family has it.'

Fizz added thoughtfully, glancing at Sylvie, 'not yet anyway.'

Sylvie nodded and then picked up the story.

'Father moves to different worlds so easily. He always knows where he is, and how to get home. So, we don't understand why he hasn't returned. While you were seeing the vortex,' she queried, 'did you have any feel for where my father was, Clare? Or David?'

'I thought I saw a man, with dark hair,' I reluctantly confessed. 'But only for seconds and I didn't see his face. To be honest, I may have imagined it. I *think* it was real but it was just before I fainted. Now, I don't know who it might have been or even if it was a dream.'

I thought that the man had been too young to be Sylvie's father, and also the wave of connection between us had seemed so intensely personal I was unable to put it into words. I felt sorry to disappoint them with so few details, but Sylvie was shining at the thought that it might have been her father and Fizz squeezed her arm, saying 'maybe next time you will see more. Whatever, Clare, you are a real find for us!'

After breakfast, feeling replete, they told me Issa needed to see me. It was overdue that we discussed the diagrams, and Issa had asked that I join her in the breakfast room. I collected my thoughts and my laptop and headed for the room.

She solicitously enquired how I was feeling, with a gentle twinkling gaze, and then poured coffee for me as she had done the first day. The two of us sat down at the table, with the coffee pot nearby and the drawings in front of us. Sipping delicious coffee once again, I opened my laptop and plunged in.

'Lady Issa, this figure represents the badge of your husband, we think. But...' I pointed to the other drawing of five birds, two flowers and a cross, '...this one I've searched online again and again and have found nothing. I'm sorry. Does it mean anything to you?'

'It may mean something, something very obscure', Issa admitted, 'but I didn't tell you because I was hoping you might be able to spot something more, possibly with more accuracy, without me putting ideas in your mind. A cross, flowers and birds could mean anything, of course. But all of those symbols appear on the flag of Westminster Abbey. In the old days, the ancient symbol associated with the Abbey was five golden birds surrounding a cross. And there are flower symbols as well.'

Issa smiled while fingering the drawing.

'It appears in many places around the Abbey. To be honest, the figure Sir Edward's artist drew looks very unlike the ones there, but it still triggered a memory with me. Now, the other figure, the cross of St Patrick, is different. We have seen that often enough, not only because it was one of Jarn's awards but also because it is in the stained glass in our library window upstairs. I am quite certain that is the meaning of that figure. With the merging of fibres, as we discussed yesterday, Clare,' and Issa smiled at me, 'it may mean that we ourselves are involved somehow in this mystery, or in its solution. But unfortunately, I am at a loss how to link Jarn's award with Westminster, if that is indeed what the other figure is showing us.'

We were quiet for a few moments, studying the drawing.

'What other names link to Patrick, Lady Issa?' I was thinking hard but not coming up with anything.

Issa bent her head over the table with her hand to her forehead, golden hair around her face, concentrating.

'Goodness, there are so many. In Ireland it could be Pádraic or Pádraig. And there were other forms in Ireland, I think. Then Patrice, or the female form could be Patricia. Originally, of course, they all came from the Latin name Patricius, which meant "nobleman". So many names now are very different from their origins,' Lady Issa mused.

But at last, the heavens flashed and I made the connection.

'Patrician Construction! One of the biggest engineering firms in the world in complex urban projects ... and I'm sure they are working near Westminster.'

I tapped on my laptop. I had seen this just yesterday while surfing for anything in London that might help, but at the time it had meant nothing.

'Yes, here we are. They're doing deep excavations near Westminster pier, to create a massive new area suspended over the Thames.'

I quoted from the article '...*giving incredible views across*

*London and leading directly to the palace of Westminster to
enable easier public access, it will also connect with underground
lines to revolutionise transport in the area for work and tourism.'*

I read more, scanning fast.

'It's going to be the centrepiece of the City of World
Culture celebrations in December. Massive fireworks and
famous artists and acts on this huge new pier, the world
watching. But work is badly behind schedule, so they are
under enormous time pressure now with the excavations, it
seems, and the crews are working round the clock. There's
the usual criticism, of course, about poor management,
underfunding, national embarrassment....'

'Deep excavations – near Westminster pier?' Lady Issa
had a distant look, trawling her long memories.

'Jarn and I were near there, in London, in the summer of
1944. The Germans were sending over huge V1 rockets, more
than a hundred each day if I remember correctly. One
evening we watched from our hotel room near the river,
they screamed as they came down and then the explosions
were enormous. Terrifying and fascinating at the same time.
We saw one detonate on land near the Thames. Jarn, with
his foresight, could see there were bigger weapons closely
following and said we needed to be ready to move. Then the
water rose up in the Thames, several times, as if things huge
and heavy had dropped in the river. I was about to grab Jarn
and step but there was no explosion. We suspected V1s had
fallen into the Thames and not fully detonated.'

Lady Issa tailed off, thoughtfully. 'At the time it meant
nothing to us, and we left the following day for France. Now,
I am wondering if whatever we saw land that evening has
come back to haunt us.'

We looked at each other for a few moments, realisation
dawning.

'They're working in the Thames and constructing new links with underground lines at depth, and all near to unexploded bombs,' I said.

Lady Issa murmured 'and if the digging triggers a series of huge explosions, it could easily cause terrible flooding. It may be why Mary saw water and trapped people.'

Then, with urgency, she said 'we need to speak to Sir Edward.'

Issa reached for her phone and dialled a number – just one, I noticed, she must have Sir Edward on speed dial, which I had not anticipated given the slight testiness in their relationship. The call was answered immediately, and I heard Sir Edward's calm voice on the other end.

Issa summarised what we had found and now suspected in a few succinct sentences. Admiringly, I thought she could have a glowing career in the Civil Service, where the ability to sum up a position clearly and quickly was both highly prized and somewhat rare, rambling verbosity while hogging the limelight being more frequent in my experience. Straining my ears, I could hear Sir Edward instantly decide to pause the excavation. He then asked a question I didn't catch, followed by Issa's agreement to meet in an hour at 17 Queens View, Embankment. She closed the phone.

'Clare, it seems it is time for your third lesson.'

CHAPTER 13
JARN, 'AFGHANISTAN', 1996

A shift. He hoped it was in the right direction. Unlike the last, when he had found himself bathing with tropical jelly fish in an apparently endless ocean.

A hard landing and he found himself surrounded by rocks, tucked into a crevasse between two huge blocks of granite and looking down on a pastoral valley far below. This was not quite his world but one very close to it and Jarn felt a surge of hope. At last, he was near home. Issa and his family would not be here in this world, but the barrier between here and his true home could be weak, and he might be able to break through. Regardless, in this new world there would likely be opportunities to replenish his strength and to find employment to obtain the rudiments of life. Clothing and food were essentials.

There had been some forward shift of time in this move. Jarn suspected he was now in the mid to late 1990's. But his musing was interrupted by the sudden whine of a shot and an explosion against his ear. Fragments of rock fell on his neck and shoulder.

Jarn ducked and edged away from his look-out point into the rocks behind. Creeping slowly around the largest rock he found himself face to face with the business end of a rifle.

'You! Stop!'

The words were in Dari, a language of Afghanistan. The rifle was clutched by a very young tribesman, wearing a mixture of Afghan tribal costume and doubtless purloined ill-fitting khaki. He could have been no more than fourteen and possibly less.

The boy spat in Jarn's face. 'Spy! You spy on us. *Taleban*!'

The rifle hovered in his face, trembling with the fingers of the child who held it.

Jarn contemplated briefly whether to melt away to another, potentially equally or even more hazardous location. But that would mean moving away from a world so close to Issa he could almost taste it. Further, there was something in the eyes of the young would-be warrior that called to him. A hint of his eldest son, when he had been of an age when he had wanted to prove himself a man. It brought out Jarn's paternal instinct. It had been too long since he had cared for a boy this age.

After a few seconds' thought, Jarn responded, also in Dari, and with care as he knew he was a finger trigger from death if he stayed here.

'No, I am a stranger here. Not one of those you and your people are fighting, my boy.'

He gestured slowly and carefully to his body. Thankfully, today he was wearing loose trousers and a light jacket – not remotely military. 'Would your enemies wear this clothing? Would they speak your language so readily? I am not one of them.'

A moment's doubt flickered in the eyes of his captor and Jarn took his moment, looking the boy full in the eye while steadily and carefully rising.

'My name is Jarn Dechar. I would ask to speak to your leader. It may be that I can help him.'

Another look of doubt, but by this point Jarn felt sure the trigger would not be pulled on him. The boy was too young and was confused by the response of his captive. The adrenaline in his blood was slowly dissipating.

'Let us go to your village, young warrior, introduce me to your grandfather.' The leader of these rebels would likely be either this boy's real father or grandfather or one he regarded as such.

Jarn could sense the intensity of the boy's relief at avoiding the need to fire. It was mingled with a memory of horror from his recent kill of a doe, for practice; he was repulsed at the thought of killing a man. Jarn felt some shame that he himself had long lost any innocence in killing. This child was too young to be a soldier.

He was not surprised when after a moment's thought the boy lowered his weapon and gestured Jarn to follow him down the slope. He could feel the child hoping that his elders would be pleased with his capture and the possible find of a strong man who might be able to help them. As they made their slow way down through the rocks to the wheat fields of the Panjshir valley, ripening in the summer heat, Jarn encouraged the boy to talk and learnt far more than his young companion knew he had revealed.

That night, he lay in the tent allocated to him and reviewed his situation. The Russian threat in this land had been in his world when he had been ejected out of it, back in 1977. It would seem that it had now been superseded in this world and this region by the group of warriors from religious seminaries his hosts referred to in Dari as the *Goroh-e Taleban*. Afghanistan had always been a melting pot of the world's troubles, criss-crossed for centuries by armies in conflict, but this particular threat seemed to be more home-grown and even more unpleasant. Territorial control was all important to this group and had been enforced with little regard for human rights. Particularly grating to Jarn were the restrictions he had learnt were imposed on the rights of women. He had seen that inequality too often over the centuries. But the massacres, the destruction of historical treasures and the denial of food aid just added to the tally of crimes.

That he spoke Dari fluently had been a point in his favour, as it seemed the enemy more usually spoke Pashto, despising Dari for its Persian origins. After some initial wariness he had been received with genuine welcome and the hospitality typical for the region. Tomorrow would be a battle, his new friends had warned him over the rice, goat stew and pomegranates they had shared this evening.

Their leader was in his forties, and his accomplishments amazed Jarn. In traditional robes, the softly spoken man was fluent in French, English, Russian and the local tongues and had a wide-ranging knowledge of classical Persian poetry, football and, Jarn was delighted to discover, chess. A man of charisma, a man being followed by thousands of his tribes-men. Jarn was intrigued. Men of power often had the attrib-utes this leader displayed, but whether they retained them once victory had been won was a different question. Or sometimes, they did not survive to demonstrate their ability once in a position of governance, as assassination was an ever-present threat. He wondered if this man would live long enough to lead his people in a more peaceful time.

So - his options this night were to shift back to the void

or to stay? But this world was so very close to the one Issa was in, his own world. He could sense it. The identification of a weak spot, one more shift, and he could be home. Moreover, he felt that fighting for his new friends was fully justified. So tomorrow he would be alongside his hosts in their battle, and he would then hope to find a way home somehow.

Twenty hours later, an impressive and completely unexpected display of high-calibre sophisticated weaponry from his new friends, accompanied by sniping from the cover of scorching rock-strewn valleys in which he had more than played his part, had left his allies the victors. They had taken a number of sullen captives and Jarn was observing their transfer to a safehouse some distance from the village, when the last spark of the conflict flared unexpectedly.

One of the prisoners snatched the rifle from a young tribesman and levelled it at his head. Even from his position of twenty feet away, Jarn could see the man's finger tightening on the trigger. There was no time to think. He did what he had done countless times over the centuries, slowing time just enough to be able to race forward and put his hands on the weapon. This time he was too slow. In the split second before time resumed its normal flow a white flash showed him the bullet had been released and was still on target for its intended victim, a boy of no more than seventeen or eighteen.

And so now there was no choice. Feeling intense frustration, Jarn captured both bullet and rifle and tumbled with them into the void where they fell harmlessly to the dark surface of the icy place.

Without surprise, Jarn found his action had indeed led to the breaking of the link between him and the Afghan world he had been in for a day. He found himself in an environment that felt European, but which he sensed was far further from home than he had been before.

Once again, it was time to move on.

CHAPTER 14
CLARE, LONDON, 7TH
JULY 2022

Just over a whirling half-hour after Issa's conversation with Sir Edward, I found myself with paving beneath my feet and the muted hum of city traffic close-by. Issa had gripped me firmly since we had stepped from Termonn and her arm was still around my waist. I opened my eyes, scrunched tightly closed for the duration of our journey, which had taken no more than a few minutes, to see that we had arrived in a quiet urban street and were hidden behind refuse bins and box shrubbery.

I took advantage of the nearest bin to discard my breakfast. I had never liked fairground rides, and this had been beyond the worst. Issa kept her arm round me and her other hand on my shoulder until she saw that I was steady and the nausea was subsiding, then she passed me a small bottle of water. I swirled and spat.

'Perhaps it would have been better not to do that just after breakfast. I'm sorry, Clare. But needs must. Now, Sir Edward has a penthouse suite here. Number 912b.'

We made our way around the bins and the shrubbery, locating the main entrance to what appeared to be an exclusive and expensive block of flats which likely had magnificent views over central London.

In the expansive and luxurious reception area of the apartments, dripping with dark wood and chandeliers, we were shown to the lifts. A perspiring grey-haired man was also waiting, having apparently been taking unaccustomed exercise. When the lift doors slid open with a quiet shush, the three of us entered it together. He punched the button for floor 9 irritably, without asking which floor we wanted, and I saw Issa's mouth curve in a serene smile.

The lift door slid open and the man stalked out, not standing back to allow us to proceed him. We followed, stepping onto thick cream carpet, and a solid redwood door marked 912b was directly ahead of us. The man gave the button next to the door a much longer and harder press than it needed, and it opened almost immediately to reveal Sir Edward, who beckoned us all inside. The expression on the face of the sweating man when he saw us following him into the apartment would have been enjoyable had the situation not been as potentially serious as it was.

On this warm summer day, glass doors were open to a wide balcony with a panoramic view over Westminster and the Thames. Stepping onto it, I could see huge cranes and a hub of massive construction facilities on the edge of the river. Men were moving far below us but there was no noise from the machinery.

Despite the urgency, British courtesy came to the fore, and we were supplied with teas, coffees and biscuits as if we were all meeting for a pleasurable social event. Sir Edward's assistant, who introduced himself as Paul Beresford, pulled out a chair for Issa, and we took our seats around a large coffee table.

Introductions were made, to the clear frustration of the

man we had followed into the lift. He announced himself curtly as Charles Delfield, head of the London Development Commission and responsible for delivery of the City of World Culture festival. Then he dabbed his face with a handkerchief, clearly about to erupt into speech. A calming gesture from Sir Edward stopped him just as his mouth opened, and he subsided, bristling.

Sitting back composedly, Sir Edward took it upon himself to summarise the situation.

'As you are all aware, I have just given the order for work on the Westminster development project to be suspended. The Prime Minister, the current Cabinet Secretary and the leader of the Opposition have all agreed with me that this is necessary.'

Delfield put his coffee down with such force that brown liquid spilled into the saucer.

'Sir Edward, I must protest, most strongly. We are weeks behind schedule. Every minute counts. Today was vital in the plans, with the Goliath crane finally in position and crews preparing to work all night. A partial breakthrough into the underground network has been made, but the next step with the mega-drills is crucial. We're losing not only time but thousands of pounds every minute the crews aren't working, it is absolutely *essential* that we restart, and now, before...'

'At the potential cost of how many thousands of lives, Charles?'

I had never before heard a quiet voice used to such chilling effect. Sir Edward had instantly taken full control of the room.

Charles Delfield swallowed and subsided, murmuring, 'a full safety assessment has been done, as you know, Sir

Edward. If new information has come to light, then of course a pause may be necessary. But has it?'

'I believe it may have.' Sir Edward sipped his coffee and replaced his cup on the table.

'This lady,' he gestured to Issa 'has come forward with information on unexploded ordnance in the vicinity of the excavation. It is possible that this is concealed at a depth far below the riverbed, at a level which would only have been reached today by the Goliath crane with its massive drills. A level which has not been comprehensively scanned before.'

Delfield glared at Issa but remained silent. Issa sipped her tea, unconcerned.

Sir Edward turned to his assistant.

'Paul, can you supply details for us, of the potential risk here?'

Paul Beresford opened his file and spoke.

'It appears that there may be considerable explosive material in this location, from World War Two, which has lain hidden for over seventy years. There are anecdotal but reliable reports,' and he glanced at Issa, 'of V1 bombs falling into the river and failing to explode. If the material is where we think it may be, and if it were detonated by the excavation, the resulting explosion would cause immense damage, not only to the buildings in the vicinity but also would be very likely to rupture water mains and the entrance to underground passages, and to breach the Thames embankment. Any, or all, of those would very likely lead to rapid flooding of the ventilation shafts into nearby underground concourses and lines, especially in Westminster and Waterloo stations, and this would be likely to spread out to other stations beyond. The volumes of water involved would be huge.'

Paul continued remorselessly painting his picture of catastrophe.

'As you will be aware, Charles, the westbound Jubilee Line platform at Westminster is very deep, over twenty-five metres below sea level, and the eastbound and westbound Jubilee platforms at Waterloo are deeper still. They are the deepest tube platforms on the network. There have been significant flooding events in the underground recently, but those would pale into insignificance compared to what could happen here. The situation is not helped by the forecast of unseasonably heavy rain in London and the South-East this evening. We think that the flood doors in the underground network would not be adequate, and the pumping stations would be overwhelmed.'

'All of this would happen too quickly for an evacuation of the stations to be possible. It is likely that thousands would perish in the surging underground waters, which could easily fill the deepest tunnels completely. The horror is almost unimaginable.'

Sir Edward's voice was still calm but also implacable as he added to Paul's ghastly summary.

'I think you will agree, Charles, that such an event would be the only thing that people would remember for decades to come about the City of World Culture festival. No financial cost matters compared to the human toll that may happen here. It would be a national, an international, catastrophe.'

Charles Delfield was ashen. It was clear he was out of arguments.

Paul added, 'we have brought in the most advanced scanning equipment we and Europe possess, and the Goliath crane is assisting with its deployment. Early results are expected shortly.'

Delfield cleared his throat and spoke. 'May I ask, Sir Edward, how the information has come to light at this late stage?'

'I'm sorry, Charles, but I cannot share that with you. It is highly classified, and that is how it will remain.'

Issa stood and walked to the balcony and I followed her. We stood looking down at the site and the huge crane, its head inclined over the Thames as if it were inspecting its surroundings. A chain and cables were suspended from it, but whatever was on the end of them was invisible below the waterline of the river. All the activity in the area was centred around the mammoth crane.

I asked Issa, quietly, 'can you remember if that was where the bombs fell?'

'The area looks very different now. But our hotel was only a short distance from here and we were in a similar position in relation to the river. Yes, I think that the construction site is very near to where the V1s fell.'

Behind us a phone rang and we turned to see Paul Beresford answer his mobile. We all listened shamelessly. Despite hearing only one half of the conversation, it was clear there had been a discovery.

After a few minutes Paul closed his phone and spoke.

'The scans are still preliminary and more will be done overnight, to a greater degree of accuracy, but they have clearly indicated three separate metal bodies. They are approximately the size and shape of V1 bombs. They were not detected earlier because they are in an unusual position, buried very deep but also wedged partially underneath land adjacent to the river, very close to the Westminster tube line.'

Charles Delfield's shoulders slumped and he put a

shaky hand to his face as Paul looked apologetically at Sir Edward.

'Apart from the scanning engineers, all non-essential personnel have been withdrawn from the area and the Ministry of Defence has now assumed command of the site. A plan is being put together for the safe removal of the weapons but it will take some time, and until then no further work can be done. They think we have been extraordinarily fortunate. The new Goliath crane in conjunction with its two mega-drills were about to start work this evening. Right where the weapons are buried.'

I moved closer to Issa, shuddering. I felt nauseous, again.

Paul continued.

'The Prime Minister is convening a COBR meeting in an hour to discuss the need for evacuation and the closing of several tube stations, he asks if you can attend, Sir Edward. Until they have reached decisions at that meeting, the news is classified. Otherwise, there may understandably be some panic.'

Sir Edward nodded, then he turned to Charles Delfield.

'I am sorry, Charles, that this impacts on your project's timescale. But you will understand that we have no choice.' Then, rising to his feet and with an air of finality, he added 'you will be kept informed of progress.'

Delfield nodded, wearily, and walked to the door, accompanied by Sir Edward.

While the farewells were in progress, I looked past Issa to the site far below. I was slowly becoming aware of the sensation when gold beams were imminent, and I felt it again now. A quick glance at Issa showed that for the moment her attention was on the door to the apartment and Sir Edward. I turned back to the site on the embankment below and saw the area criss-crossed by golden lines. But, weaving through and through was a fibre that was different. Thicker, not gold but iridescent, with colour that graduated along its length from pale to darker. How odd. I reached out to it to explore more, my fingers twitching for information.

Suddenly all sound and movement stopped. The distant thrum of London and the faint sound of classical music from a far-off apartment ceased, as did the conversation behind me, of Sir Edward having a last word with Delfield. All gone. I looked down at the site below me, where tiny people and traffic were now still, and heard Issa's voice in my ear.

'Goodness, Clare, you have stopped time.'

I spun to her, aghast, my hand to my mouth. Over her shoulder I could see Sir Edward unmoving, his hand on the door handle. Charles Delfield stood next to him, frozen.

'What have I done?'

The only sound left in the universe was the noise of a distant straining, as if machinery was under a load and it was increasing. My fear grew.

'Well,' Issa remarked, placidly, 'that is amazing. None of our children have ever done that. Jarn and me, yes, of course. And Jarn fiddles with time just for fun, I keep telling him not to. But you are so young. It's really extraordinary.'

I clutched her arm; the tiny part of my mind that was not succumbing to terror thought this was really not the time for Issa to be gazing at me with surprised maternal pride. The sound of grinding pressure was now uncomfortable.

'What is that noise?', I gasped at her.

'That is time complaining. No-one can hold this for long.'

'Issa! Help!' I was close to panic.

'Ah, child, no need to worry. Here.'

A waft of her fingers in the direction of the site and the groaning ceased as it was replaced by the normal sounds of London. I had never been so happy to hear them. Far below, tiny distant movements showed the site was working as normal. I drew a huge and shaky breath of relief.

'But Clare, this is something we need to investigate. Not now though.' She turned to the door as there was a click of the catch. Delfield had finally left. We were still standing near the balcony, but Issa now walked to Sir Edward.

'Sir Edward, and you also, Clare, I have a favour to request.'

Sir Edward smiled wryly. 'After your service today, Lady Issa, I think the government would find it hard to decline any request you might make. A little souvenir from the Crown Jewels perhaps?' His eyes twinkled.

'You should know, Sir Edward, that it was Clare who succeeded in linking the clues and I do not think we would have averted disaster without her. But although the task you gave Clare has now been accomplished, I would be most grateful if you would permit her to stay with us for some more weeks. I am wondering if her skills can help us with the question of my husband's disappearance.'

Sir Edward's face showed his enthusiasm for the idea but he turned to me with his usual courtesy.

'It depends on Clare. I am entirely willing that she remains with you as a secondment posting, in fact I would strongly encourage it. But Clare may wish to return to London for personal reasons?'

My heart had leapt at the prospect of returning to Termonn House. It seemed far too early to break my link with the home and the family living there. Even more so, given what had just happened. I nodded my agreement, saying I would be delighted to stay if Lady Issa could accommodate me. Issa and Sir Edward beamed.

Outside the apartment block, Issa searched the street.

'Now, Clare, Mordecai will hopefully be on his way with the car. He may have been caught up in traffic. But I thought you might prefer a more traditional mode of transport home.'

I certainly did, and I also very much liked the use of the word 'home'. We stood close together on the kerb, scanning the traffic, and I noticed the attention Issa was attracting from passers-by, her elegance and beauty setting her apart. She appeared unaware of it.

A few minutes later a polished black vintage Jaguar pulled up next to us and Mordecai stepped out. He opened the rear doors and ushered us inside. Within moments we were heading into the traffic of central London, relaxing in the leather seats.

'A good day, your ladyship?'

'A truly excellent day, Mordecai, and in more ways than one.' Issa answered. 'Thank you for coming at short notice to collect us.'

'A pleasure, ma'am. The old girl hasn't had many trips of a decent distance for quite a while.'

I guessed 'the old girl' was the car, as Mordecai was lovingly patting the steering wheel. 'His lordship loves this car, we've kept it up over the years, but annual trips to the garage and little drives round, just not the same, is it? She wants to stretch her legs. Well, her wheels.'

We relaxed and I found myself dozing as the car made its way through London and headed for the motorway.

Waking when we were past Oxford and only miles from Termonn House, I asked a question that had been nagging at me.

'Issa, if we hadn't solved the puzzle of the diagrams today, would you have foreseen the actual event in time to stop it? It may only have been a few hours away.'

Issa regarded me from her seat and answered thoughtfully.

'Probably, given it was so huge. I had already felt something approaching, but I couldn't pin it down until you connected the figures. It is possible I may not have been able to act in time. Sometimes it is better to resolve issues by more normal methods, Clare, and I think this is one of those times.'

She turned to look out of the window, at the countryside passing us.

'It is true that we do foresee events, and regularly, but to be honest we have never been able to do it consistently. The universe is too subject to change from so many possibilities, and things may happen to avert any event at any point, from the time we try to predict it through to the last minute before the happening, whatever that is. For example, the crane today could have broken down, or the bombs not triggered for a while or maybe not at all. And it is not always a good idea to intervene anyway, events when they happen in sequence are unpredictable and we could often make things worse unwittingly.'

'Sometimes it is only in the second before an event that all the lines of fate coincide. We see what we had sensed approaching, but without enough knowledge to avert it, and in that moment everything becomes clear but it is too late to stop it.' A shadow passed over Issa's face as she patted my hand.

'It has happened so many times, all the events you recall as tragedies we have seen coming in the last seconds but too late to change. This may have been another. We have averted many, but unfortunately many others have still occurred.'

Issa looked out again through the car window. 'So we have never seen ourselves as some sort of emergency service either for Britain or the world, although I am sure Sir Edward - and his predecessors - would rather like us to be that. I suspect Mary is more reliable than we are in some ways. And she is certainly more effective than most of the previous Cassandras. The woman appears genuinely talented.'

'Will Mary still have nightmares?' I didn't like to think of her needing constant sedation. The gates approached as our car turned into the estate.

'Not unless the government's measures are unsuccessful, as that line of the future has been taken away. But more visions will doubtless arise. They are lucky to have her, although I am not sure she is as fortunate to have them.'

The car crested the slope and Termonn basked below us in the valley, moat and windows reflecting gold from the evening sun and welcoming us home.

CHAPTER 15
JARN, 'GIZA', 21ST AUGUST 2010

Jarn gazed at the painting admiringly. It was only small but the yellow flowers dotted with red posies were brilliant against a dark, almost black, background. Issa would love this, he thought, to brighten a corner of their manor house, illuminated with subtle lighting. And it was Impressionist, a style they had always both liked. In his memory he recalled escorting an elegant Issa on his arm as they promenaded through the galleries of Paris, so many years before.

But a glance at the description below the exhibit had him smiling ruefully. Back in his home world he was quietly wealthy, but certainly not rich enough to decorate their walls on a whim with a Van Gogh. This small museum, the Mohamed Mahmoud Khalil Museum just outside Cairo, appeared to have an impressive number of famous artists on exhibit.

Always curious, he looked towards the elderly steward seated in the room. The man had been paying him very little attention, his gaze fixed on the sporting pages of his newspaper. There were, admittedly, no other visitors in this room and no visitors were anywhere nearby, as far as Jarn could tell. He assumed that the locals had only a limited interest in Impressionism and the majority of tourists would focus on the ancient treasures of the Egyptian pharaohs so close by.

Jarn's Egyptian Arabic had never been fluent and was now rusty as well, but he mentally dusted it off a little and pulled words together.

'Excuse me, sir,' and the man looked up, reluctantly. 'This is by Van Gogh?'

'Yes, indeed, as you see.' The man's hand wafted towards the description. 'It is very famous, painted by the master in 1887. Even more famous since it was stolen from here just over thirty years ago, and eventually recovered.'

The man would have returned his gaze to his paper but Jarn politely pressed him.

'It was stolen? And then recovered?'

'But yes. It was returned from Kuwait ten years after thieves took it from us. It has been requested by other countries on loan many times since, but our director will not release it. It is too precious.'

Jarn turned his attention back to the painting, indulging in a dream of having it in his library. It was lovely, and it drew his gaze. Van Gogh.

But... ah, no. Reaching out, it was as clear as day to Jarn that this painting was not over a century old. He delved and decided it had been not much more than two decades since paint connected to canvas. Expertly done, but definitely not by Van Gogh. Well, that was interesting. The painting recovered from Kuwait after the theft was not the original but a brilliant copy. Perhaps the museum were unaware?

He wandered into an adjacent room, cogitating. Art theft was a major business in the crime world, he knew, but the deliberate insertion of a fake was surely less common. No matter how well done, it would be spotted before too long, perhaps when the painting was loaned out for an exhibition. But the room steward had said it had not been allowed to leave since its 'recovery', which certainly suggested at least one person in the museum was aware of the deception and wished to keep the painting hidden from expert examination.

He heard the steward in the room behind him depart, presumably for a tea-break, and turned his attention to the paintings in this new room. Gauguins, a Monet, and a Renoir. Jarn moved to examine the Monet. But he was immediately aware of footsteps in the room he had just left, and a whispered conversation. He moved back towards the connecting door and shifted between realities, careful not to push too far and be lost once again in the whirlpool of the void. The rooms in front of him and behind him faded a little but he stretched his hearing.

'This one.'

'We will be seen.'

'No, the cameras are all switched off. And most of them do not work anyway.'

Jarn moved undetected into the room and saw one of the men push a couch under the so-called Van Gogh and then stand on it. His accomplice handed him a box cutter, and with four quick slices the canvas was freed from its frame. The square was quickly rolled up and stuffed into a narrow tube, and then Jarn watched in amazement as the tube was pushed under the small gap between a radiator and the parquet floor, well out of sight. Only tatters of canvas remained in the frame.

To Jarn's astonishment the first man then ran out of the room to the top of the marble staircase and bellowed 'Thieves, thieves! Secure the doors!', before turning and smashing the security alarm on the wall with his fist. The alarm started to wail shrilly.

In less than a minute, security officials and museum administrators rushed into the room and began to bewail the theft. Security cameras were consulted without success, as none had apparently been functioning. Over the next hour, an army of police arrived, adding to the mayhem. Photographs were taken. The room was dusted for finger-prints. The steward mentioned the presence of Jarn himself, just before he had left the room for his break, but little notice was taken of him as two potential perpetrators had already been identified on the basis of suspicious behaviour elsewhere in the museum. Security forces were already on the way to the airport to apprehend them. Jarn stood well back, invisible, and watched the scene with amusement. He had not expected his short Egyptian sight-seeing trip in this reality to be quite so entertaining.

Finally, the room quietened. The man who had liberated the canvas from its frame was left with a balding man.

'How tragic,' the balding man said. 'To be lost again, so few years after its recovery.'

'The French will no longer be able to request the loan of it, now.'

'Indeed not. And they had apparently become ... press-ing. There are only so many times a museum can refuse.' The man looked at the empty frame. 'But even a copy of such a masterpiece is beautiful. When the situation quietens, bring it to me. In the meantime, leave it where it is.'

'Of course, sir.'

Both men left.

Feeling absolutely no compunction against theft in this particular circumstance, Jarn stepped fully into the world and moved to the radiator. He reached for the roll lying beneath it and extracted it.

He would need to consider carefully where to store it in this world until such time as he could have it reframed and hung at Termonn, whenever he succeeded in returning there.

Jarn chuckled to think of the real thieves wondering where the copy had vanished to, while the rest of the art world would doubtless question for years where the original Van Gogh had vanished to after its second theft. Jarn suspected that particular painting was securely hung somewhere in Kuwait, where it would doubtless remain undetected for centuries.

But, at some point, the masterly copy would look absolutely splendid in his own library.

CHAPTER 16

A MEDIEVAL MANOR HOUSE
IN SOUTHERN ENGLAND,
DECEMBER 1651

Even as she reached out to the scraps of meat from the roast
in the hearth, she knew she had made a mistake. She was
so hungry, the burnt remnants of the meal near the edge of
the fire in the great hall were too alluring to resist. But a
sharp crack on her wrist and the cry of 'damn witch!' from
the worst of the rabble of men around the fire confirmed
that she had shifted too much and too fast. For a fraction of
time she must have lost presence, disappeared, and then
reappeared a little closer to the food. She could never
control it. Couldn't move when she needed to but moving
without intention when it was much better that she should
not. Being exhausted, beaten and starving didn't help any
control she may have attempted.

Punishment and then sport for her persecutors were
inevitable and the beatings and assaults began again as
they had countless times before. No-one would save her
this time; no-one had saved her for weeks. The lord of the
manor had protected her while he was young and healthy,
but he had sickened during the war and had died at Ware-
ham. The worst of his men, without true allegiance to

either Crown or Cromwell, had returned without him to fight over the pickings still to be had in the old Dorset manor house. There were only a few other servants left in the decaying place, the others drifting away over the years when the menfolk had been away. Most of the servants who remained looked at her askance, content for retribution against the favouritism shown her in the past and wary of her strangeness. 'Witch', she had been called for years now. She should have left while she had the chance and cursed herself for her stupidity. Only remnants of loyalty to the lord who had given her a home had persuaded her to stay.

Diving within herself, she tried to shut out the worst of the pain of the attacks. Her efforts at least numbed it, but this time the agony forced her to plunge deeper and travel further in her mind than she had ever done before in the desperate hope of disappearance, although she had never yet been able to do it when she needed it and had no hope now. But this time through the darkening mist came a voice.

Who are you?

The hills of northern England, December 1651

A hard frost glittered in the moonlight around their camp-site in the hills. Jarn had enjoyed a dinner of roast boar and had made sure that his men had eaten enough to satisfy them. Men served him best when their bellies were full. And it made them less likely to rebel over commands, not that he had ever had much difficulty in that regard. The men were his, to serve his purposes and Jarn was more than powerful enough and charismatic enough to be able to enforce his decisions. But over the years it could not be denied he had grown fond of at least some of them. Somewhat fond. Well, perhaps a little.

He edged his wrap closer to the fire. The night was bitter. To the far north, shimmering lights in the sky showed that the earth gods were walking again, and there was a whiff of sulphur on the breeze. He knew that he was the only one in the camp to sense it. But it was too far away to be any threat to them, and in any case there was little that could threaten himself, although none of his men were aware of that.

He relaxed into his bedding and briefly recalled the warmth of the last woman he had taken pleasure with. No woman was within leagues of their winter camp. There was nothing for him tonight other than a blanket near the embers. But as he curled into sleep an insistent discomfort nagged.

A dim sensation was coming from another of his kind. Of his many talents, empathy with others of his nature was the one he found the most irksome, and it seemed to be growing with the years. Fortunately, there were so few like him that he was rarely troubled, but tonight was different. As the minutes passed the discomfort grew to something more akin to pain.

Fully awake now, he rolled on his back and opened himself fully, stretching his perception. To his astonishment, he recognised familiarity. Many years before he had felt a call from one of his kind and had searched for the source without success. Over time, the call had become less obvious, less insistent, until it barely existed. Eventually he had put it out of his mind.

Now, it returned with massive force. Torture, intrusive and invasive. With the pain came clarity. The call came from a woman, and he knew with certainty that she was no more human than he was. She was akin to him, and yet not fully like. Similar but offering things he didn't have. The tantalising meshing of two interlinking puzzle pieces.

The recognition thrilled and exhilarated him, after so many years alone. Jarn felt a huge, an overwhelming, surge of need, although now was not the time to fully identify its nature.

Who are you?

There was no answer. By now, given the pain he had felt the reflection of, she was probably no longer conscious. But he had learned enough to know roughly where she was. The hunt would start at daybreak. They would move south.

A medieval manor house in southern England, January 1652

Pain still beat, drummed through her body. No part was free of it. But at least there was no fresh torture. She had slept the sleep of exhaustion and the start of recovery last night and for much of the day.

Waking amid nightmares, the sound was still ringing in her head of the sword and dagger fighting when a small army had burst into the manor yesterday and had slaughtered her tormentors, or at least all those who did not flee to save their skins. Her mind was unable to accept that yesterday had ended the hell of her existence as the rabble's entertainment; within her, terror still bubbled just below the surface, although she fought to subdue it.

Now, through a haze, she heard steady steps approaching the tower chamber to which she had been carried only partly conscious the previous evening. The steps sounded firm and with some weight.

Male.

Not again. Under her bedding, she grabbed the old dagger that had been hers previously and which a maid had newly restored to her. She fingered the blade absent-mindedly, her nails running over the fine lines carved on both flat surfaces.

Her slashed arm protested but she ignored the pain. With the dagger gripped in her hand she edged to a more upright position and pointed the weapon towards the door of her dingy chamber. Pushing dirty golden hair out of her eyes, she tried desperately to sharpen her vision, aware of her young maid stepping closer, but still sheltering behind her pallet. She clasped the blade with shaking fingers but deadly intent. Further captivity and renewed torment would not happen. She would kill to avoid it. And no-one would hurt the maid if she could prevent it.

The door creaked open.

The man who was now standing on the threshold was the tallest and broadest she had ever seen. The leader of the men who had freed her yesterday, he blocked the doorway and dominated the room, magnificent but deadly. She had seen glimpses of his ruthlessness when her persecutors had choked on their own blood not many hours before.

In the late afternoon light from the tower windows, his hair and trimmed beard glinted black. His eyes were similarly dark but held a gleam of amber. They regarded her calmly and steadily.

As their gaze connected, she was overwhelmed with a bone-deep sensation, the innermost parts of her awakening, stirring, shifting and growing. Reaching out to new paths barely suspected before. Merging. Without comprehension, she recognised the elemental force of the link between herself and this man. An altered perception in his gaze showed that he too had felt - something.

Regardless, her grip on the weapon tightened, and she raised herself a little from the pallet. Pain from her stabbed leg shot excruciatingly through her. She could not help wincing.

The man spoke.

'Be still, my lady, there are no longer any here who will hurt you.'

His voice. Deep, resonant, it rolled between the stone walls of the chamber. His gaze on her was intense. Deeply curious, but something else. Compassionate?

She sat up a little straighter and grimaced but managed to pull the woollen blanket more firmly around her. It was irritating that her words came out in a croak, but for weeks she had not used her voice other than to scream.

'Easily said, lord, but I can hear that this place is now full of your men. My maid is fearful. I will not allow you to harm her.'

She very much hoped the threat was sufficient, as with injured limbs and other wounds too many to count, she doubted she would be able to do much more than scratch his hide. Perhaps she could inflict more damage if her first aim was good? She readied her dagger and tried to look more intimidating than she felt.

There was a spark of something deep in the darkening eyes, but what it meant she couldn't summon the energy to determine. The strain of clutching the dagger and of preparing her broken body to fight him was starting to tell. After months of near starvation, she had little physical strength left and with deep frustration she felt her head droop a little.

His voice was low. 'They are, all of them, under my command and I am never disobeyed. There is no one here who will hurt you or yours. And all those who injured you are dead or fled.'

The giant of a man took one more step inside the door, and then to her astonishment knelt one knee on the floor so that he was more on her level.

Without taking his gaze from hers, he said, 'in two days we will leave here, for a place where there is peace and no stench of death and evil. A place where you will be able to heal. I need you to be well enough to travel with me. And I will take any you wish to accompany you.'

This with a nod to the maid still skulking in the corner shadows. The young girl flinched and cowered. There was no chance of her leaving the village she had been born in, her attachment to her mistress did not extend so far.

'Try to rest and heal as well as you can, for the journey will be long.'

He rose to his feet, still watching her intently, as if he was trying to assess the temperament and qualities of an unknown horse, she thought uncharitably. She did not expect the way he lowered his head in respect.

As the door closed behind him, the room seemed both emptier and darker.

Jarn made his way down the stairs, his mind in a turmoil never experienced in his long centuries.

She looks like an angel, she has the heart of a lion, her body is shattered but she would still try to spit me to save her servant.

And the link between them. Unbelievable. Unexpected. His strengths merging with hers, widening, deepening, and rippling through dimensions never before suspected. Interlinked with such union, and such desire. He knew his life had changed, forever. His mind replayed their last words.

'Who are you, my lady? By what name should I call you?'

'My family called me Nerissa. But now my name is Issa.'

CHAPTER 17
DAVID, 'RUSSIA', 30TH JUNE, 2022

Snow crunched under his feet and dark trees surrounded him. The cold scent of pine reminded David of winter forests in the Russia of his childhood over two centuries earlier.

His discussions with the gatekeeper of the world he had visited which had been so similar to the Dodona of his own reality, had changed his plans. Instead of heading for home, he had on impulse extended his search further and wider than he had ventured before, propelled by a new sense of alarm and urgency. There was a threat, the gatekeeper had said. To his father, specifically. Someone was targeting him, and the separation of Jarn from his family and his home came from that. And the threat was deepening, spreading. The joy David had felt in hearing that his father was still alive had been tempered by concern; what was the threat, and was Jarn in imminent danger?

So, David had passed through the void to a group of worlds he had not visited before, and felt the unmistakable draw of the lines to one which felt quite distant from his own world. Stepping to where his senses told him the gatekeeper resided, he had emerged into a setting that most definitely was not Dodona or anything remotely like it. He shivered and promised himself to step quickly to a world, any world, of warmth if he couldn't find the equivalent of the Dodona temple in this chilly place. Snow was starting to fall.

But ahead, between the trees, he could see lights, and what appeared to be stone walls. He quickly did a small step, and in seconds was in front of a large stone dwelling surrounded by glowing lanterns. It was a cottage from a fairy tale, with carved wood under the eaves and steps leading up to a wooden veranda of knotted tree trunks. Smoke curled from ornate chimneys set in the snow-covered roof. David walked up the steps and crossed the snowy veranda to the carved wooden front doors. He was certain this was not the residence of a gatekeeper but perhaps he could ask for directions.

There was no doorknob or bell, but the door opened just as he raised his hand to knock. A pretty young woman clad in an embroidered blouse and full dirndl skirt beckoned him to enter, with a welcoming smile. When she spoke, her voice was musical.

'*он приходит*'.

With some surprise David recognised it as Russian, or something very similar. '*He is coming.*'

She waved him forward again and David stepped inside.

The girl disappeared through another door, and David took stock of his surroundings. A large rustic room, stone walls decorated with woodcarvings, a paved floor covered in bright rugs. Comfortable leather chairs, shelves full of books. And in the centre an enormous stone hearth and a chimney rising through the high beamed ceiling. Logs were burning brightly, and David started to thaw.

Another door opened and a youngish man strode in. Tall, slender and dark-haired, he was dressed in a tunic with a sash, loose trousers and high boots, and David was again reminded of the clothing of nineteenth century Russia.

The man spoke. '*Твой язык?*' '*What language?*'

David responded, 'I am at ease with quite a number, but English comes most readily these days.'

'Then, my friend, we will converse in English. Ah, refreshments.'

The girl had returned with a tray on which were pottery tankards, a jug, and a plate of small cakes. As she approached, David recognised the honeyed aroma of hot *sbiten* rising from the jug, and the cakes looked very much like *pirog*. This world was indeed similar to the Russia he remembered from so many years ago. His host gestured him to an armchair, and David sat as the man poured steaming drinks and moved the cakes towards him with a genial 'please, partake,' before sitting down himself.

'Thank you. My name is David Dechar. I appreciate your hospitality.'

Sipping his drink – it was indeed *sbiten*, with the welcome addition of some kind of alcohol which tingled down to his thawing feet – David continued.

'I hope you may be able to help me. I seek the gatekeeper of this world, and I understood this was the correct direction. Is she close by? Or perhaps I was mistaken in the path I took?'

The man laughed, his handsome face creasing with a grin. 'Not mistaken, except in one assumption. I am the gatekeeper you seek.'

With difficulty, David managed not to choke on his *sbiten*. 'I apologise, Gatekeeper. But I thought all gatekeepers were ladies.'

His host chuckled again, clearly relishing the conversation. He rubbed his hands and leaned forward. 'It is true that nearly all of our kind are women. Not all of them are ladies, David! But in this world and close ones, the gate-keepers are men. It has always been so. I am Oleg.'

He took a hearty swig from his own tankard.

'So, now we have cleared up that small confusion, how may I assist you?'

David was well-practiced at his explanation of the search for his father, and he repeated it yet again. It had been fruitless nearly everywhere, with the sole exception of his visit to the version of Dodona a few weeks previously, and his expectations were low this time, especially as this world appeared so remote from his own. But as he explained his search there was a spark in the eyes of this most unusual of gatekeepers.

'I have no information myself, I regret, other than that deriving from rumours. Tales of a man thrown into the void decades ago and now a traveller of worlds in his search for home. An odyssey, it would seem. Also, tales of damage done to some gatekeepers and their temples, apparently resulting from the same event. Ah - but here is one who maybe has more for you.'

The door to the veranda was opening and in a blast of icy air and a haze of snow another man stepped into the warmth of the room, well-wrapped in furs. He stamped his boots and took off several layers, revealing his face. David goggled as a man virtually identical to Oleg stood before him, his eyebrows raised at David quizzically. Oleg stood and passed the newcomer a steaming full tankard. Then he grinned at David.

'Permit me to introduce you. This is Orel. Orel, this is David Dechar. He searches for his father, and I see from the lines that they are from a reality you have visited. The world from which you returned with Baranan.'

David's gaze moved from one to the other. Looking carefully, he could see that they were not identical, there were some small differences.

'Are you brothers?'

'Not exactly!' Orel's laugh sounded identical to Oleg's. 'But we regard ourselves in that light. Oleg is gatekeeper of this world, while I was gatekeeper of a very similar one, which split from this over a century ago. As there were only small differences between them, the worlds were able to slide back together decades later, and so one of us could no longer be a gatekeeper. When our world splits again, as it doubtless will, I will go to the new one.'

'And in the meantime, he is my trouble-shooter!' Oleg chuckled. 'It is the same in your world? Your gatekeeper discourages *gerasi* transgressions and punishes those who overstep?'

'Yes,' David nodded. 'Our gatekeeper occasionally disciplines my kind. She is... quite strict. Meddling in other worlds is one of the acts that provokes her to intervene.'

David was only too familiar with the centuries-old difference of opinion between his father and Melite on the matter. Jarn had complained about Melite's constraints and sanctions often enough.

Orel took another swig from his tankard, and grimaced, finding it too cool. Striding to the hearth he took a poker from the fire and put it in his drink, with a sizzle. Steam rose again.

'Meddling, yes, unfortunately there have been several incidents of that kind when we have had to intervene. The one Oleg refers to was the most recent, when I located a runaway from our world in your own, some years ago.

During our... recovery of the man, I had the opportunity to meet your gatekeeper. She was a most interesting personality.'

Orel stretched back in an armchair near the fire, his gaze frankly appreciative as the young woman returned with a fresh steaming jug and slid more hot cakes onto the plate. Leaning forward, he grinned at her as she passed his chair and she pushed him gently back in his seat with the edge of her ladle, giggling. His eyes followed her out the door.

The evening passed with easy conversation, and a constantly refreshed supply of increasingly alcoholic drinks and food. David reflected that this gatekeeper was about as different from Melite as it was possible to get. She had always put him in mind of an elderly and particularly grumpy crow, and the thought of her supplying such hospitality was unimaginable. He suspected that even his father secretly found her a little intimidating.

He was thinking it was time to step into the void and either return home or continue to one last world, when Oleg spoke. He had been silent for a while, while David and Orel had discussed the differences between the Russia's in their worlds. Oleg's hand was under his chin and his brows lowered in thought. Now he gestured towards David.

'Your father, David. Is it not strange he has not returned? He has been missing for decades, and yet we have heard he is especially adept. Such a shift is simple for most of your kind, and it should be trivial for him.'

Oleg was voicing the mystery that had perplexed David and all his family for many years, the thought underlaying their worst fears.

'We do not know, and it has puzzled us. It should indeed be child's play for him. But I recently spoke to a gatekeeper in a world similar to ours, and she believes that something is preventing him.' The gatekeeper had actually said 'someone', but David decided to not be so explicit.

But Oleg saw beneath the surface of his words. He passed a thoughtful hand over his beard. 'She suspects it is deliberate?'

'Yes,' David confirmed with some reluctance, 'although it hardly seems possible. Father is a strong personality, but I am not aware that he has an enemy who would target him so malevolently. Or, indeed, one who would have the power to do so.' He saw a look pass between the pair seated around the fire. There was communication between them without words. David sensed curiosity and some concern, but his telepathy skills were too immature to provide details.

Orel spoke first. 'There are rumours, and also some things we have experienced ourselves. They may be unconnected to your father's disappearance.'

Oleg continued. 'But, then again, they may be part of the same tale. Firstly, the void is altering. In some parts, it is growing. My fellow gatekeepers, in realities near to us, are concerned. Measures have been taken to check such growth, but it then rebuilds elsewhere. Again and again, it is stopped and then it regrows stronger than before. We are not sure our measures will ultimately be sufficient.'

He stood and approached the massive hearth, looking directly at the fire still burning brilliantly. The golden haze of the fire leapt and for the first time David saw within the flames the outline of the vortex. He suddenly understood why there was no temple here. This room itself contained the sacred fire and the vortex. Now it had stirred to golden life and was reaching out to Oleg, sinuously edging towards him. It reminded David of a cat. The gatekeeper's gaze was almost affectionate as he reached a hand into the swirling radiance.

'And also, we suspect there is some evil intention at work within the void. We have both felt it. And on several occasions we have actually exerted ourselves to repel it, while we have been travelling. This is not a recent development, we were first aware of a threat over a century ago, but like the void itself this presence now seems to be increasing in strength.'

There was no longer a hint of laughter on the faces of the two men, they both looked solemn, their handsome faces reflecting the firelight. The vortex swayed out towards them both but seemed reluctant to stir too much this evening.

'If these are indeed related to the search that brought you here, we advise you are very watchful within the void, David. The evil may be directed not only to the father but also to his son.'

CHAPTER 18
JARN, 'ISTANBUL', 26TH SEPTEMBER 2020

Jarn recognised the place the moment he stepped. The sensory overload he had always felt in this city in centuries past had not changed, despite the passage of years. He knew exactly where he was.

He was in a strange world, not his own, but this city was still the old Constantinople. The new Istanbul. For millennia on the cusp between Europe and Asia, it remained so even today. Ottoman, Turkish, Roman, Greek. First and foremost, Byzantine. All were here, with the sights, sounds and aromas the mixed heritage brought with it.

But, to Jarn, there could today be sensed something else: a distinct awareness of approaching danger.

He knew himself to be in the Sultanahmet, standing on the concrete balcony of a block of modern apartments. In the heart of old Constantinople, the apartments lay between the Bosphorus, the Golden Horn and the Sea of Marmara. From the balcony he could see the minarets of the Hagia Sophia, that astonishing core of the city; in some centuries a Christian church, but currently wavering between museum and mosque. With a vision focussed on the crucial fulcrums of his world, Jarn had always sensed what this place was, what it had been and what it might become. Although precisely what, even a *gerasi* could not see.

Beyond the Hagia Sophia, he knew from old memories, was the Topkapi palace and his last official visit to the palace in his own world flickered through his mind. One of the most astonishing trips he had undertaken for the Tsar; the formal procession through the palace, dressed in *hil'at* robes of honour, the grand vizier in full state. After the ceremony in the audience chamber and having been invited to view the Imperial Council chamber, he had been aware of unseen but watchful eyes from behind a golden grill. Jarn still wondered whose eyes they had been. He suspected the Valide Sultan, the Queen Mother, but an inquiry at the time could have cost him his head, ambassadorial representative or not.

But for now, ancient history was overlaid with twenty-first century noises, blaring traffic and distant music, mixed with calls to prayer. It was after noon, so this would be Zuhr prayer time. Around him, skyscrapers jostled with centuries-old bazaars. This old area had many new buildings, jarring against Jarn's memory of how it used to look. Tourists, taking in the sights and the sounds of the city, were starting to head towards restaurants for lunch, spiced cooking aromas wafting in the late summer air, as the faithful heeded the call to prayer.

The alarm Jarn had felt from his arrival, minutes before, was growing in magnitude and intensity. He was alert to a rumble in the earth deep below. Pressure was building, with irresistible strength. Catastrophe felt imminent. It was in that second that he recognised a familiar swirl in the threads of fate, far more complex than was apparent from the circumstances. Lines were surrounding him and brushing together, interweaving.

He stilled time to reach for more information, and the balcony around him receded into dimness. Himself, obviously, yes. But... *Issa*? How was that possible, here? She was not in this world. The other lines were unfamiliar, and Jarn sensed they were important but he could grasp no meaning from them. Time complained as his hitch continued, the delay could not be held much longer. Utterly perplexed, Jarn relaxed his grip and time flowed on.

He stretched his vision to explore the threat more thoroughly and was profoundly shocked. By all the old gods, Jarn thought, this was huge. More than he had ever perceived before. His thoughts reached out to Issa, although he knew she could not sense him in a different world. Yet again, it was time to step away, while he still had chance. Disaster swirled through the lines, glistening. All too obvious and only seconds away.

Nearby in the adjacent apartment he became aware of the sounds of children and the voice of a woman; their mother, Jarn guessed.

'We will eat the *menemen*, it is good. Then Miray will return from her friends' house, and she will have what is left!'

Jarn looked down from the balcony and saw a little girl of about six approaching the apartment block on the street below. She was looking about her in fear, despite the still-normal street scene.

With utter astonishment he realised why. She was aware of something approaching, something that she could not understand but which terrified her, because the child was *gerasi*. Dark haired, with a lower lip that was trembling and now with wide tear-filled eyes as the threat loomed closer, she was, incredibly, one of his own kind. And he recognised in her another of the strands he had seen moments earlier.

Jarn had long accepted that he could not save everyone from an oncoming fate. Some people, over the years, he had indeed saved. His lovely daughter-in-law Fizz had been one of them, one of many in a single blood-soaked night in the India of partition. But if he had tried to help everyone, it would have been never-ending. And one disaster so often simply replaces another. For the sake of his sanity, he had had to stop listening, to avert his senses. But today Issa was in his thoughts even more than usual and with this little girl so close and apparently interwoven with both of them, this time he couldn't just move on. He knew that her human family, in the room behind him, were not going to survive the enormous event and there was no time to avert that, but this frightened child did not need to die.

His action needed no more thought and, indeed, there was no time for any. He stepped down, grabbed the little girl and pitched both of them headlong into the void. As they vanished, the city around them shook as on an early day of creation, the fault line under the Marmara Sea just south of Istanbul rupturing catastrophically as continental plates shifted.

The Hagia Sophia had seen it all before. Soundly built seventeen centuries earlier by ancient architects and engineers who knew and understood earthquakes, her massive walls had resisted the trembles of the earth ever since and would do so again. But now she looked upon the city surrounding her, with its teeming modern buildings built with fragility for profit, and saw the world around her crumble, burying more than a million of her sons and daughters.

Three months later

The sun lowered behind the distant hills. Sunset was coming earlier now.

Birds flew to their roosts as Jarn watched, with his back against a tree, the small child he now regarded as his newest daughter sleeping in the bed he had made for her, bracken as the base, softer plants above, and then his own jacket around her. In truth, she looked very comfortable.

Jarn had pulled the girl out of her home world in the nick of time, but the worlds they had shifted to, again and again, had all been inappropriate. Some blazingly hot, some icily cold, some with hostile predators, some with malevolence hidden growling in the trees. Time and again Jarn had whisked the child away to heaven knew where, as his movements were without any control.

But finally, they had arrived at a peaceful beach. Waves splashed and Jarn had seen wood he could make both fire and shelter from and had heard fish leaping. More importantly there was no evidence of humans or *gerasi*, no animals and no threats, no matter how far Jarn stretched his senses. He had carefully placed the exhausted child on the sand and set about making a home, of sorts, and dinner.

That had been weeks before. It had taken many days before the child had snuggled to him one evening and started to talk of her family. Over many more evenings, Jarn had gained insight into Miray's home, made up of her mother, two little brothers and a chaotic but loving extended family. Miray's father had disappeared before the girl's birth and she knew nothing of him, although Jarn was aware the man had to be *gerasi*. But her mother had married when Miray was tiny, and that man, the father of her half-brothers, had been kind to her until his death in a motorcycle accident the previous year. Apart from that event, her life had been happy and normal until the September day when the earth broke apart. But the girl had no idea of the abilities that were hers by birthright.

In turn, Jarn described to her in stories akin to fairy tales, where he had come from and who the members of his precious family were. Miray listened night after night, captivated, until her eyelids drooped. Jarn had delighted in the telling, every story seeming to bring him closer to his beloved home.

The child was so young, not yet seven. A *gerasi*, but one with no training. And the little girl was terrified of the void, having never shifted until Jarn had whisked her from the path of death. He felt a stabbing pain as he was reminded of Sylvie, his adored younger daughter, who had always been fearful of the void. A fear Jarn could well understand, given the dead blackness and lifelessness of the icy place. But now, Miray was another young *gerasi* fearful of her heritage and, unlike Sylvie, Miray had had the trauma of losing her mother and brothers, her entire world. Her nightmares about the loss of her family and her home recurred again and again, night after night, reminding Jarn of the ones Issa used to suffer after her rescue, and with each night terror he felt fresh stabbing pain as he comforted the little girl, stroking her back as she sobbed.

Now, Jarn leant back against the tree and wondered for the hundredth time what Issa would do if she were here. His mate had a nurturing nature, and he knew without a doubt she would absorb this child into their family with no thought or care for the lack of direct lineage. The girl would become theirs, just as their birth children were and just as Jarn now saw her as his.

But what would she do to treat the trauma, the nightmares? Jarn thought she would, at the start, have the little girl sleep in their bedroom every night, relieving the fear just by her presence. And she would ensure that Miray's days were filled to exhaustion with exercise and learning and fun, from dawn to dusk and beyond. Stuffed with a healthy diet, endless mental stimulation and racing around in the lands of their estates, he couldn't remember any of their children ever struggling to sleep. They were more usually begging for bedtime. He chuckled to himself as he remembered the evening when David had pitched forward into his soup, exhausted into sleep by his first day of hunting in the fields around their Russian home. Jarn still remembered carrying his young son to bed.

Such treatment was harder under the current circumstances. Jarn knew he had to try again to return home. More than anything, he wanted to take this child with him. She had become his daughter. But he could not drag her through shift after shift. Each trip to the void terrified her, and who knew what menaces awaited her in every world they catapulted into? In their journey to this world they had already met dangers enough. So, he had to move her to a place of absolute safety while he continued his attempt to return to Termonn. Then he would, beyond any doubt, return for her.

After yet another fish supper, Jarn tried to explain this to a small girl who was already traumatised. They would leave this place and travel to somewhere safe, then he would find the way to his own home, and without any doubt he *would* return for her. Jarn's mention of returning to the void had the girl terrified again but she had finally slept. He gently wiped away the tearstains remaining on the girl's cheeks and started to plan. Tomorrow they must step, again, together, but not to the void.

It needed a gentle, fun introduction.

And so, for the next few weeks they did small hops, going nowhere near the void. Turning it into a game, Jarn would ask how many birds Miray could count before they moved again? How many trees? How many people? One day, giggling, she said 'two birds, lots of trees, and four humans,' as Jarn surveyed the landscape in front of him and thought he may have finally found a solution.

The land looked Mediterranean. There was a substantial stone farmhouse a short distance away, set among olive groves. He could see people working the fields and, as Miray had said, there were three of them. And approaching them was the fourth person, a middle-aged man with a face alive with curiosity.

But the man was not quite human. Neither was he fully *gerasi,* but he had aspects of their nature. He reminded Jarn of Mordecai, a man who was also not human but who was also not *gerasi* except for his longevity. Hettie was similar. Jarn knew the man walking towards him had recognised Jarn for what he was and accepted it, was even honoured by his presence. He gestured that Jarn and Miray accompany him to the farmstead, and they followed him over paths rutted with white stones, the scent of baked earth and herbs in the air.

Jarn stayed for weeks, ensuring that Miray was safe here. He could see no possible threat, the land was peaceable and Athan and his wife Thera, childless, had both come to adore Miray and could readily provide for her. It was the perfect solution, but Jarn was agonised the day he finally came to leave. Miray's lower lip trembled in a heart-breaking reminder of how he had first found the little girl, but she was steadfast as she looked at him with eyes older than her years.

'I know you will return for me, Jarn. And I know you can't stay. When you come for me, I will be waiting. Bring Mother Issa with you?'

It was the last request that broke Jarn's resolve. His descriptions of Issa had always enchanted Miray and her desire for both new parents broke his heart. He pulled the small child into his arms, his mouth against her hair. Somehow, he *would* get home, he *would* solve the problem of directionless travel, and he *would* return, with Issa, to reclaim this lost child. It would not be an empty promise even if it took him millennia.

'We will both come for you. And you will be our daughter.'

CHAPTER 19
CLARE, TERMONN HOUSE,
8TH JULY 2022

It was again breakfast time in the kitchen and Maya was clearing away my plate. It seemed I was now a resident in the house, one who was permitted to eat in the family kitchen, and no longer a guest who required serving in her own bedroom. The feeling of acceptance was pleasant, but I didn't want to be waited on.

'Maya, let me do that,' I urged. It felt wrong on many levels, but especially that this silent gentle lady should be my servant. But I was deposited back in my seat with a little push, and Maya moved the coffee pot closer to me. Giving up, I topped up my cup. Sylvie and Fizz were late this morning, either having a lie-in in the lodge house or perhaps already about village chores. I missed their chirpy, sisterly presence.

Sipping my coffee, I searched online for the events of yesterday and any speculation on the reason why the Westminster construction work was suspended. The closure of major tube lines near Westminster was indeed frontpage news.

The Patrician company had made a statement saying

that due to indications of World War Two ordnance in the Thames they were proceeding with extreme caution; building work would continue once the site had been declared safe by the Ministry of Defence. No risks would be taken with public safety. Controlled explosions may be required, in which case there could be a need for some limited evacuation of the area and possible prolonged closures of part of the underground network but, it was repeated, there was absolutely no risk to the public. The Mayor of London confirmed the messaging. Residents and workers in the area should remain attentive to the news but should be unconcerned for their safety.

Perhaps it was so, now, but it could have been so different yesterday. Images of what might have happened played through my mind as I remembered Mary's graphic warnings. Suddenly, I felt the need for fresh air. The kitchen was warm because of the ever-hot range and the morning indicated yet another brilliant English summer day, although the air was more humid than previous days and thunderstorms were forecast. I thanked and hugged Maya, who nodded sedately and patted my arm, and headed for the stable door.

Once outside, the air felt fresher but clouds were looming to the east behind St Michael's tower. I had not yet walked in that direction and set off around the east terrace towards the track leading up through the pasture. I found myself accompanied by Sergei, the Tibetan mastiff. Sergei was a huge and powerful dog with a black and tan coat, looked after by Mordecai at his home in St Michael's tower. Hettie had told me the breed were flock guardians, mostly sleeping during the day and alert at night. Clearly Sergei had decided his night-time duty was over and so he was at liberty to escort me back to his tower home this morning.

We crossed the ha-ha and continued up the track. After ten minutes, I was feeling the heat and wishing I'd brought a sun hat. But we continued up to the tower, which loomed over us at a surprising height when we were close. From a distance it had seemed smaller. Looking back down towards Termonn House, I admired again the beauty of the manor nestled in its valley. Lawns and flower borders surrounded the golden stone house, with its edging of moat: it was a truly beautiful setting, at the centre of the cross of paths. Tourists would rave over it, if they were aware it existed, but it was not open to the public and seemed to have been overlooked by most guides to the Cotswolds.

A door behind me opened and Sergei bounded towards it. Mordecai had emerged from his apartment on the ground floor of the ancient tower. The huge dog licked his face affectionately with both front paws on the man's shoulders. A smaller human would have been knocked over.

'Get inside, daft pooch'. A soft push persuaded Sergei to trot inside to find his breakfast and presumably his bed. Mordecai turned to me.

'Good morning, ma'am. Sounds like a good job done yesterday by you and the lady.'

'Thanks.' I was still not entirely sure I'd done much to deserve praise. I added, 'it was good of you to pick us up.'

He produced an expression that on most people would have been a grimace but on Mordecai was a smile.

'A pleasure driving that car. The lord would be pleased to see her exercised, not standing idle. But she's a good girl, always rises to the occasion.' I thought that to Mordecai the car was an animal, perhaps even a pet.

'Now, weather's going to break soon, ma'am. P'rhaps best to be making for home? Either straight back down or, if you want to cut round by the beacon, you could take the track opposite.'

He gestured behind me, and I could see a path that curved through woodland up to the beacon.

'Thanks, I will!'

The path was shady between the trees, the bleating of sheep more distant in the wood. It curved round to the right and the cool under the trees was welcome. The path then climbed quite steeply before levelling out and running along the edge of a large tree fringed lake, presumably the one Issa had mentioned, which had fed Jarn's water powered turbine before it had ceased to work. The sun dappled through the trees as I walked, but with every step I could tell it was becoming weaker, as the sky above became more overcast.

In the distance I could see grass, and the beacon beyond. I was surprised when I emerged from the wood to see just how cloudy it had become in a short time. The clouds had scurried in. My path led towards the beacon summit, just a few hundred yards away, and with a glance back over my shoulder at the black gathering clouds, I decided it was best to get indoors. I walked smartly through the wildflower meadow and then turned right, onto the path which led from the beacon down to the house.

After a minute of brisk walking, I felt a wave of the sensation Issa had called *jamais vu*, my surroundings looking for a second unfamiliar to me although they were actually unchanged. Issa had explained it was due to my sensitivity to a nearby world. I stopped and looked around me. Shards of sunlight were falling upon both the path to the house and the path to the beacon, both glowing. From this height I could see the track beyond the house leading to the old gates and again it gleamed, burnished against the dimming sky. As black rainclouds approached, the golden paths became even more striking, the manor house below me brilliant against the now darkening valley around it. There was a rumble of thunder in the distance as I turned my back on the beacon and started again down the path to the house.

Suddenly I became aware of someone or something behind me. I spun.

The track to the beacon and the beacon itself, were now ablaze with fire. And out of the golden flames a tall man stepped. Dark-haired. I experienced again the over-whelming sense of familiarity I had first felt in the vortex days before. This was, I knew, the man who had half-turned to me.

Neither of us moved, for what seemed like hours. Rain-drops began to fall, in the distance came another rumble of thunder, but for me the world was still. I felt no fear of the man in front of me. Instead, a sense of stretching, of completeness. Of pieces joining, slotting into position. Paths, worlds, whole dimensions, coalesced into sharp focus in the golden clouds around me.

The man came closer, and I could see wonder in his eyes, which I thought must be reflected in my own.

'I am David. *Who, on this earth, are you?*'

CHAPTER 20
JARN, 'DEDONA', 18TH MAY, 2022

Jarn was thoroughly fed up, irritated beyond measure by travelling endlessly through worlds but being unable to shift to the only world he wanted to be in. Moving, every time hoping to be near home. Sometimes sensing he was close, trying to make the final shift, which should have been so easy for him, he had been doing it for centuries. Knowing exactly how to do it, where to direct his movement. Approaching the void with certainty. Stepping. And then an uncontrollable spinning and finding himself worlds away. Again, and again.

Over his long lifetime he had travelled with pinpoint accuracy and a profound knowledge of the shifting worlds as they altered, developed and coalesced around his home world. Human decisions were constantly made, futures altered, new worlds created, spawning a multitude of even newer worlds around them. But Jarn had foreseen all of them, had always known where he was each time he emerged from the void, and with his ability it should have been but a shift or two to get home from anywhere even vaguely close. He was still at a loss to understand why all his attempts were now random, out-of-control. So often, to be so close, only to be spun off on his next attempt into a world even more distant, just to grit his teeth and have to try again. Concern not only about his family but about Miray, who he had left approaching two years ago, nagged at him and increased his sense of urgency.

But finally, he knew he was in a world very close to home, the closest he had ever been. It looked, smelt, felt, so similar in nearly all respects, only a few differences. He thought he was in a Mediterranean country, perhaps Spain or Portugal.

Jarn approached with supreme caution the frontier that lay between himself in this world and what he felt beyond doubt to be his home world. So near, so very near. But he felt trepidation at the prospect of being jettisoned again into a world of never-ending glaciers or deserts, and only to have to painstakingly rebuild his attempt yet again.

Probing carefully, a step at a time, he knew with complete certainty there was indeed a strong barrier in front of him, barring him from the world of Termonn. He knew that with just another step he would be repelled again heaven-knew where.

Withdrawing, he thought carefully. Trying to get to his home world from here would be no more successful than his other attempts. Why not try a different approach? Try to step to the site of Dodona in this world?

He pulled the familiar energies together and shifted, emerging into a damp, overcast plain, with drizzle in the air. The landscape, through mist, was the familiar valley of Dodona, with the ancient amphitheatre to his left. He looked hard to the right, where he knew the temple had been in his home world centuries before.

Many worlds had a portal in a similar location, some the

residence of gatekeepers and some not. Jarn knew that not all gatekeepers were friendly to *gerasi*, and none – absolutely none - would assist in transfer between far-distant worlds or would assist in meddling in the affairs of other worlds. Such things were strictly prohibited. Jarn doubted a gatekeeper would even assist him in shifting to an adjacent world, but perhaps he would be lucky.

After intense concentration, the landscape shimmered and the ancient temple appeared before him, rising from the few remaining stones littering the ground in this area. So familiar. And his heart leapt even more as he saw the gatekeeper, who was turned away from him, facing the entrance to her temple. A woman very similar to Melite. Not Melite herself; like *gerasi,* she existed only in her home world. But most likely a twin of hers, created in a past split of realities from Melite's own world. Jarn hoped that was the case, as it would be a further indication he was close to his home world.

The gatekeeper turned at his approach and Jarn forced himself not to recoil. She might have once been much alike to Melite, but her face was horribly scarred, as if it had been severely burnt on one side. The remaining side of her face twisted into an expression of recognition when she saw Jarn.

'Madam.' Overcoming his shock, Jarn knew well how to approach gatekeepers, and the honour due to them. He bowed. Deeply.

'Jarn Dechar.'

She approached him, and the scarring became even more visible. It appeared as if one side of her face had been subject to intense heat. The surviving side of her face was accusing.

'It was *your* action that wrought havoc on us, decades ago.'

Her words meant nothing at first, but as he looked at her face the truth slowly dawned. The force of the nuclear explosion in the void, the void to which he had sent the exploding weapon, must have rippled through the darkness and into the gatekeeper's portal in this world, so alike to his own.

His face showed his horror.

'Yes, you are correct. One day, an immense burning power came through our fire. We were surrounding the vortex, in the midst of our devotions. There was no warning. It burned me and killed several temple maids.'

Her face twisted in grief.

'We knew then that an event had occurred in the void. But it has only been recently that the power of our temple has returned, and through it I have seen in the flames the action that triggered the explosion. And I have seen you. As you fled from it.'

Her scarred face contorted into the approximation of a grimace. 'Only just in time, I might say. You, at least, were fortunate.'

Jarn was genuinely, deeply, contrite. He had not thought such things possible.

'Madam.... it was never my intention to hurt you. Or your temple. Events moved so fast. I had no time to think of the consequences...'

'That sounds almost human, Jarn. They rarely think of the consequences of their actions for others either, do they? Or at least, not when self-interest is uppermost in their thoughts.'

The gatekeeper walked into her temple, and two maids approached. At a word, they disappeared into the further recesses, emerging almost immediately with a flagon and cups. The gatekeeper lowered herself to a stone bench and poured wine, passing a cup to Jarn.

'But I do understand your action. The lives of many humans were at stake, and your own family not so very far away. Yes, it was understandable and also courageous. I do not really reproach you for it. And neither does Melite, I believe. I should introduce myself. I am Melisse. A sister of Melite, created centuries back, when her world split and this one was born.'

The gatekeeper sipped from her cup and continued.

'So, why are you here?' Her gaze on him was penetrating. She seemed to be searching for something.

'That is simple.' Jarn tried to fix his gaze on the undamaged half of the gatekeeper's face, as the horrific scarring was too vivid a reminder that it was his action that had caused it. He was trying to avoid being overwhelmed by guilt.

'I am trying to find my way home. I seem unable to take the final step. Although it should be easy for me. I do not understand why it seems impossible.'

'Ah, yes, returning home may indeed be a problem.' The gatekeeper had a steely gaze in her remaining eye, and Jarn was briefly reminded of Melite.

'Firstly, you need to understand that it was not only this world's temple that was blasted, it happened in other close worlds as well, with similar damage. However, the effect for you personally...'

Jarn stood suddenly and moved away, turning his back on the woman. Dread filled his mind as he realised that his inability to return might not be due to himself or to some strange physical cause but instead be because his world was no longer there. The thought hadn't occurred to him before. He found himself unable to ask the only question that now mattered, feeling numb. True despair threatened to over-come him for the first time.

But he heard her voice behind him. 'Your world was not destroyed, no. It is more complicated than that. Have you looked into the vortex recently, Jarn Dechar?'

'No, this is the first time I have got as close as this to a temple, or to home.' Jarn turned to her, hope slowly returning.

'Then let us look now.'

The gatekeeper beckoned him towards the cauldron in the centre of the stone temple. The embers within were merely glowing, only small flames flickering with shades of blue and orange. She took a handful of herbs from an earth-enware bowl on the rim and scattered them into the embers. Flames instantly flared, spitting, and a shimmering gold and silver vision rose up, reaching a height which towered over them. Jarn instinctively fell back a little. It had been decades since he had viewed a vortex, but the sight was as awe-inspiring as ever. And the Dodona vortex was exceptionally powerful.

'Do you see anything unusual?' The gatekeeper was watching Jarn rather than the swirling creation she had conjured.

Jarn looked carefully and his attention was caught by the black centre which stretched from top to bottom. Black was a poor description; it was a shape that seemed to suck in and capture all the glittering light around it. An emptiness.

'The void seems bigger than I remember.'

'It does indeed seem to be growing somewhat, which concerns all of us. It is encompassing whole worlds through its expansion, dragging them into the dark. Anything else?'

Jarn examined the vortex carefully and saw nothing else unusual. Melisse reached a hand towards the vortex and with a gesture rotated it, bringing a section closer to where they stood. This part grew and blossomed under her hand, more and more swirling detail becoming visible. One world in particular came into sharp focus, gold and silver clouds spiralling.

'What is that?'

Jarn pointed to a tiny dark brown spot amid the swirling mass. Despite its minute size it was noticeable because it was the only feature of that colour in the vortex.

'Ah, yes. This is the world we are currently standing in,' the gatekeeper's one-eyed gaze became hawk-like in its focus, '...and *that*, Jarn Dechar, is the part of the void which is now around you.'

Jarn thought he had misheard. 'Around me?'

'As I look at you now, I can see it myself, from here. But it is probably not visible to you. You are, after all, not a gatekeeper.'

This was said with an air of condescension and Jarn found himself unexpectedly submerged in a memory of Issa joking that Melite made her think of a supercilious vulture. A wave of nostalgia flooded him. The way his wife's eyes would shine and her lips curve as she laughed or giggled. Her low chuckle, which he had always found incredibly seductive. It had been over forty years since he had last seen her and these days she was even more in his thoughts than before, as he comforted himself with recollections.

Jarn lost himself in memory for a moment before forcing himself back to the conversation.

'How can one person be surrounded by part of the void? I have never heard of such a thing.' And Jarn did not really believe it. The physical damage inflicted on the woman had clearly disturbed her judgement, if not her mind.

'We do not know, we only suspect. But we think that the

event at the airfield which led to the explosion in the void, and which rebounded on other worlds through their gateways, was not an accident. We think that someone or something was behind it, guiding it. Guiding it to you, very specifically.'

'No, Gatekeeper. It was just an accident. A bizarre one, I agree. But an accident nevertheless.'

'Jarn, you are not a fool. Suspend your disbelief and consider. Firstly, the chance of the lightening hitting that particular aircraft were low. Then, we understand that the likelihood of such a thing actually triggering the weapon is miniscule, and yet it happened. And finally, you are unable to control your shifts, are you not? And whenever you get close to home, you rebound further away?'

'All of those are true, I believe.' Jarn spoke grudgingly, but his mind was whirling.

'Then, it is our opinion that some sentient being is behind this, one who has the aim of either destroying you, entrapping you or both. It would appear they failed in the first goal but they have partially succeeded in the second. They were able to use the force of the explosion to detach part of the void and to shape it around you, to frustrate your movements. We have never heard of such a thing before, but it seems the only explanation.'

Jarn struggled to grasp this new perception of his problem. He suddenly recalled with dread a feeling he had experienced in a fleeting trip through the void years back, a sense that there was some evil there, searching blindly but seeking him specifically. Coming closer and closer. He had lurched out of the void with his heart hammering but had subsequently dismissed it as imagination. It had, after all, only happened once.

The gatekeeper continued remorselessly.

'To be clear, we believe that the barrier around you has been constructed deliberately to stop you returning to your home. Either to keep you away from your family…'

'Yes…?'

'Or to draw you back to the void and some sort of meeting or confrontation.'

Both thoughts were deeply unwelcome. But the theory indisputably had some logic behind it. Why else was he unable to shift home?

'So, there is no way I can return home at present, Gatekeeper? And my family are likewise trapped?'

She quirked her remaining eyebrow at Jarn. 'No. Your son has demonstrated that they, at least, are not trapped.'

'David?' Jarn's heart soared. Oh, to see his son again, or any one of his children. 'David has been here?'

'Yes, David. He passed through several weeks ago, searching for you. We spoke of these matters and I showed him the expansion of the void and the worlds it has consumed. I believe he will return at some point. However, we doubt you can be here when he is, should he reappear. The malevolent deliberation behind this has created a barrier around you which is strong. The action to separate you from your family will likely not permit you to be in the same world as them. We suspect that is the purpose of it.'

Disappointed by the lack of attention being shown to it, the swirling gilded vortex sank back towards the embers, settling into them with a small huffy hiss. Jarn didn't notice, he was prowling around the cauldron. His frustration erupted in one growling question.

'How do I get home?'

'It may not be possible.'

The gatekeeper took a speedy step backwards at the

expression on Jarn's face. The answer was clearly not accept-able to him. She raised a placating hand.

'Now, my boy, now... there may be possibilities. If you travel to the site of your home, either in this world or another world very close to yours, you will be near to your power there. Your home is on the strongest conjunction of lines in your world, apart from those running through Dodona, and the lines give energy which help travel across worlds. You know this, it is why you made your home where it is, after all. On what humans call ley lines, may the gods help us.'

Melisse poked the embers irritably.

'Give a human two points and they have to draw a line between them and count up the ancient sites nearby. They then happily disregard features that don't fall on their lovely straight line and ignore modern features like power stations which do. And then they say they have *proved* the existence of these magical lines. And most of them are complete twad-dle. But the Termonn intersection is perfectly genuine. And powerful.'

He agreed with the theory, but surely it was one thing to travel to the site of his home in this world and quite another to expect a gateway to magically open once he got there.

'And once I am near the site of Termonn?'

'After that, we cannot say. A gateway may exist where your lines cross, in all nearby worlds, or a new passage may be opened which is strong enough to destroy the barrier around you. Although we suspect that would take immense power.'

'What sort of power? Another of those infernal bombs?' As if there is any chance of me finding another of those damn devices he thought, bitterly.

The gatekeeper turned back to the embers and gave

them another energetic prod. 'The power you and other *gerasi* possess. It is immense, you know. The transfer of power when one of you leaves your life may be enough to create a new door if it is directed suitably.'

'So, I just need to wait until one of my family dies, or sacrifices their life to get me back? You think I would accept that kind of gift?'

'It may not need such drastic action, but you will not know without travelling there. But for the gods' sakes do not travel via the void in future. Now depart, Jarn Dechar, I am weary.'

No, this gatekeeper was not very different from Melite after all. The two might not have been the same person but they clearly shared a common heritage. Jarn had noticed before that the servants of Zeus had a certain air of entitlement. And he had never been sure that the gatekeepers were merely the servants of the old god. He had wondered idly more than once if they had originally been offspring.

Finding himself dismissed, Jarn moved towards the great temple door. The temple edifice was already starting to shimmer away. A thought struck him and he turned back to Melisse.

'Should my son return, reassure him. Tell him I will never stop trying to come home.'

Then he was back in the drizzle and the mist. Behind him were only a few stones, almost submerged beneath the soil of millennia.

'...and tell him I love them all.' But the temple had vanished.

CHAPTER 21
CLARE, TERMONN HOUSE,
8TH JULY 2022

We crashed through the stable door and stood there, dripping rain onto the stone flags of the kitchen floor and panting, as rain and hail pelted on the path outside and onto the kitchen windows. We had run at speed down the path from the beacon to avoid the worst of the storm, my hand in David's. I jogged frequently in London and was grateful for it now. Fortunately, David appeared to be just as fit, keeping pace with me easily.

Hettie had been mixing something at the kitchen table, but at the sight of us blasting into her kitchen she dropped the spoon and gave a small squeal. Maya, stirring a pot at the range, turned and, although wordless, her hands clutched to her chest were as eloquent as the sound Hettie had made. Within moments we were folded in warm towels and Hettie was rubbing my hair. Maya pushed David to a chair and placed a cup of hot tea in front of him. Then the door from the hallway opened and Issa sped in, to stop abruptly as she took in the scene before her.

David stood and held his arms out to his mother as she ran to him. I averted my gaze, thinking this was a private moment that needed no observers, but I was aware of Hettie pausing in her rubbing of my hair and Maya watching the scene with the closest to a grin I had yet seen on her inscrutable face.

A few moments later Sylvie flew in, closely followed by Fizz. Issa relinquished her hold of David and stood back to allow him to be swamped by his sister and her partner's embraces.

A delicious lunch with something sparkling had us all crowded around the kitchen table, Maya and Hettie included. Halfway through, Mordecai and Adam came in and were both sat down with full plates and glasses. Gossip was exchanged about Michaelcombe, the country and the world, updating David, but I noticed that he was quiet. Presumably having spent months in other worlds, it was difficult to contribute items of relevance to the conversation, and he was also trying to adjust to being back home.

For me, I was too shaken by the sensations that had overwhelmed me, and my new vision of an entire creation linked to David, to be able to do more than try to follow the talk around the table. I felt in a new reality, my under standing and perception of the networks between worlds entirely changed. All I could do was gaze speechless at him when I thought no-one was looking. My glances revealed more of the man I had run down the hill with. Tall, broad and with features that were a mixture of the charismatic but somewhat scary Jarn I had seen in the drawing room photo-graph, and his more delicate mother. But a strong person-ality all his own. I drank him in, my heart beating fast. My new awareness of him told me he was feeling something of the same. I was intensely aware of his gaze on me whenever I was looking elsewhere, just as mine was on him when he was talking to his mother or sister.

I had had one significant relationship before, but it had been nothing like this. Now it was as if David and I had swept past weeks of 'getting to know you'; we somehow knew each other deeply, despite only meeting an hour ago. Then my eyes met David's. For a moment time stopped and I saw it all reflected in his eyes.

But the world of Termonn was moving on, despite our private earthquake. House-keeping arrangements followed. It was best, Hettie suggested, if I stayed on in my current room, and David remained in the stable apartment where his possessions now were. I felt guilty and said so, but everyone else very much agreed with the proposal. David belatedly caught up with the conversation and nodded to the new arrangements, with a last look at me.

Hettie went over to the stables with David to make sure the water heating was on and to refresh linens and towels, and I was left sitting at the table trying to make sense of the surge of sensations and emotions that had hit me. Issa placed a gentle and understanding hand on my arm and withdrew, as Sylvie and Fizz ushered me upstairs with our coffees to the library, a room I had not been inside before.

It was a large and beautiful room of double height, facing north, with what seemed to be thousands of books, and on the higher levels folded manuscripts. The magnificent window was topped by stained glass and I noticed the central pane was indeed the badge of St Patrick, as Issa had said.

On the marble fireplace was a framed and tinted daguerreotype photograph of a seated Queen Victoria with a balding and worn-looking Prince Albert standing behind her. Seated next to the Queen, who unbelievably was managing a demure smile rather than her usual forbidding expression, was Issa. In a crinoline which still managed to be elegant, her hair held up by combs and a lace cap on her head, she was half-turned towards the Queen as if listening to her. Behind Issa and standing next to the Prince, was Jarn, his eyes focused on the camera. Despite his conventional pose and the formal correctness and suave precision of his attire, there was something about the directness of his gaze and the challenge in his eyes that made me wonder how the royal couple hadn't noticed they had a tiger standing next to them. The inscription under the photograph said 'Windsor, October 1857'.

I became aware of Sylvie at my side.

'The Queen and Prince really enjoyed having Mother and Father visit them in the late 1850's. The Prince enjoyed talking to Father about science and engineering, and the Queen loved Mother, with her gentleness and her experience of the world. In fact, earlier in the year this photograph was taken, Mother had held the Queen's hand when her last child, Princess Beatrice, was born. Of course, it all came to an end when the Prince died in 1861 and the Queen went into seclusion. My parents did see her afterwards, although not so frequently, but their royal service and connections continued into later reigns. And still do.'

Sylvie pointed to framed photographs of Issa, and occasionally Jarn, with members of the Royal Family over the last century. I recognised Queen Mary, looking quite grim, seated next to Issa, who was demurely embroidering a cloth, and another photograph of a grinning King George VI offering Jarn, clad in jodhpurs and a polo shirt, a trophy of some sort. There was Jarn again, swinging a young prince in the air, Issa sitting laughing on a tartan rug on the grass with Queen Elizabeth. Another frame held a very recent snap of Issa with the present monarch, by what appeared to be a Scottish loch.

Sylvie then led me to some of the most important items in the Termonn collection, the celestial and terrestrial globes near to the desk and a beautiful antique orrery. She gave brief descriptions of all of them, and Fizz chipped in with dates and details. I knew they were giving me time to adjust from meeting David, and I was very grateful.

After a while, we sat sipping our coffees on the large sofa, Sylvie on one side of me and Fizz on the other. I thought of trying to put my feelings into words, but my thoughts stumbled. It was too much to describe. After companionable minutes, Sylvie simply said 'we know. We remember when we first met.'

CHAPTER 22
JARN, 'AUSTRALIA', JUNE
AND JULY, 2022

Oh please, not more sheep.

After leaving Melisse, the gatekeeper of this world, Jarn had taken her advice and had eschewed the void, simply stepping to new locations within her world. Even when stepping, his movements were unpredictable, but at least he was not propelled out of this world, which he knew was close to home. He had spent weeks working in this reality's equivalent of South America. Somewhere where there were more sheep than humans, by a very large factor.

Taking casual work as a hired hand, he had assisted with herdings, shearings, the transfer to abattoirs, and then early births. If he was never to see a sheep again in his existence it would be far too soon.

Then he reflected with considerable guilt that his greatly missed English estate possessed his own very substantial flock of sheep. But they were usually at a distance in their green pastures, there were far fewer of them than here, and somehow the little blighters were more acceptable because they were his own. And they had character.

He had turned his hand to lambing on many occasions,

as had Issa, her midwifery skills and slender fingers being very useful. Jarn recalled wistfully from years past how his wife had nurtured tiny new-borns near the warm kitchen range, wielding the milk bottle with dexterity as snow fell outside. She had been very good at it, his memories reminded him, although it had sometimes been difficult to extract the small creatures from her care and return them to the juvenile pen in the stable block. If Issa had had her way the kitchen would have been full of small gambolling lambs. And their droppings.

So - what did he find on emerging from his last stepping away from what had appeared to be South America? Another landscape of sheep. Bloody sheep. Blasted woolly sheep. Baa'ing and endlessly bleating.

Jarn had begun to wonder if one of the many deities of the old world he had offended in centuries past had taken deep umbrage and was determined to make his life a misery from now onwards. If so, she was succeeding (and Jarn had little doubt that this particular god was female).

However, this did not look like South America. It was emptier, flatter, pastures penned with white fencing disappearing into the far distance on all horizons, except for a red-roofed building about a kilometre away. Jarn gritted his teeth and set off in that direction, sheep skittering away from him as he stalked. They must have sensed he was not to be meddled with as they kept well clear, although he had noticed that the average sheep seemed to have little concept of self-preservation.

As he approached the red-roofed building he could see that it was a ranch, and a substantial one. Several men were working in the vicinity. A man who might have been a manager approached him from a nearby shed with a suspicious 'G'day to you but how the hell did you get here?' and

Jarn realised he was in a version of Australia. Oh great. Australia. And sheep. Could life get much worse? His heart sank.

His visit to Australia in the 1830's, in his own world and with Issa, had not endeared him to the Australian settlers of that time. He and Issa had rescued Maya from men doing their best to slaughter her in the most degrading and painful way possible, simply because she was a native and did not speak their language. To them, she was sport, similar to the game they had been hunting, and in their view she was far less than human. They had already succeeded in killing her husband, barbarically in front of her, before Jarn and Issa had arrived. Jarn had cut Maya down from the noose that was close to strangling her and had left her to Issa's care while he turned to her would-be murderers.

Jarn had not dealt kindly with the men, unreasoning cruelty being a trait he had no patience with. At the time, he had tried not to take pleasure in the punishment he had meted out. That would have resembled what the men had been doing to Maya, what they had done to her husband. But to this day he was not sure he had entirely succeeded, no matter how justified he had felt at the time. It had left a tarnished memory that was tinged with guilt in his mind, and he had preferred not to visit the continent again. If Issa had not been present his retribution would have been even more severe. He knew that at his core he was a much less civilised creature than his wife. Her caring and humane nature was one of the many things he adored about her.

'Good afternoon' – the sun was past its peak so it seemed a fair guess – 'Do you need any hired help, I'm looking for work?'

'How'd ya get here? We're a long way from any road.'

The man was understandably suspicious, and Jarn was fixed with a piercing stare from under bushy eyebrows in a weather worn face. He thought the man was looking at him oddly. Unusually so.

'Cutting across country with some pals in a 4x4, heading for the water' – Jarn really hoped there was a river or lake or even a dried-up riverbed of some description not too far away – 'we got a bit lost and then we had quite a bust-up and I decided to cut loose and walk. Really glad to see your place.'

He hoped that would be sufficient. And hoped to heaven there hadn't been any recent serial killings in the neighbourhood.

'Okaaaay...' Jarn was looked up and down like a piece of cow flesh but fortunately his physique seemed to impress.

'I'm Mark Driffold, station manager. We're a bit short at present, so if you come in and talk to Mrs B, if she likes you there may be a chance of a few days' work.'

An assessing stare. 'But any trouble and you'll be out, clear?'

'Yes, sir.' Jarn was grateful to have the prospect of work so speedily, and in such a location. But, he thought, he really did need to get home to his own estate, where he could do the hiring and firing himself. He was getting fed-up with being ordered around.

It transpired, from station staff chatter, that he was in Queensland, Australia. An area of heat even in the Australian winter, and deep in savannah country. The owner of Belaron, as the station was named, was a Kate Borman.

Jarn had a short interview with Kate Borman. Mid-thirties, fair-haired and willowy, with a complexion that in England may have stayed pale but with the Australian sun was golden. Her husband was no longer on the scene, it seemed.

He had noted her look of shock when he first introduced himself, in the house office Mark Driffold had led him to, but had decided to ignore it. Her face had actually whitened under her tan. Perhaps she just disliked tall men. But he was aware that Kate was assessing him shrewdly in much the same way as her manager had, and with more perspicuity than many had before.

He explained that he was from England but had moved around a lot. And, certainly, he reflected, that was nothing if not the absolute truth. At the end of the short interview, he found himself hired for a week.

Several days of hard physical toil followed. Jarn was fit, but the weather was hotter and more brutal here than he had experienced for some years, and by the end of each day he looked forward to a sluice in the farm hands' shower and his bed in the staff quarters. He was relieved that his duties didn't seem to involve sheep, being more in the nature of fence repair and outbuilding maintenance.

On the fourth day he was tasked with repairing clapperboard facing to part of the main house and became aware of three pairs of watchful eyes on him while he went about his tasks. He stretched out and sensed that all the pairs of eyes had female owners, and two were regarding him with blatant interest. One was Leila, the maid, and another was Clary the cook. The third was undoubtedly Kate Borman herself, and Jarn felt her feelings were more complex.

By mid-afternoon the clapperboard was mended, the holes were filled and the surfaces sanded. The following day he would paint both clapperboard and front door to match the rest of the building.

'Mr Dechar.'

Kate's voice called up to him from the drive below his ladder.

'It's a very warm day. Would you appreciate a cup of tea? I thought you could tell me a bit about England?'

Jarn knew that the England here could be quite different to the England he had left over forty years before in a similar but different world. He would have to be careful. But he was good at prevarication and a cup of tea would be welcome. A cold beer would be even better. He descended the ladder and accepted the invitation with a nod and a grateful smile.

The large drawing room of the house was a mixture of colonial, modern and 1970's English. Kate poured tea into a china cup from a silver teapot that would have fitted well in houses in Kensington or Richmond. But Jarn saw with contentment that she also had chilled beer glasses and bottles with moisture condensing on their surfaces, recognising that a man who had been working outside in the heat for much of the day would not have his bodily needs met by a cup of Earl Grey. He accepted a filled glass with real gratitude.

An hour later they were well into a discussion of nineteenth century literature and England's castles, topics apparently of interest to both of them. It seemed that there were indeed very few differences between his world and this one, and the conversation was easy. Kate was on her third cup of tea and Jarn had lost count of his beers, but it was probably his fifth. His hostess was charming and well-informed, with intelligent eyes and a flashing grin when he made her laugh over some recollection.

Jarn sensed an underlying sense of loss about her but was steadfastly not probing beyond the surface. Anything deeper would be snooping and he had no desire to spy on his employer. Besides, Issa had told him for centuries that it was rude to delve, a talent he had exploited readily and without the slightest qualm in the centuries before they had met. But perhaps Kate sensed some similar loss in her guest, as she put her cup down and looked him in the eye.

'Is there a Mrs Dechar? Or is that too intrusive a question?'

Jarn slowly placed his glass on the coffee table. He looked for a few moments at the floor-to-ceiling windows and through them to the house lawns and the paddocks beyond. Apart from Miray, it was the first time in decades that anyone had asked him about his family. The first time he had the chance to open up the chasm he kept hidden, the deep agony of the endless separation. The loss of his mate, gnawing at him every day, waking him every night with dreams, and nightmares of what might be happening to her in his absence. The endless stomach-churning loneliness of life without her. Suppressed during the day, far too vividly alive every night.

The simple question suddenly hit him hard, very hard. He felt his eyes grow moist and blinked to clear them while still looking out of the windows. He didn't trust himself to speak, knowing his voice would break.

After the moments had extended into several minutes without him being aware of the passage of time, he felt a hand on his arm. Kate had moved from her chair to be next to him on the sofa.

'I'm sorry. I wouldn't have asked if I had thought it was so – so painful.'

Jarn swallowed and pulled himself together with an enormous effort.

'You weren't to know.' His voice did indeed break on the last word.

How could he explain? Should he invent a death? Deep within himself he felt that was wrong. This woman had unusual empathy, he could sense it. She deserved more than a lie, and some deep instinct warned him that a lie in these circumstances would have consequences. But to tell the truth was inconceivable. Perhaps a half-truth would suffice.

'It's difficult – impossible – to explain. But we are separated. I can't go back to our home, to my wife. I haven't been able to go for quite some years now.' He looked into grey eyes that were deeply sympathetic, and it encouraged him to go further.

'And I miss her, every day.' Again, his voice cracked.

Kate simply squeezed Jarn's arm, the gesture more than words. After a few minutes, she refilled his glass and her cup, and they sat companionably together in silence.

Jarn found that his hire was extended for a month, with some indoor work on files and accounts in addition to outdoor tasks. As the season for lambing was approaching in the southern hemisphere, he was relieved to be at least partially avoiding the sheep.

He had been asked to tea twice since the first visit, the one which had led to him coming close to breaking down. On the last of these, Kate quietly told him about her husband Gerald. Jarn had assumed she was separated, widowed or divorced, but the truth was worse. Gerald had been in a truck on the edge of their land, a year ago, and while crossing a river swollen by flood rain had slipped over the edge of the pontoon bridge. The truck overturned into the water, the doors jammed and the inside flooded. By the time help arrived Gerald had been deprived of oxygen for long enough to cause massive brain damage but not quite long enough to kill him. He was cared for in a nursing home in the nearby township. There was no hope of recovery.

And, Kate murmured, she had been shocked on first sight of Jarn because of their physical and facial similarity. For a moment, she had thought it was Gerald, or his ghost. It explained Driffold's reaction on first seeing him, as well, Jarn thought. A coincidence, but an odd one.

Jarn had held Kate's arm as she had done for him, but she had turned to him fully so he could hold her close as she cried quietly against his shoulder. While in this position the door had opened and Mark Driffold had entered. He had closed the door immediately but not before a flash of anger had crossed his face. Jarn regretted that the manager should have gained a false impression, but his regret was more for Kate than himself. He needed to move on in his search for Termonn, but he now felt a responsibility to this woman.

They met again for tea and beer on the day before Jarn's employment ended. He was pretty sure that Mark Driffold had no intention of renewing it this time, presumably deter mined to protect his vulnerable employer from the wiles of unscrupulous strangers.

Kate wasted no time in getting further into the details of her family, clearly longing for Jarn's advice.

Gerald, she told him, had an older brother, George. And Kate was contemplating selling the station to George. He had long had thoughts of moving to Australia and had dropped hints for years. He would be able to sell his own property, the family house in England, and she knew he would give her a fair price for the station. Kate hoped that George would keep on the staff she had here. And she could perhaps find somewhere else, in Europe, possibly Switzerland or Austria, where there were mountains. Gerald would be more content in fresh air, cared for in a place with the best medical facilities.

'It sounds a great idea, for you both.' And Jarn genuinely thought it. She needed a fresh start, and the hope of finding happiness elsewhere. This station wasn't going to give that to her, it was too remote.

'Yes.' Kate touched his arm again. She revelled in even a slight touch of human warmth. 'I feel it is the right thing, for both of us. And for George, as well, he has been talking of moving out here for years. This could be the new Termonn House.'

It was a heart stopping moment.

Jarn had long been aware that what most people would dismiss as coincidence or serendipity was more often the merging of lines of time and space interwoven through the fabric of the universe. When lines crossed, even fleetingly, the impression of extraordinary coincidence could arise, but it was seldom the coincidence it appeared to be. And it was for those with abilities such as his to spot these events and to bend them to their will. This was clearly one of those crossovers and it was down to him to make full use of it. He knew, in his bones, it would lead him towards Issa.

'Termonn House? Near Oxford? Or near Dublin?'

'Near Oxford, in the Cotswolds. Have you heard of it? The family bought it from the Clarendons back in the mid 1850's. I think that was how George got his name, after the 4th Earl. The family was distantly related, and the Earl was the British Foreign Secretary, I think. And yes, I believe there's another house with the same name near Dublin, the history of them is connected somehow.'

Kate proffered Jarn another biscuit, which he declined, his

mind churning over the new information. What it meant, precisely, he didn't know. What he felt, and felt to his core, was that he needed to be at the site of his and Issa's home in England in this world. Here, the ownership was in the hands of Kate's husband's family. There would never have been a connection with the Dechars. But the crossing of lines would still be there, as the gatekeeper Melisse had said, and there may be a weakness he could exploit. This coincidence reinforced the gatekeeper's suggestion even more. He had to attempt it.

How to get there? He could no longer use the void and it seemed stepping wasn't much more controllable than void shifting had been. His next step could end him in the Arctic, for all he knew. But the link between this station, Kate's family and the site of his old home was undoubtedly not to be ignored. As thoughts flew around his mind, he became aware Kate was watching him closely.

Hell, he thought, coming to a decision, this was going to take hours.

It did. But over two hours later, and a heck of a lot more tea and beer, they were both quiet on the sofas of the drawing room. The sun was lowering to the horizon and Jarn was dimly aware he hadn't yet fed the yearling stock in the house pasture and that Mark Driffold would be unimpressed and onto him as soon as he left the house.

No matter. This was more important.

Without a word, Kate suddenly stood and went to the computer in the corner of the room. She started pressing keys.

'There's a flight from our nearest airport, which

connects to a flight to Heathrow, in 11 hours. If we drive all night, we can make it. Do you want me to book you on it?'

Jarn felt stunned. This was a woman with his own decisiveness, but still, it was an incredible leap for anyone to make. Then he nodded, without words.

After minutes, as Kate tapped on the keyboard with various expressions of frustration and satisfaction, he said quietly, 'I only have the wages from the last three weeks. And some South American currency which you would have to exchange somehow.'

'This is what friends are for, Jarn.'

Jarn lowered his head. It went through his mind briefly that he needed to do something, somehow, in some world, for this wonderful woman. What, he didn't have a clue. Perhaps Issa would know.

'Come on, get your bag.'

'I don't have a passport,' Jarn said, reality seeping in.

'No, but I have Gerald's and you look enough like him to get away with it. Heaven knows, he doesn't need it now. I've booked the ticket in his name. What's the worst that can happen?'

Well, I could be arrested for impersonation, thought Jarn, but he accepted it was not a risk that troubled him. The stakes were too high.

CHAPTER 23
DAVID, TERMONN HOUSE,
8TH JULY 2022

In the drawing room, David stood close to his mother, both of them looking out at the rain still drumming down outside although it was now late afternoon. St Michael's tower was obscured in an unseasonable mist.

'Mother, how long is it since you saw the vortex?'

'I have not called it up since you left. It rose for Clare a day ago but had sunk before I saw it.'

'It rose for Clare?'

'It seems she is adept. She did it without meaning to. Without even knowing it existed. But it was too much, for such an inexperienced one, and she paid the price with a collapse.'

David looked at his mother, astonished. The vortex would instantly leap upwards for his parents, but they were extraordinarily powerful. For other *gerasi* it would be sluggish. Its almost child-like characteristics had made the family laugh when it had deliberately ignored Sylvie and later did the same to Fizz. Even for David himself, he remembered often sitting patiently in the Undercroft before it would appear before him. Yet it had risen immediately for Clare, without any summons.

He recalled just a few days previously feeling a strong call from a vortex. One that he had spun to identify but had found gone just moments later, before he had traced it. He now knew it was his first ever link to Clare, and their connection had shaken his world. Some concern washed over David as he struggled to understand why the vortex had responded to her so quickly.

But at the moment there were more urgent things to speak to his mother about, and he forced himself to shrug off his disquiet about Clare for the time being.

'Mother, I need to show you something.'

Issa nodded briefly and turned toward the hall. She led the way to the passage and then down the staircase. David followed, descending the old stone steps until they were in the Undercroft. He inhaled sharply, the scent of herbs and the chamber's otherworldliness striking him afresh.

They moved to the central pedestal, and took up positions opposite each other, placing their hands on the engraved surface. Immediately, the carvings glowed gold and a white light grew, centred above the stone surface. Issa and David's attention on the light was rapt as golden clouds merged with the whiteness and took a more solid form, of starry worlds and connections between them. A shimmering matrix coalesced, each point and line now in brilliant gold. The shifting shapes whirled, grew and shrank, stars swirling within white clouds, reforming and distorting, growing and flexing. The connecting lines formed multiple shapes which danced, each spinning on its own axis.

Within the white gold brilliance was a deep blackness. A core, running from top to bottom like a huge blot of light-absorbing ink, leaching through the dimensions. In parts it was growing outwards, the bulges splitting the vortex into multiple sections.

Issa gasped. 'It has grown, has it not? The void?'

David, opposite her on the other side of the pedestal, nodded gravely. 'Yes, it has grown, and it is still growing. And the split into these subsections is new.'

Issa's face expressed her shock.

'I have never seen this before. It has always been steady. Permanent. Everlasting, we thought. Just a means of transfer between distant worlds. A channel down the centre. But this...?' Issa pointed to the darkness, her astonishment evident.

'About two months ago, I travelled here, to this adjacent world' - David gestured to a globe - 'and I spoke to the gate-keeper of that world. Melisse is her name, and she is a sister of Melite. She told me things about the event in '77, and how the detonation had rebounded through the gates of worlds. She was herself terribly injured and her vortex has not long since repaired itself. With the new vision it provided, she saw that it was Father's action that had inadvertently led to the destruction of her temple and the injury to herself. But she understands it, she feels no anger towards him.'

Issa listened intently, it was valuable information after so many years with none. But she also felt a wave of fear. Was it possible that Jarn could have survived the force of such an explosion. Or...?

David was now gripping the stone with both hands.

'Melisse told me that the void is now encompassing whole worlds through this recent expansion. Do you remember when I was little, you and Father took me on a trip, and the world had beaches with sunshine and the bluest sea?'

'And a brilliant moon over the sea at night.' Issa remembered the holiday, so long ago.

'And the wonderful porpoises, friendly as puppies?'

'You had your own. Partridge, you called her. She came whenever you were on the beach.' Issa smiled faintly at the memory although her gaze had not wavered from the vortex and her thoughts were still on Jarn.

'That world was here.' David gestured to a point in the swirling shape, but it was one where there was only inky blackness. 'Melisse showed me that it has gone. That location is now within the void.'

'The void has engulfed a world? How? It cannot absorb worlds; it is just a transit between them.' Issa sounded deeply shocked.

'And I'm sorry, Mother, but there is more. See here.'

David gestured towards a golden globe, swirling very close to the black.

'After talking with Melisse, I travelled here, and they have experienced strange things. Creatures, mostly very unpleasant, have been seen which have never been seen before, and sometimes the world goes dark for days. The Shamen are working night and day but now they can barely hold their own. They are begging for help.'

'Dear gods. What help can we give them?'

David looked at his mother but had no answer. There was none.

'Is that all, David? Enough bad news for one trip? Nothing of your father?'

'I've saved the best till last, Mother.' David had a bit of zest back now and grinned.

'As the world of Melisse is close, and she was compassionate, I went back just yesterday and she said' – David drew a deep breath – 'that Father had been there, and very recently. Just weeks ago.'

Issa gasped and took her hands away from the pedestal to cover her mouth, her eyes now fixed on David.

'At last, David? He is still alive?'

Despite all her apparent assuredness, and the brave front presented to her family, David saw that Issa had lived with the possibility that her husband had perished nearly half a century earlier, or in the decades since then. He caught her hands and gently placed them back on the stone, as the glimmering vortex had sighed and lowered a little without his mother's touch.

'Yes, he is alive and well. Melisse spoke to him; they had a lengthy conversation. He said he had tried repeatedly, ever since he was lost, to get back to us but could not as there was some barrier in the way. Melisse told him, as she told me, that he is indeed surrounded by a wall. It seems in many ways to be an extension of the void but it is around him alone. She could see a dark layer clearly, although Father could not. Melisse is convinced that the barrier has been placed deliberately and with malevolent intent. She told Father as much.'

Issa shook her head, clearly struggling to comprehend. 'There is a void *around* him, and it is deliberate? But who? And how?'

'I don't know, Mother. Neither did Melisse. But she said Father was determined to thwart it. And lastly, she said it was his wish that if it ever became possible to get a message through to us, he wanted us to know he loved us all and would never stop fighting to come home.'

Issa bowed her head and took a deep shuddering breath, with her hands gripping the stone. David watched her compassionately, his own eyes moist.

After some moments she raised her eyes again to David's.

'This is consistent with news Clare has brought me, from the weapons specialists here. She told me they are now convinced that your father's accident wasn't bad luck, it was a deliberate plot. But no country has the ability to prime the weapon in the way it seems it was primed to explode.'

Her gaze was steely as she looked at her son.

'Your father is being targeted by someone from beyond this world.'

***

Later in the day, Issa and David were sitting in the drawing room, watching the pastures darken with the setting sun. The rain had finally stopped, leaving Termonn damp but refreshed.

David sipped his wine and then ran a thoughtful finger around the rim.

'So, Mother, who is she?'

Issa had been expecting the question, given the immediate and obvious connection between her son and her guest. It had happened precisely as she had foreseen before Clare had even arrived at Termonn.

'I don't know, my boy. I sensed her existence months ago, and I now know I felt something when she first came into existence decades before, but then I did not recognise it for what it was. And neither then, nor more recently, did I know where she was. Neither did I know the extent of her abilities. Or, until recently, her connection to your line.'

'But you found her.'

'It would be truer to say that she found us. Or perhaps

that the strands we have created over time led her to find us.'

Issa added, thoughtfully, 'I have never come across one quite like her before.'

'She seems very much like us. She is *gerasi*, it is obvious, and that is incredibly rare. But is she unusual other than that?'

'There is something different about Clare, something I cannot put my finger on. Perhaps your father could if he were here.'

'In what way, Mother? She seems very normal to me. Wonderful, but normal nevertheless.' David found himself wanting to protect Clare as well as understand her and was wary of his mother's perception.

Issa stood and moved to the window, and after a few moments David joined her. They gazed out at the tower, now red in the setting sun. Issa spoke.

'I have asked her about her family. It appears her mother had talents, although I do not think they were as Clare's are. And her mother is dead, but I do not know the circumstances except that I could feel Clare did not want to talk about it.'

Another wave of concern washed over David. Over the evening dinner table, he had asked Clare an everyday question about her family and had immediately sensed a reluctance in her to share her background. It seemed his mother was also aware of it.

Issa continued, thoughtfully. 'She has mentioned her grandmother, I believe her mother's mother, who seems to have been an unpleasant person but not one apparently gifted in any way. So, Clare's mother does not seem to have acquired her abilities through her own mother. Everyone we have known of our kind has had at least one parent similarly talented or, occasionally, has been of unknown parentage. So, it seems likely that the father of Clare's mother must have had abilities, but he is unknown.'

'And not only is her grandfather unknown, so is Clare's own father. The important point is that although she is untrained, she has extraordinary ability. She actually paused time, quite unwittingly, when we were in London the other day.'

David gasped. But his mother continued, quietly, on her own line of thought.

'Her talents appear to be such that I feel she must have had either two skilled parents or skilled grandparents, on both sides. At the moment, we don't understand where her mother's skills came from and we have no idea about her father. It is a mystery. And if Clare knows anything of it, she is reluctant to share it.'

She sipped her wine, her eyes looking outward to the lands of Termonn but also inwards. David waited patiently for his mother to complete her thought, his own wine in hand. The evening light glinted through the old glass of the windows.

'So much is now moving, after so long. Perhaps Clare is the reason.' Issa paused for another long moment, looking at her puzzled son.

'Mother, how can Clare possibly be influencing Father's loss or return?'

'Do you remember when I travelled to see Melite, in 1979, and begged her for help in finding your father?'

David nodded. When Jarn had failed to return after nearly two years of absence, the family's hopes had been centred on Melite: the lack of help from the gatekeeper had been crushing at the time, Issa white and trembling when she returned.

'Melite said something then, and I did not understand it. She said that she could not help, she could not see him. I was in despair, I thought she meant he had died. So, I only half heard her next words, but I remember she looked into the vortex and saw something that fascinated her. She gazed for a long while, moving her hands this way and that, bringing parts of the vortex into focus and moving other parts back, all in absolute silence. Then she said, very quietly, 'τα σκέλη είναι ομιχλώδη αλλά θα καθαρίσου' - 'the strands are misty but they will clear...'

Issa sipped her wine, her thoughts in the past as she recalled her meeting with the gatekeeper.

'Her next words were indistinct but I thought I heard 'με σαφή'. It means 'with clear', so I thought Melite was saying again that the strands would clear. But Σαφή is also a version of the name Clare, and I now wonder if I misheard her, or that Melite herself had misunderstood. And whether she was saying that the strands would clear with Clare.'

CHAPTER 24
JARN, 'TERMONN HOUSE', 6TH JULY 2022

Jarn paid the taxi driver who had driven him from Heathrow with currency Kate Borman had dug out of a drawer, left over from the last trip she and Gerald had made to the UK. Yet another debt he owed her. She had also rung her brother-in-law George, with a request that he look after her friend Jarn and give him a base for a few days while he found his feet after the long flight. Termonn House, or at least the Termonn House in this world, was now close.

Jarn had decided against asking the driver to take him to the door, instead requesting to be dropped near the old gates. He lifted his backpack over his shoulder and made his way up the slight slope to the summit. From there, he gazed down at Termonn.

Both the landscape and the house were heart-breakingly familiar. Not entirely the same as his own house, as the rill was not there and there were slight differences in windows and the style of the front entrance. The courtyard buildings were also different. These appeared to have been converted to offices, and the cars in the courtyard suggested that the stable block may in this world house small businesses. But he still found himself swallowing a lump in his throat as he walked down the approach road towards the house. It hurt knowing that this was not his own property, no matter how similar it looked. Just the same location but in a slightly different world, and that made all the difference. It wasn't his home, and his own family were not here, had never been here.

He was received with a warm welcome from Laura, George's wife, who conducted him upstairs to the room he had been allocated. It was the room that in his own Termonn House was David's, overlooking the courtyard, the room he and Issa had determined back in the 1850's would be for David, as it overlooked his line of power. An emotional wave crested over him which he managed to conceal.

Laura chatted about the family, asking after Kate and how Jarn had met her, and Jarn supplied the back story he had agreed with Kate during the long drive from the outback station to the regional airport just twenty-four hours ago.

Under the surface, Jarn was struggling. Fatigue from an arduous trip combined with finding himself in such familiar surroundings but knowing it was merely in a near world rather than his own, were both taking a toll. Laura nodded understandingly, promising to send up refreshments, and issuing over her shoulder an invitation to dinner with her and George if Jarn felt up to it later.

He collapsed on his bed, and put his arm over his eyes, finally finding himself alone without the need to keep up appearances. Moments later there was a knock on the door as the young housekeeper brought up tea, sandwiches, and cake. Jarn devoured the lot with gratitude and put the tray outside the door before returning to the bed and closing his eyes. He was asleep in moments.

He slept through dinnertime and most of the night, waking disoriented at 6am. Taking a shower in the bathroom attached to the bedroom, he could see that the luxurious fittings were a big improvement on the styles available in the 1970's. In his past, in the room that had been David's, this had been a dressing area, but he vowed to install a similar bathroom at home if Issa hadn't already done it. Then he set off to see how different this house was to his own.

He found his host at the kitchen table, stirring coffee. George did a double take at Jarn's appearance in much the same way Kate had on first meeting him. Clearly George was also struck by his facial similarity to his brother. Jarn wondered if George and Laura were speculating whether Kate's fondness for her new friend had something to do with him looking so like Gerald.

The similarity in their appearance didn't extend to George, who was slighter than Jarn, with hair that had a hint of ginger and a beard of the same. But George grinned a welcome, sticking out his hand and shaking Jarn's warmly, offering a tour of the house and grounds before breakfast. Jarn smiled, thanked his host and accepted the offer with alacrity. This was exactly what he needed.

Following George out of the kitchen and back towards the hall, Jarn noticed there was no passageway like the one in his home that led to the Undercroft. That was a disappointment, but even without that focussed centre of power he could already feel the strength of the crossing lines. They heartened him. It was not surprising, really, that the subterranean room had not been developed here, as without their perception of the power of the lines, Issa and himself would have doubtless remained unaware of the huge chamber under their own home. Jarn suspected that something similar nevertheless existed here, hidden away under the flagstones of the hall since the Reformation. The lines of power were exactly the same.

As George showed him round, good-naturedly chatting about this and that, Jarn could see that the structure of the ground floor of the house was almost identical to his own, and even some of the furnishings were similar. He didn't know whether to feel pleased or sorry about that. But he knew he was starting to feel homesick.

George led him outside and on a tour of the path around the house. The gates appeared identical to his own, as Jarn had seen the day before. St Michael's tower was there, again looking the same. The tranquil moat reflected the old house, as it did in his own home. There was no rill, and no statue, but a path still led from the house into the western woodland. A smaller tower rose on the summit beyond the courtyard but was not topped by a beacon structure. Perhaps it had existed previously and had been removed. Then, Jarn reflected, it had been himself and Issa who had been responsible for the rill and the statue on their own estate, and they had also restored the old fire beacon. The differences between his own Termonn and this one was largely due to the differences he himself had made, with his wife. Even down to the differences due to the furnishings Issa had introduced. Could it be possible that it was his own and Issa's existence that had split this whole reality from their own?

Jarn felt a strong urge to explore what might happen if he tried to step from here to his own world, in this location so familiar and with the energy from the lines flowing around and through him, but he resisted it. If successful if would be traumatic for George to have his guest vanishing before his eyes. Best to try it somewhere private. He turned his attention to his host and concentrated on what he was saying.

'...so, yes, if Kate is willing, it seems the best option all round. Poor Gerald. The accident was a terrible shock, of course, but Kate has done everything possible for him. She deserves some life of her own, poor girl, not stuck away by herself miles from anywhere.'

Jarn could only nod in agreement. He had thought the same thing and he said as much, telling George how well Kate was managing the station and how impressed he had been with her staff.

'That's good to hear. And for Laura and me, well we've fancied trying Australia for ourselves, ever since Gerald went out there. We've always liked his place. And we do have experience of farming...' he gestured at the land around him '... so now the children are off our hands, it seems a good time to have a go. Either Australia or back to the old house near Dublin. Big farm there as well, and there is talk of it coming on the market.'

Jarn's ears pricked at the mention of the other Termonn House, close to Dublin, where he and his family had once lived. So many interconnecting strands here.

He mentioned Kate's idea of bringing Gerald to a sanatorium in an alpine location and George nodded.

'That would be great for Gerald, and Kate as well. She will feel better knowing he has the best care possible.'

They had arrived back outside the kitchen door and Jarn followed George through, back into the kitchen. George headed for the fridge and took out eggs and bacon, then turned to the range and lifted one of the lids.

'Breakfast, Jarn? I need to get my cholesterol in before Laura gets up and feeds me oat bran and low-fat yoghurt.'

Jarn chuckled and accepted happily. Having missed dinner, he was now ravenous. George put a pile of bacon to cook in a huge pan and started to whisk a massive number of eggs. Jarn watched him and wondered just how many people he was preparing breakfast for. Was he doing it for the staff as well? Slices and slices of bread went in the toaster, marmalade, butter and jams were put on the table, and more coffee was brewed. A jug of orange juice was poured as a healthy afterthought.

It turned out that there were only the two of them eating, but they still managed to make substantial inroads into the meal before Laura came in. Hands on hips, she looked accusingly at her husband who smiled at her guiltily.

'And we're eating out tonight at the Bellamy's', she said, with mild reproof, 'and you know she always produces too much rich food. Your diet re-starts tomorrow!' A finger waggled in George's direction.

Then she grinned at Jarn and said, in a completely different tone, 'I'm glad you enjoyed your breakfast, Jarn!'

Jarn spent his day contentedly painting fencing. It reminded him of his work at Kate's, but the task was far more pleasant away from the eagle eyes of Mark Driffold. He had been keen to do something to repay his hosts' hospitality and had finally persuaded George to give him a task. While outside, he had gently prodded the barrier for weaknesses, and was rewarded when he felt patches that did indeed feel much less substantial. One in particular, just outside the kitchen door, was fragile. He would investigate once George and Laura left for their dinner party.

Itching to do it, the day passed slower than he would have liked, but eventually he heard the front door close. It was early evening and a meal had been prepared for him and left in the fridge for reheating, but Jarn was too impatient to get to the weak spot he had found, and he walked rapidly through the kitchen.

Drawing fibres together, and seeing lines start to glow around him, he concentrated on the patch that showed no lines at all but which was instead a cloud of pale gold. He grasped the edges of the area with his mind and pulled.

The house around him blurred as a new space formed. Jarn felt no sense of threat, no sign of a malevolent void, and there was no longer a barrier here. Heart thumping, he stepped through the gap and found himself in the kitchen of the house he knew with certainty was his own.

The sense of elation was so great he had to stop himself falling to the stone floor and kissing it. At last, thank the gods. Home. Finally, home.

Looking around him, he saw that Issa had made some changes. A new and huge range cooker occupied one wall. In fact, none of the kitchen equipment was as he remembered. But then, it was over forty years ago, things would have worn out, and probably more than once. The old kitchen clock was the same, a slow rhythmic tick, the huge pine table was just as he remembered. Evening sunlight spread on the stone floor from the light through the door, unchanged.

He stilled as footsteps and the sound of voices approached from the hall. Things were happening too fast. Jarn had not given any thought to how he would deal with meeting Issa again, or any of his family. It would be a shock for them, but they would deal with it as a family, as they always did. He felt his face breaking into a huge grin as Issa entered the kitchen, Hettie behind her with a tray. The woman always seemed to be moving a tray from somewhere to somewhere else, he thought, with deep contentment. He stepped away from the kitchen door and walked to his wife until he stood at her side, arms outstretched.

Issa looked towards the door behind Jarn and turned to tell Hettie that the outdoor planters needed watering and that she would do it. Meanwhile, could Hettie check whether Clare was awake and needed any supper?

Then she walked straight past Jarn and out of the door behind him.

CHAPTER 25
CLARE, TERMONN HOUSE,
9TH JULY 2022

The morning after David's return, we sat close to each other at the kitchen table, without words, hardly even exchanging glances. After our connection of the previous day, words and looks were not necessary. I believe we drank coffee. We may have had toast, and possibly eggs. But the golden haze that surrounded us was food enough. I knew him, and he knew me. Our new world had started with the bonds we had made yesterday. They were bonds that linked us irrevocably, and we both knew it. That Hettie and Maya also knew it was clear from the way they each shovelled food onto our plates, grinning, with the expectation it wouldn't be consumed. After a silent half hour they urged us out of the kitchen door.

And so we found ourselves sitting companionably side by side on a fallen log that had been carved into a seat, next to the track leading to the beacon.

I knew questions were coming. In the first instance, courtship always revolved around background and family, didn't it? I already knew some aspects of David's background, and now it was only natural he would want me to share mine; he had already asked about my parental home, yesterday, a question I had ducked. Although we already knew each other at a much more basic level, my background would fill in gaps for him. Despite that, I couldn't respond to the questions I knew were in his mind. A barrier flashed up between us.

Something in our connection must have told David that discussing my home was beyond me. Instead, he felt my curiosity and the need for me to have information and he courteously side-stepped his own questioning.

'Where would you like me to start, Clare, I can feel a tsunami of questions in that mind of yours!'

There were so many aspects of my new life I still didn't understand. Where to start?

'You are all so long-lived. How do you deal with that? And how do you live, do you have careers?'

'We do, all of us, have careers. We try to move around professionally every twenty or thirty years, though, giving each place the chance to forget us. If we return after decades, to a university for example, we can say 'Oh yes, I do look very much like my father'. Or grandfather, depending on how long ago it was. Before mass photography, it was easy to explain away a physical similarity.'

'But...,' and I thought David looked a little embarrassed, '...we have been very much helped by Sir Edward and his predecessors. Father has been of such value to the government since Victorian times, they would do anything to keep him and this family on their side. Over many decades, we have been issued with whatever certificates our lives require. Birth certificates, school certificates, university degrees, regularly updated passports, NHS numbers, driving licences. You name it, we have it, and they are regularly refreshed even though Father hasn't been here for a while.

Actually, we even have death certificates, to suggest that we have passed on and any similarity of name is just due to its use in a new generation. I have to say, it's a little creepy to possess your own death certificate!'

David glanced at me.

'Clare, our false educational qualifications are not a lie. We have all qualified many times over, at university and postgraduate levels. I have three doctorates. Fizz and Sylvie will go back to Oxford in a few weeks for yet more postgraduate study, for what must be the third or fourth time. And that is on top of their qualifications from other universities. Our genuine degree certificates could paper a wall.'

David chuckled, gazing at the house below us.

'In fact, I am surprised Mother hasn't already done that. It is just difficult to explain why you are applying for admission to a university or for an academic post or a research grant when your birthdate was over two hundred years ago. That is what the government helps us with.'

'Why is your father so important?'

I could tell from his photograph and the descriptions I had heard of Jarn Dechar that he was charismatic and apparently powerful, but it wasn't obvious to me how he was a governmental asset.

'Father has never, since about 1860, stopped working for the British government. Partly because it appeals to his need for adventure, partly because a powerful governmental ally is always useful. He knew it was important to our lives to have the documentation that the modern world increasingly needs, and the British government supplied that. So, he looked after all of us, with his foresight. As long as we remain resident in the UK or in countries which are now part of the Commonwealth, the support for this family continues. Over the years it has been essential, and the knowledge of us has been passed down from government to government, together with the need to look after us.'

David grinned. 'The royal family have been amongst our greatest supporters. Father, and Mother, have helped them many times over the years. Mother has been a lady-in-waiting to several Queens, and she still is. She is very good at it.'

'But what service does your father provide to government that is so valuable?'

David rested his back on the seat and contemplated.

'The last one, back in 1977, is an example. Father and Mother saw a threat looming, a big one, and notified government. Not surprisingly, Father was then called upon to assist. The Ministry of Defence in Whitehall schooled him on what he could expect, in conjunction with his perception of possible events, and then he went to the airbase to try to avert the most obvious future. The result was a partial success – the event Mother and he had foreseen was averted – but also a failure, in that Father was lost.'

David looked at me to see how I was taking this.

Reassured, he added 'so, you can imagine how useful such skills might be to any government. And not only to avert a foreseen threat and future, but on top of that Father has more traditional skills, as a spy and a warrior. They have asked for his help many times, around the world, in trouble spots. Sometimes in places only Father knew would lead to trouble if events couldn't be averted. The role was a great match for his talents and abilities, and it was also exactly what he enjoyed doing. Through all the early centuries of his life, long before he met Mother, he was essentially a mercenary, leading small armies in conflict and usually to reward. *Gerasi* talents are enormously advantageous on a battlefield, of course – the abilities to vanish, and to spy - but

Father is also highly skilled in the more traditional fighting techniques. After 1860, what the government offered was almost perfect for him, and had the advantage that he was protecting Mother and the family at the same time.'

David continued, thoughtfully.

'But Sir Edward must have struggled in recent years, since Father disappeared. With no-one else able to fill the role, Sir Edward's predecessor back in the 1980's tried, at the encouragement of the then prime minister, to persuade Mother and me to take on the service Father had provided, but neither of us was keen. We were canny and never said 'no' categorically, so our flow of certificates and passports continued, fortunately. Life would be difficult for us without them. And Mother did undertake some tasks for Sir Edward. I did one or two myself.'

I was fascinated, wanting him to continue with his background. Instead, he reached for my hand and raised it to his lips with a gentle kiss and I felt his eager need to find out more about me.

'And you? Where have you magically appeared from?'

No. It was impossible. I wanted to tell him but the barrier was too strong. The life, the people of Termonn were too important to me, and rejection was more than I could face. So I looked away, over the peaceful land around us, while squeezing his hand to let him know I wasn't rejecting him. I could feel his gaze on me for long moments, as he studied my averted face and then he continued, as if nothing had happened.

'Do you want to hear some history?'

Turning back to him, I nodded, eager to hear more and also to turn David's attention from me.

'Well, I was born in England just after the French revolution. Mother and Father had left France decades earlier to avoid civil unrest in Lyon, and they had made their new home in London. But we moved to Russia in 1806 and that is where I grew up. We lived near St Petersburg throughout the Napoleonic wars, in a big house in St Petersburg itself during the season, but we also had a country home an hour's ride away. An elegant house in a park, warm and beautifully furnished as all Mother's homes are. Surrounded by forests for hunting, lakes for swimming and fishing. We were very happy there.'

David gazed over the land in front of us, but his gaze was distant. Rather than sheep grazing, I thought he was seeing a scene of endless steppes and snow.

'I was a young man when we were in Russia, really only a boy by our reckoning, and I misunderstood the relationship between my parents. I thought Father was all that was splendid, so tall, imposing, good-looking. He excelled at sports, hunting, he was always well informed and clever. He was so strong, and not just physically. Everyone seemed to respect him, look up to him and ask him for advice. He was my hero, really. And he was a wonderful father. Loving, as many fathers were not, back then.'

He looked at me almost apologetically.

'In those days, in Russia, society was dominated by men. Women, even those of the highest rank, were expected to be beautiful and accomplished but no more. So, being young, I misjudged and misunderstood Mother, even though I loved her very much. I thought she was a sweet natured and beautiful woman whom my father loved, and that she was the weak one and he the strong one in their marriage.'

'Mother was a brilliant hostess, and the most glittering and wealthy of Russian society would seek out invitations. Their balls were unbelievable, glittering with lights, uniforms, silks, jewels, the most delicious food and delectable wines. And Mother organised it all. But eventually I realised that during the nights following each ball, each soirée, she would go to the poorer houses herself, to redistribute whatever foods were left, and to give blankets and the medicines of the time, not that those were very effective. My parents even then were worried about the gulf between the rich and the poor in that society. It was unusual - most of St Petersburg society didn't notice and weren't bothered even if they did.'

'To go out, as she did, night after night, took courage. I know Father was unhappy about it, he often went with her and when he could not, he sent guards to accompany her. But Mother usually gave them the slip, I think. Sometimes she would be away all night, if there was someone sick or if a baby was being born, returning only in the morning.'

David looked over the grounds into the far distance.

'And in 1823, my brother Daniel was born.'

I gaped at David. A brother?

'My parents doted on him, of course, we all did. Our kind have children rarely, usually only one a century is born to a mated pair, if that. And I was only just over thirty when Dan arrived, a curly haired baby with Mother's colouring. But almost from the start we felt something was wrong. He was unstable and had to be watched constantly.'

'Unstable? Was it some kind of physical problem?' I looked at David, concerned my question was too intrusive.

'No, he was perfectly normal physically and he was a clever little chap. But I sensed that he was born a wanderer. I could have been mistaken; my empathy was very new at the time.'

I felt David was not telling me all he had seen with regard to his brother, but I decided to say nothing.

He continued, thinking back two centuries.

'The problem was that he would fade from the world. We assumed he was travelling to the void, or at least stepping to neighbouring worlds. There were old tales of such things happening, but it is incredibly rare. *Gerasi* children usually only travel once they are older and able to control it, during adolescence or more usually adulthood. To have a baby disappearing was terrifying for Mother and Father.'

I tried to imagine what it would be like to have a baby capable of vanishing and world-walking by themselves and was unable to.

'How did they cope? They must have been frightened all the time, that he would go without them noticing.'

'Yes, they were. I remember once, when Dan had been chortling in his cot and playing with a toy, a little rabbit, he suddenly looked to one side as if he heard a distant call, and in an instant he had vanished. Mother called Father, and Father rushed to the cot, I could see he was tracing the eddies around it, then he too vanished. I tried to follow, by this time I was learning how to move and control my movements, to follow the flows between worlds. But Mother held me and wouldn't let me go.'

'After about ten minutes Father reappeared, with Dan in his arms. I never heard what happened, but Father was soaked from the waist down and Dan was wet and sobbing and clinging to him. Father passed him to Mother and she held him for a long while, comforting him.'

I was engrossed in the tale. But as I had never heard of Dan before, I had a horrible premonition the story would not end happily, and David saw me putting two and two together. He nodded.

'Yes, unfortunately. Nothing happened for several months after that but then he started to disappear again. A few times he simply reappeared, presumably having not travelled too far and being able to sense his way home. On one other occasion, he vanished, Mother disappeared almost simultaneously and a few seconds later they were both back, with Mother clutching Dan in her arms and shaking. Dan looked happy, he was smiling and I remember he was kissing Mother as she returned with him. But after that, my parents took it in turns to watch him in his cot at night.'

'And perhaps it was inevitable, it happened again and this time no-one saw it. My father was doing the night watch but he'd been working all day until late in the evening and was tired, he fell asleep. And when he woke in the early morning, the cot was empty. Dan did not return and has never been seen since.'

David drew a shaky breath. It had been nearly two centuries, but the loss of his little brother clearly still affected him deeply.

He went on, after a few moments.

'The whole household was distraught, and my parents were traumatised, of course. Father travelled day after day, night after night, until he was exhausted. Mother usually stayed behind, in case Dan found his way home. It was during this time that I realised how resilient Mother was, how she supported Father and how she kept our family together despite her own grief. In those months, she was the strong one. Father was despairing, he blamed himself, but everyone has to sleep some time. We never blamed him. Mother never uttered a word of criticism, she comforted him.'

'We stayed on through what was left of the reign of Alexander I. It was only in the spring of 1826 that we left, after the Tsar died. We had been there for twenty years, and people were beginning to remark on how young my parents always seemed, that they hadn't aged at all. Father was well known at court, he was an advisor to the Tsar, so my parents were very visible, not exactly low profile. When Mother had Daniel in 1823, after over seventeen years in Russia, society thought it was her first baby, as my parents had always said that their children were Father's from a previous marriage - one of whom was me, of course - but even then, it must have seemed odd for Mother to have a baby after so many years. So, we didn't want to attract any more notice and when the Tsar died it seemed a good time to move on, although none of us really wanted to leave our homes.'

After a pause he continued.

'Anyway, in 1826 we left Russia. We travelled for several years. To the east, mostly, India, China and then Japan. My parents still searched for Dan but eventually, over time, our hopes faded. A small establishment was kept in St Petersburg for many years, long after we had left, in case Dan somehow found his way back. As far as we know, he never did.'

I put my hand on David's arm, although it was odd to offer comfort two centuries after a bereavement. 'Did your parents have any idea what happened?'

'I don't think so. They travelled to the worlds nearest them at that time, of course, and left messages with those very few individuals who could return to us with any information, but nothing ever resulted from it. I suspect they think that Dan wandered to a world very different to ours, perhaps with water or great heat, and ... did not survive long enough to come home. I still think of him, a frightened baby, lost and so far away from us.'

I looped my arm through David's, and we slowly made our way back to Termonn through the summer meadow.

It was later the same evening when we were ensconced in deeply comfortable winged leather chairs in the drawing room that David finished his tale.

'After leaving Japan, I made my way back to Europe and studied at universities in Italy and France for a number of years. I was fascinated by archaeology and anthropology, and it is still my specialism, my fascination, and my career. Meanwhile, my parents travelled to Australia. That was my mother's idea, I think she felt Father needed something very different to help him recover from Dan's loss, and also the role he had taken on for so many years in Russia. And they had heard a call which they thought came from one of our kind, and they do not ignore those, they are so rare. But that is a different tale and one I can't tell, I was not there.'

'By the mid 1840's they were back in Europe and their main home was in Ireland, at the original Termonn House just outside Dublin. The house had been established, at my parents' command, by their household from Russia, and when they arrived there in 1846 it was already a comfortable home. Father travelled to Europe regularly though, he had business interests there, especially in Paris and Berlin. And he would meet people he knew from their later days in Russia. One of those was Lord Clarendon, who became Lord Lieutenant of Ireland in 1847. He and his wife were great friends of my parents, and they often stayed in each other's houses. My mother could tell you many tales of Ireland in those years, some terrible of course as they had arrived in the time of the famine, but also some marvellous stories of the people and the folklore.'

David stood and beckoned me to a framed print hanging over one of the smaller bookcases. The drawing showed a regency style house set in what appeared to be a park, with cedars of Lebanon in the grounds, and gentlemen and ladies in nineteenth century crinolines sitting under the trees. In faded script, the print was entitled 'Termonn House, Dublin, 1848.'

'Then', David continued, taking a sip of brandy, 'in the 1850's Father was asked by Lord Clarendon to help out with a visit to Paris of Prince Bertie, the eldest son of Victoria and Albert, and Father not only helped out but saved the life of the prince when a display at the Paris exhibition exploded. It was not much reported at the time, only Lord Clarendon and, I believe, a French journalist saw the event before Father... altered things. But it was that event that led to my parents being close to the Queen and the Prince Consort and to my father receiving his title. It also indirectly led to my parents selling the house in Dublin and purchasing this house. But that is yet another story for another day.'

'Are you and Sylvie their only surviving children?' I was sad to think of just David alone with his parents after the disappearance of Daniel.

'Oh no, they had Henry in the seventeenth century. Henry is the oldest of us.'

The seventeenth century. Jarn and Issa were married at least three centuries ago and had had a child. I shook my head, astonished.

'What does Henry do, where is he?'

'Henry is a she, not a he. Henrietta. Named after Henrietta Maria, the Queen of England. My parents knew the Queen in Paris in the late 1660's, towards the end of her life when she was in exile, and Henry was born there in 1668. Nowadays she is probably the most over-qualified doctor on the planet. Every thirty years she re-invents herself and starts again at a different university and a different medical school.'

David chuckled. 'But she is a fantastic person, the most empathetic of all of us. Everyone loves Henry. We all wish she could find her partner. But these things happen when they happen. Sometimes out of the blue.'

He put his head close to mine and pressed a gentle kiss to my forehead. I looked at him, still rather overwhelmed by the last few days, but returned a kiss to his cheek. His good looks staggered me, and the interwoven links between us were even more astonishing. Then I thought back, digesting the information I had just been given.

'If Henry was born back in 1668, has she not been married in all that time?'

'Oh, indeed she has. Three times, or is it four? Yes, it must be four because there was Owen who died in 1919 of Spanish flu. They'd only been married two years. Met in France in World War One, at a casualty clearing station. Henry was a nurse and Owen was a doctor. By World War Two Henry was able to serve as a doctor herself, it was more easily achieved by then.'

David added, thoughtfully, 'all her marriages have been to humans, of course. But marriages, no matter how much Henry has loved her husbands, are not the same as matings between *gerasi*. Perhaps she will never meet her mate. Or maybe he or she has not been born yet.'

A woofing and yelping came from outside. David moved to the doors leading to the terrace and called to the dogs, Sergei and Kimi, who were chasing rabbits in the field. Sergei came back obediently and flopped down at David's feet. Kimi, in the way of her breed, totally ignored David and carried on pursuing her prey.

'Where is Henry now?'

'She's in Africa, in Cameroon, a gynaecologist working under a Médecins sans Frontières scheme. And before you ask, no, she isn't quite like us. Apart from longevity and empathy her abilities have never fully developed, although she can still influence the lines. Mother thinks it's just because she has never met her true mate. My parents believe she is very talented, but that her talents have not yet blossomed.'

David looked thoughtful.

'Unlike mine, and yours, Clare. My mother finds your abilities astonishing, and she is a very good judge.'

Now was the time to confide at least something of my history, my family. I looked into his perceptive eyes, his gaze gentle and supportive. But words would not come.

David put a warm arm around my shoulders and pulled me closer to him, my head on his shoulder.

'When you feel ready, Clare. Only when you are ready.'

CHAPTER 26
JARN, 'TERMONN HOUSE',
6TH - 9TH JULY 2022

Jarn saw his wife walk past him, first with incredulity and then with utter shock. She had been within an arm's length; how could she not have seen him?

He spun and followed her as she walked to the stable door, putting his hand on her arm. It passed straight through her. Jarn turned to Hettie as the older woman brought a bottle of plant feed and handed it to Issa. It was clear that Hettie, just a few feet away, could not see him either.

He was not fully in their world.

Jarn stood motionless for long moments. Then, desperately hoping he had been wrong, he followed Issa out to the path and stood next to her, his face inches from hers, watching her face avidly for the slightest sign she could see him.

She had filled a watering can from the outside tap and was adding some drops of feed. Then she lifted it and watered the hanging baskets, water running down onto the path below and drips trickling down her slender arms, wetting her sleeves. Jarn realised that the sound of the water splashing on the paving was not as sharp as it would be if he were fully present; the noises of a world not fully stepped into were always less distinct. And his surroundings were paler, less clear than they would have been if he had succeeded in fully stepping.

Without any true hope, but now desperate, he stood as close as he could and called his wife's name again and again. Then he tried telepathy. Nothing. Issa moved from basket to basket, watering, refilling, and watering. She clearly heard nothing, was oblivious of his nearness.

The pain caused by his wife being utterly unaware of his presence was indescribable. The disappointment, of being so nearly home but failing to be visible there, crushing. All he had desired was to scoop his wife into his arms, to bury his face in her golden hair, breathe her unique scent, feel her caresses, see her joy and to know he had finally returned to his mate. So close and all shattered.

For over two hours he stayed in his house, searching for any additional place of weakness but finding nothing. He watched Issa and Hettie drink tea in the kitchen, Maya cooking at the stove. He saw his adored Sylvie come in and wheedle a biscuit out of Maya as Issa chuckled. None of them could see him, no matter how much he called. He stood on the old stone floor, the same here as in the other Termonn he had stepped from, with his mind a chaos of despair.

Eventually he had no choice but to return to the other Termonn House, Laura and George's home. He walked straight through their kitchen door into the late dusk, and on to the paths outside, without thought or direction. Tears ran down his cheeks as grief overwhelmed him.

At last, he found himself sitting on grass close to where the beacon was in his own world, and where the beaconless tower was in this world. Night had fallen fully by now, and there were very distant lights from the few houses and cottages in the landscape below. Owls hooted as Jarn played over in his mind every second of his move to his home, the sight of Issa, Hettie, Maya, Sylvie. Following Issa outside, talking to her. Watching incredulously as she was oblivious to his presence.

What was she doing now, in their Termonn? Taking a shower? Preparing for bed? Was she thinking of him? Seeing her again for the first time in so many decades, beautiful and healthy, had his thoughts whirling and passion surging despite his anguish. If he been able to break through, they would be together now, with the family, celebrating. The magical day would end with them being in each other's arms, in their own bed again after so long. He would be able to hold her, kiss her, she would kiss him, wrap her arms around him, he would...

Gods.

Jarn threw himself back on the grass, feeling dew seep through his shirt, and wrenched his mind away from fantasising. He had to work, had to think.

So, *think.*

The part of the void around him was, unbelievably, still preventing his full return. He was invisible in his own world, although he had doubtless vanished from Laura and George's house as well. He had simply shifted between two adjacent realities, with a physical presence in neither, the strategy he had found so useful in the past. The only difference now was that he was unable to take the final step and move fully into the other world.

In his mind he returned to his conversation with the gatekeeper of this world, Melisse. She had suggested that the barrier around him was a construct, made deliberately to trap him, to prevent him returning to his home and to separate him from his family. This now appeared to be true. But the gatekeeper had also said that his best chance was to be at this place, with the power of his own lines. And that events may lead to the barrier being broken. It had already partly worked, as he had got far closer here, at Termonn, than he had ever managed before. It was the final step that had eluded him.

But he knew he could get no further until he had rested, the emotions of the day had drained him. Jarn returned to the house and felt some relief that Laura and George were still out. The friendly housekeeper, Jo, reheated his meal and Jarn headed back with it to what was David's room in another world, finding some relief that at least in this world he was solid, see-able. He soon fell into an exhausted sleep.

Over the next few days, he thought constantly of what had happened and he very slowly started to emerge from despair to achieve a clearer understanding of his situation. With that came the faintest glimmerings of hope. He had been so close, only one tiny breakthrough step was needed. He would explore more, he would search the whole estate. Perhaps he hadn't found the weakest point. He refused to accept that the only way to complete the step was through the death of one of his kind. Other ways must exist.

Jarn came to feel enormous gratitude to both Laura and George, who had extended their welcome indefinitely, it would seem, and treated him as a family member, as a friend. He felt a twinge of remorse that this may have resulted from the idea that he and Kate were in a relationship, even if it was at an early stage, but that couldn't be helped. In the meantime, he could still step over and see Issa and his family, even if they could not see him, and that was worth a great deal.

Jarn found himself unable to resist stepping to his own world frequently, when the kitchen was empty and he could step without his disappearance being observed. He took so many 'jet-lag naps' in his room that he felt his hosts must be suspecting he was suffering from some sort of sleeping sickness. He also explored, repeatedly, the house and the estate and was rewarded with the discovery within the house of several other areas of weakness.

One, in the drawing room, was especially large and fragile, which Jarn suspected was due to its position directly on his line of strength to St Michael's tower. He was grateful to have several alternative locations from which to step, no longer having to wait for the kitchen to be empty.

In his visits to his own world, Jarn gradually became reacquainted with his house and saw with admiration how it had altered in the last half century. Issa had updated rooms and their furnishings without changing the fundamental nature of their beloved home. The outside he examined little, preferring to be indoors where he could see his family, but the odd foray out of doors showed tended gardens and well-maintained land. Although the number of sheep had apparently increased, blast it. He applauded the introduction of what looked to be new rare breeds, and the care that the farm manager and their tenant farmers were giving them.

He was not surprised to recognise the manager as Adam Simpson, who he had last seen as a teenager. Jarn suspected his wife had done some nurturing and support of the baby she had delivered back on that snowy night in 1963. But he thought he saw a sadness surrounding his manager and vowed to look into it when – it had to be *when* - he got home.

Jarn saw with especial fondness that Mordecai and Hettie continued to serve his wife with the loyalty he had seen from them over many years. Neither of them were gifted with *gerasi* abilities other than extreme longevity, but to him they were now family and not servants. He and Issa had selected them carefully and wisely over the years and were being rewarded; he would make sure these friends would be rewarded in their turn.

The inscrutable Maya, with her scars both visible and hidden, he deeply wished he could assist more, but he had always been at a loss as to how to do it. He had sensed such deep grief within her from the death of her mate, he had never known how to help her and the same was just as true today. The woman's grief had not changed. Jarn hoped that Maya's love for Issa, which he sensed was her strongest remaining emotion, might be helping her find purpose.

Some changes he viewed with more resignation. The laptops which seemed to have invaded every room, like some pervasive alien species. His family endlessly tapping on what Laura had referred to as smart phones (Jarn had suppressed surprised curiosity and had simply nodded sagely in a manner he hoped implied he had a bunch of them himself). The log fire in his beautiful and extensive library on the first floor had been replaced by a log burner powered by gas and he saw with horror it was also controlled by one of these little electronic devices. Admittedly the room was now less smoky, which was good for his books.

And most importantly he watched, again and again, his family and their partners. Sylvie and the lovely Fizz, together and their mating even stronger than when he had left. David, and his obvious fascination with the visitor to the family, the dark-haired Clare. Jarn saw clearly that David and Clare had a deep connection which strengthened daily. Clare was an incredible addition to the family, however she had arrived here. Her powers were an intricate and ideal mesh with David's, a match the universe had created with perfection, just as his and Issa's had been.

And Issa herself. Jarn watched her insatiably, returning time and time again just to see his wife, seeking her out every moment he could. The sight of her thrilled him but he knew deep frustration in his inability to touch her or to speak to her. And every time it was harder to leave her.

It was no surprise to him that Issa was isolated despite the love of her family. He knew that no matter how many centuries passed she would not re-mate, as he would not. But the loneliness he could see she was hiding, every day, was very hard for him to swallow.

Late one night he could not resist the urge to find her, to watch her sleeping. He stepped and in moments was in the bedroom that had been theirs for so many years. Very few changes had been made here. The huge oak four-poster bed was still there, large enough to easily accommodate a man of his size with comfort. The frame had, he recalled, been specially crafted for them in St Petersburg, with superb carvings showing scenes from Russian folklore.

A fire glowed low in the marble fireplace and Jarn was mildly irritated to see that this again was now a gas-fired log burner. But then he recollected that the old wood fire had made everything smell of woodsmoke, had led to the room needing redecorating every year, and had spat sparks to Issa's beloved Chinese rug leaving tiny holes. Yes, perhaps it had been a good idea to change it.

In the dim glow from the fire Jarn moved to the bed and

was overwhelmed by emotion when he saw his wife asleep, her arm thrown over her head in a position he knew well. She often slept with one or both arms raised on her pillow. It was a warm night, as it had been in the world he had just stepped from, and Issa was wearing only a short thin nightdress, with delicate straps over her shoulders. No sheet covered her body and he gazed avidly, a starving man seeing a feast for the gods spread out before him. His eyes travelled over her slender feet, golden legs, the gentle curve of belly, and the swell of her breasts. Her neck, cheeks and closed eyelids. Her mouth, with softly parted lips. Golden hair spread over the pillow.

If he had been fully present in her world, he would have pounced on his mate heedless of waking her, smothering her with kisses. As it was, to his enormous frustration, he couldn't touch her; he wasn't fully in her world and he knew from centuries of experience that touching living creatures in a world not fully stepped into was impossible, his hand would pass straight through. But he could at least lie next to her.

Jarn stretched out his length, next to his wife after so many decades, and gazed into her sleeping face. Up close, she was even more beguiling. Thick curling eyelashes, slightly flushed cheeks, golden curls drifting around her face. He even fancied he could detect a whiff of her familiar scent. In what reality, Jarn thought, could any man be expected to resist the mate he had not seen for nearly half a century. He expected no answer and would not have welcomed one. He already knew he could not keep from his beautiful wife, even if they were not in the same world.

Jarn raised himself over her, careful not to let his body touch where hers appeared to be, so his illusion wouldn't shatter. He moved his mouth to a few millimetres above hers and imagined the contact of their lips. Losing himself in imaginary kissing for minutes, Jarn tried to ignore the increasing desire now surging through him.

Suddenly, with shock, he realised Issa's eyes had fluttered open. She was gazing directly into his face. Wasn't she?

After a few heart-pounding seconds he saw that she had simply woken, or perhaps it was truer to say she had slightly woken, from a dream. And it had been a delightful dream, judging by the gentle smile on her face and her deepening breathing, her chest rising and falling more rapidly. Her eyelids half closed, stretching both arms back on her pillow, she moaned '*Jarn.*'

From so many years of marriage he knew exactly what his wife wanted and needed at this moment, and had they been together he would have taken the greatest delight in satisfying her, to the intense pleasure of them both. As it was, it was impossible. But his own need was now peaking with the vision of his mate so close, and he reached down. As he did so, Issa's body arched upwards, and he had to quickly lift himself to avoid her rising hips and the illusion of her being lost. Her breathing more rapid, he knew she was as close to the edge as he was and despite the desire now exploding through him, he found himself still able to admire her ability to crest without any direct stimulus, just one of the many advantages a woman had over a man, he remembered. Then all thoughts vanished as he surged, Issa tipping over the edge at the same moment.

Each gasping the other's name, in different worlds, their breathing finally slowed.

CHAPTER 27
CLARE, TERMONN HOUSE,
10TH JULY 2022

Over breakfast with David, we had discussed the Undercroft, and my reaction to it. The brilliant light, my sudden awareness of other worlds, and then my collapse. David had touched my hand sympathetically and I could see he was not surprised by my reaction. He knew the Undercroft and the vortex very well. But he was determined to help me with a gentler reintroduction to it, so we headed towards the breakfast room to see Issa.

'Mother, I am planning to take Clare to the Undercroft today to show her the lines. Do you object?'

Issa raised her head from her newspaper and looked at the two of us. She had been deeply absorbed in an article.

'No. Not at all. Good idea.'

'Would you like to come with us?'

'No, off you go. Have a good time!' Issa turned back to her paper. 'Don't lose her.'

'No chance of that.' David's hand was warm on my back and his eyes were twinkling.

'Oh, and David...,' Issa's voice followed us as we headed

towards the door. 'Watch Clare's fingers. She is like a child with a new toy, can't resist touching all the pretty things.'

I felt mildly told off, but David grinned. 'I remember you saying the same about Sylvie, a sign of intelligence and a curious mind in a toddler, you said.'

'Yes, very true,' laughed Issa. 'Of course, Sylvie actually was a toddler at the time, whereas Clare is a toddler in her twenties!'

We made our way down to the Undercroft. I felt some qualms, remembering what had happened on my first visit, but David's solid presence was deeply reassuring, as was his warm hand in mine. With that, I felt absolute trust.

Once on the stone floor next to the pedestal he pointed to the seat on the lower floor nearest the stairs.

'This is my seat, the one in line with the beacon. And that,' he pointed to the chair opposite, 'that is yours. That is nearest the old gates. It is opposite mine, so completing our line of power. Father's seat is between you and me, in line with St Michael's tower, and Mother's seat is opposite, in line with the rill and the statue.'

'What about the upper seats?' I asked, looking at the other four chairs on the higher level, each positioned between two seats on the lower level.

'Well, they have shifting ownership,' David looked at them, gazing above us to the next level. 'When Henry is here, she tends to sit between Mother and you, but of course she doesn't have a mate yet so her line isn't as strong as it will hopefully be, one day. We think that Maya has strengths which are very much aligned to Henry's, and she could complete the line by sitting opposite Henry, but the vortex frightens her, so she has never done it. Mother and Father have never been able to persuade her, perhaps there has never been a need important enough. The other two seats are currently Sylvie's and Fizz's. They are both young, and only fairly recently paired so their lines are rather weak. But they will strengthen in time.'

As so often, I didn't fully understand this. 'But I'm younger still, why am I stronger than them?'

'You have amazing potential, Clare. We are not sure why you are as you are, but we guess that it is something resulting from your heritage. You were gifted enough for my mother to sense your arrival the night you were born, back in the 1990s.'

Issa hadn't mentioned that to me. It seemed extraordinary that she should have sensed my birth, but Sylvie and Fizz had told me how powerful she was.

David's eyes had taken on a faraway look, and he added, 'I was in the US at the time, and I was conscious, as well, of something happening that day, but it wasn't clear enough for me to identify exactly what. I puzzled over the feeling for a couple of days and then put it out of my mind. My father sensed when Mother was born, hundreds of years ago, but he was older and more empathetic than I was back in the nineties.'

His hand squeezed mine. 'Anyway, you are as you are and personally, I am very grateful for it. Now, let's play with the lines. And if you are very well behaved and promise not to fiddle with your fingers, we might get the vortex up as well.'

'Should I sit in my chair?' I found myself reluctant to move away from him.

'No, as there are only the two of us, we will just stand on either side of the pedestal.'

David placed his hands on the surface. I was about to do

likewise but he shook his head. 'Don't touch just yet. Let me go first.'

The room seemed to lighten as fibres started to glow in the air, centred around David and his hands on the surface. He half turned so I could see behind him. The channel from him leading along the floor behind him, to the front of his chair, was glowing.

'Now, give me your hands.'

He placed them on the pedestal, so our fingertips were touching. The room filled with beams as still more fibres glowed and danced. I looked over my shoulder and saw my channel was filled with burning light, rippling and eddying as if it were liquid. Peering past David, I could see that his channel was also now burning liquid as mine was.

Beams swerved and danced round the pedestal, lighting up the carvings on the surface, which looked as if pure gold had been poured into them. I looked into David's eyes. The connection between us was magical and immense. His power flooded through me, and I knew my own was surging back to him.

I didn't understand what was happening, but I no longer cared. Yes, we were perfectly matched. I knew that for certain now and so did he. We grinned uncontrollably at each other, overwhelmed with joy, and he gripped my hands across the stone surface. Moments passed as we gazed at each other amid the sparkling golden fibres. Our future glowed as bright as the threads around us. I felt David's fingers stroking my hands.

'Shall we try the vortex again?'

I nodded, eager now.

As we reached out to it, the brilliant vortex rose from the surface, encompassing our hands and shining on our faces. It grew until the shimmering mass towered over us, but now, despite the multidimensional swirling and eddying it made more sense to me. Somehow, I understood, if only partially, the dimensional flows around the worlds and the silver links joining them. It was as if a network of connections had blazed into existence in my brain.

The vortex even seemed to welcome us and to reflect our joy, as if it had a personality of its own. I still recoiled from the black centre at its core, which seemed bigger than before, but the tiny shifting golden globes were enchanting. I fought not to reach out and grab, and David saw my struggle. He chuckled and held my hands more firmly in one of his own while with the other he pointed towards a section of the vortex.

'This area here, Clare, these two tiny globes.'

There were so many, hundreds of thousands of them moving through shifting dimensions in a never-ending dance and I was at a loss to know how he could distinguish between so many sparks and globes. It was like finding two tiny villages on the surface of a map of the earth. But he continued to point.

'This is our world and the adjacent one is where Father was seen just a few weeks ago. I had hoped these two worlds might merge, as they are almost identical, and perhaps Father would be returned. But it hasn't happened yet.'

I studied the two golden worlds intently. I still expected them to look like planets but there were no features on their surfaces. David saw my wonder and explained again, as Sylvie and Fizz already had.

'No, they are not planets. Each globe reflects an alternative reality of our own world, created through choices or events. The interconnections between them,' and he pointed to the shimmering silver threads connecting the globes, 'they are simply reflections of the similarities between the worlds. The connection between our world and the one Father was in is strong and bright. It shows that there are many similarities and few differences. The separation between our worlds is recent, so there are few changes.'

The vortex was a construction of beauty, like a fine piece of intricate filigree jewellery. It was mesmerising.

With a deft movement of his hand, David rotated the vortex and part of it expanded, showing more detail, more globes and many more shimmering connections.

'We can expand the vortex almost infinitely, drilling down further and further into separate worlds, all breaking away from a parent world, millions and millions of times. The more we do it, the further we move away from our own reality. Some of these worlds are very different to ours, they may have split from this world millennia ago. And they have a whole host of gatekeepers, some related to Melite, the gatekeeper of our world, and some not. Some have no gatekeeper at all.'

As I gazed, I saw two tiny shimmering spheres move closer and closer to each other, until in a sparkle of white brilliance they exploded into one. David had followed my eye movement and he smiled at me.

'That happens very often. A new reality is created because of a quite minor difference. Perhaps in one world someone chose to turn left and in the other world they turned right. But ultimately it makes no real difference to the future, so the two realities just shift back together. Unless the change is really significant, there is an attraction between neighbouring worlds, almost a magnetism. Realities seem to want to merge back if it is possible.'

He shifted the vortex back to the original view, and the two worlds, ours and the one Jarn had been in, appeared again before us, magnified.

I was suddenly aware that David was focussing more intently.

'I don't like the look of that. Do you see the black threads?'

I peered and could see what he meant. Black strands were interspersed with the silver, close to the two globes.

'What are they?'

'I think they may be coming out of the void. There are two. Here and here. Emerging from the dark, like filaments and approaching our world and the one Father was in.'

'And what is that?' I asked. 'That tiny brown spot.'

It was within the globe David had said was the adjacent world, the one where Jarn had been.

David suddenly saw what I was pointing to, and I heard his intake of breath.

'I have never seen anything like that before. But it may be the void barrier which the gatekeeper of that world, Melisse, said was around Father. If so, he must still be in that world.'

We looked at the vortex, focussing on this one small area, and the two globes with their dark fibres suddenly seemed to me to hold a threat. I felt revulsion.

It would seem that David shared my apprehension. 'I don't like this, Clare. Let us go and find my mother.'

The flames in our channels died down and the vortex folded back to the surface and sank within it, as we lifted our hands from the pedestal and walked to the stairs.

A short while later, Issa, David and I were gathered around the pedestal, now three pairs of hands on the hard stone. The golden mass arose before us, murmuring contented recognition, and we examined its shining surface and the endless shifting galaxies of bodies within it. David enlarged the area of our world and the adjacent one with the tiny dark spot and Issa's attention was rapt. We all thought the tiny mark might indicate Jarn's presence, and Issa was transfixed.

'Mother, do you have any idea what would happen if the void reached our world?' David was looking at the black filament extending to our tiny glittering globe.

'Nothing good, I fear. It is impossible to say with certainty. Perhaps for many there would be no discernible difference, at least at the start. Or perhaps it would be as in the world with the Shamen, and we would experience strange darkness.'

Issa shivered, her eyes fixed on the sphere that was our reality, with its black tendril.

'But if two adjacent worlds were both close to the void ... Jarn once speculated about this, based on an experience he had many, many years ago. Two worlds were on the brink of joining back together but were unstable because of their proximity to the void, alternately attracting and repelling each other. The pasts and futures of the two worlds combined and split, time and time again and he told me there was a strange series of unexplained events. Actions and consequences were no longer linked, there was no logic between an event and what should have followed that event. Things could happen in reverse order, against all nature. Jarn told me it was quite terrifying. He foresaw that both worlds were descending into chaos and would ultimately destroy each other. He left just before that happened.'

She added, 'I must confess I have wondered afresh about his experience, since we thought the void was expanding and swallowing realities. It is mere guesswork, but it seems possible that the same thing may happen here, and in the world Jarn is in.'

David and I looked at each other, horror evident on both our faces. Issa continued to gaze stoically at the vortex before her, deep in thought and studying the pulsating shape closely. I saw her gaze flit again to the tiny brown shape we now thought marked Jarn's presence.

She added quietly, 'and I have been reading just now about several odd events, things happening with no apparent cause. A small dam burst in Indonesia but there was no reason for it as the rains didn't fall until two days later. And there was a destructive wildfire in Australia yesterday, very much out of season. I wonder if it is the start of more. The start of events happening out of sequence.'

David gripped my hand and fixed his gaze on Issa. 'How do we stop it, Mother? We must at least try.'

With a small wave from Issa, the lower part of the vortex magnified still more. The fibres extending in inky darkness towards the two glowing orbs could now be clearly seen. There were filaments at the end of each fibre which flicked and twitched. Whenever the apparently random movement led closer to a globe, a tiny whisp minutely extended itself in the same direction. It made my skin creep.

'It's like a snake's tongue,' I whispered.

'Very astute, Clare. Yes, that is exactly what it is.' Issa's lovely face expressed part fascination and part revulsion. 'Its purpose is like the forked tongue of a snake. To detect prey and then to devour it.'

Then her expression changed to one of determination. She turned from the pedestal, and the golden shape shrank back with a deep sigh of disappointment. 'This is an adjacent world, and it seems your father is there. I can step to it. I am going.'

'No, Mother, we must think about this.' David put his hand out to stop her, and Issa moved it away, gently but resolutely.

'My son, I have spent half a century, thinking, dreaming and waiting. Now is the time for action. He is so *close*.'

David reached for his mother's hands, gripping them to stop her movement to the stairs.

'There are two tendrils there, shifting and searching. One towards this world, one towards the world probably closest to ours, where we think Father is. What do they have in common, these worlds?'

With reluctance, Issa stopped and thought. 'The worlds are almost identical; they have much in common, and few differences. Maybe whoever our enemy is cannot distinguish between them.'

'Or maybe, the truth lies in that you are in one world and Father is in the other?'

David went on, remorselessly, 'and we know the entity appeared to be targeting Father, and not with any good intentions. What if it is targeting you as well? What if having both you and Father in the same place would simply present a bigger target than if you were separated?'

Issa looked at her son and finally gave up trying to pull her hands away from his.

'Yes, my boy.' Her shoulders sagged a little. 'It is only that I am desperate to see him again, and he is alive and so near, it is clouding my judgement.' After a few moments of gazing at the vaulted roof above her, she added 'what do you suggest?'

'If you go, it will leave us vulnerable. You are the strongest of us and we need you here to protect Termonn. I think it would be better if I step to that world rather than you, aiming for the place where Father's own personal void'

– this with a dry smile – 'seems to be. It may show us something. I would have no need to go near the void, there would be no danger.'

'Except a tendril from the void is clearly approaching that world, as well as our own. If there is something malevolent there, it could reach you now, even if all you do is step.'

'I will be careful, and fast, Mother, don't worry.'

Issa gazed at the slumped vortex. It now seemed to be dozing, gently rising up and down from just above the stone. I thought there was even the hint of a snore. Issa turned back to her son and it was clear she was biting back disappointment and longing.

'Take Clare with you, David.'

'Clare? Mother, no!'

'If it is as safe as you say it is, she will be in little danger. And if it is more dangerous, your combined strengths may be needed to get you both home. You have the potential to be as powerful as your father and me, and even now your skills together are strong.'

David struggled, but I saw the moment when he accepted the logic of his mother's argument. He looked at me questioningly and I nodded without hesitation.

'Very well. Clare will come with me.'

Once the decision was made, we moved to the drawing room and stepped quickly. David's arm was around my waist and his strict instruction to touch nothing, absolutely nothing, no matter how tempting and glittery, rang in my ears. I was not to reach out myself, he would control the stepping, he said. We would stay between worlds and just observe.

And as before when I had done this with Issa, the drawing room blurred before coming back into focus. But this was a different room. The shape was the same, the windows still looked out over pasture and the view to St

Michael's tower was identical. The furnishings were mostly different though; curtains, carpets and sofas all changed. It somehow wasn't as harmonious as the lovely room Issa had created.

The similarities and differences were disconcerting, but my attention was riveted by the three people already in the room. They were seated on the sofas, but they all watched the wide screen television in the corner, a feature Issa's room did not have.

A middle-aged woman and man were seated together, the man holding the woman's hand with his other arm around her shoulders. In an armchair nearby, a man was sitting, his eyes also on the television, and I had my first sight of Jarn Dechar.

I knew immediately it was him, not only because of the resemblance to the photographs at Termonn but also because David's arm tightened around me, and he moved automatically towards the man who was his father, with a gasp. Jarn did not see us, any more than the other couple did.

Even seated he was imposing, broad and of a height that would be extraordinary had he been standing. Deep mesmerising eyes, hair so dark it was almost black, a trim beard of the same colouring. Both very lightly tinted with silver. His complexion was slightly olive-toned, suggesting an origin in a more southerly country. A face of angles, shadows and immense character, with some small scars. A man used to power and command, I thought.

The voice from the news reporter filled the room, the pictures on the screen moving from one scene of extreme devastation to another.

'...reports are still coming in, but the current situation is that at least three high rise buildings, all apparently of steel construc-

tion, have collapsed, and all of them are in Southern California. There are fresh reports of the partial collapse of a large number of concrete buildings and bridges across the state. Emergency services are at multiple scenes and people are being brought out from the debris, but it seems inevitable that the death toll will rise considerably over the coming hours. It is known that several thousand people worked in these three buildings alone and the collapses happened mid-morning when the offices would have been fully occupied. We're now going to our correspondent in Los Angeles. Paul, do we have any idea what could have caused these terrible events?'

'No, Lisa.' The reporter's face on the screen looked professional but also shocked. 'It is being widely reported that this is consistent with earthquake damage, from a big earthquake of at least 8 or perhaps even 9 in magnitude, but the seismographs show no sign of an earthquake or any other surface event. Geologists here in the US and across the globe are working on it, but at the moment they have no answers.'

David and I exchanged glances, and he pulled me even closer to his side, my own arm around his waist. Was this the first example of what Issa had feared, that actions and consequences would no longer follow in a logical order, but could actually be reversed? Would the earthquake that caused these events occur in the next few days? Would our world be the next to suffer something as catastrophic?

'It reminds me of 2001, George, and Maura is in San Francisco,' the woman whispered, and the man squeezed her hand reassuringly.

'We'll ring her in a few minutes, love.' George comforted the woman who appeared to be his wife.

Meanwhile, Jarn's attention was fixed to the screen, his expression one of deep concentration.

Next to me, I heard David's voice. 'Father?'

But there was nothing more to be done here. We had the answer we were looking for, depressing though it was. As we turned to step back to our own world, I thought I heard a faint response.

'*David*?'

CHAPTER 28
CLARE, TERMONN HOUSE,
10TH – 11TH JULY 2022

On our return, after only a few minutes absence, Issa walked up to us, her face showing her relief. David reached for his mother and hugged her.

'You are very wise, Mother, it seems that things are indeed happening without apparent causation.'

We described what we had seen, not only the Californian damage but Jarn, his appearance and his companions. I could see Issa sucking in the information like a parched sponge takes up water.

She rained questions at us. How did he look? What was he wearing? Did he look well? Was he thinner?

She visibly had to force herself to stop asking for more details of her husband, and she turned her face away from us, her shoulders trembling. For her, it was the first true confirmation that her husband was currently alive, albeit in a different world. I couldn't stop myself moving to her and putting a tentative arm round her. She smiled gratefully and returned my hug, but I could still feel her tension.

'David,' I asked, 'did you hear your father say your name, as we were leaving?' I was wondering if I had imagined it.

'Yes, I think so, just as we were stepping away. It is hard to believe though, he clearly did not see us. And I am almost sure that if we had taken the final step and appeared in the room, he would have been dragged back into the void, with who knows what consequences.'

'But hearing is possible,' Issa said meditatively, turning back to us. 'Perhaps the filaments of the void stretching to both our worlds and being interconnected are partly breaking down the barrier. Jarn may well be able to hear us. Sounds and scents are always the first thing, they come more quickly than vision, although they are a little muted.'

We left Issa pondering and went to the kitchen, where we updated Sylvie and Fizz, both stirring bubbling saucepans of summer fruits on the stove, on the developments. Sylvie beamed with sheer happiness, her eyes filling with tears, and Fizz hugged her.

'It is so good to know Lord Dechar is well and close by,' Fizz said. 'If only we could get him back here.'

'But we do need to do something, David,' Sylvie urged in a voice that shook. 'We can't leave him there for the void to grab him. And we may not have much time.'

David put his arms around his sister.

'We will do something. We just need to plan things out. I think we will all need to collect in the Undercroft, soon. It may be that together we can repel these void filaments.'

'Without Father, would we be strong enough?' Sylvie looked doubtful.

David answered, 'we have Clare now, thank goodness, and perhaps we can persuade Maya as well, as it is an emergency. We have long thought her line is similar to Henry's. She would give us at least some strength on that axis.'

Fizz looked out of the kitchen window, where Maya was watering the hanging baskets. 'She is so frightened of the vortex. I think it is something to do with when she lost her husband. They were true mates.'

Sylvie looked at her in puzzlement. 'How do you know, Fizz? She has never spoken in all the time we have known her.'

'When we were first together, you and I,' Fizz said, 'Maya mimed for me. She put her hand on her heart, and then put her other hand over my heart, and nodded. She looked so sad but also happy. I knew she was telling me that she had once been as in love as I am, and she was pleased for me.'

Sylvie visibly swallowed back emotion. Her voice was husky.

'Her husband died, he was murdered, right in front of her. Mother once told me, when I was young and was being horrible to Maya as teenagers can be. Mother and Father knew there were people with abilities in that area of Australia and they went looking for them, back in the early 1830's, I think it was. They found the most terrible scene. Maya had been tortured, it is why she is so scarred, and the men were about to hang her, in fact her neck was already in a noose. Mother took care of her while Father dealt with their attackers. But it was too late for Maya's husband. And she had seen him die.'

The conversation about Maya had triggered a thought in my mind. 'Would it be possible to get Henry back, do you think? She would give us more strength, wouldn't she? Especially if she joined with Maya opposite her?'

'I will ring her, that's a brilliant thought, Clare.' David drew his phone from his pocket and punched a button. 'But she would have to travel very fast, and she can't step as we can.'

A distant voice answered quickly.

'Hi, Sis! Got time for a chat?'

Henry's flight would land at Heathrow at 8am tomorrow, and she would be home before lunchtime. In the meantime, there was nothing to do but think, study the vortex and watch the news. We were all looking out for events which had no cause, hoping that nothing major occurred before we could make our attempt to fight the filaments in the Undercroft.

In the late evening, Sylvie and Fizz took Sergei and Kimi out for a long walk in the grounds, as Hettie and Mordecai made their way back to their apartments in the Tower and Maya headed to her rooms in the stable block. David and me watched them leave. Then, we were alone in the silent kitchen.

Our eyes connected and we moved into each other's arms. I stroked David's hair and his cheeks, as his hands pulled me close.

An extraordinary understanding had grown between us over the brief time we had known each other, together with a dynamic attraction. It mattered not a whit that we had only just met, we knew each other as if we had dated for months. He tilted my chin up, our lips hovering close, then our mouths drew together as if magnetised. For long moments the kiss deepened, our bodies entwined and our hearts pounding. But we both felt it at the same time, the enormity of the threat facing us resurfacing, and we reluctantly returned to reality.

The stillness of the old house surrounded us as we remained wrapped in each other's arms, but the tension of needing to do something, anything, grew. We disentangled ourselves reluctantly and hand-in-hand went to find Issa who, after a brief compassionate glance at us, led us to the

Undercroft. We brought up the vortex between us, which glinted and flickered a welcome as it rose above us.

Again, we concentrated on the two tiny globes, which were the worlds we were fascinated by. Ours and the one Jarn was in, so similar. The black tendrils had stretched, and both now touched the sparkling orbs, which were no longer completely golden but had patches of black on their surfaces. Issa brought up the vision in closer detail and we could see that Jarn's world was now tightly gripped by the black vine. It explained why we had seen the catastrophic scenes in America, in the other world. But the filaments were stretching out towards our world, multiple lines extending like a spider's web.

'Sylvie is right, there is very little time left.' David's tone was anxious.

'I have warned Sir Edward, and he is coming to us tomorrow morning,' Issa said quietly. 'I felt some guilt at telling him what disaster seems to be facing us when I had no solution for him, but he wanted to be here in case he could provide any human resources or assistance.'

'Did he have any inkling, Issa?' I asked. Sir Edward was usually remarkably well informed on nearly everything.

'Not about what is happening here, of course,' Issa said, with a gesture at the vortex. 'But he says there is concern internationally about recent unexplained events which have happened and seem to be gaining in frequency. Several incidents have been covered up, I believe, to avoid panic. One was the loss of a plane from radar in the South China Sea, but it was a plane that had not actually taken off – it just appeared briefly on the radar a thousand miles away and vanished moments later, only to be found on the tarmac of the airport immediately after but with all the passengers and crew dead. Drowned, it would seem.'

We looked at Issa in horror.

'So yes, I think it is safe to say that Sir Edward does know that things are very wrong.'

In the late evening, I stood in David's arms at the foot of the stairs, leading to the room that had been his and was now mine. Neither of us wanted to be apart. But reluctance to share my past held me back from the final step for us. I was at a loss for words, having no idea how to explain my reluctance, given the intimacy of the bond between us. But my David knew. He cupped my cheek in his hand and said 'we will wait, Clare, until you are happy to share what is in your past. All I ask is that we are not apart tonight.'

And we were not. I lay in David's arms all night, in the room that now belonged to both of us. Worry about how events would enfold tomorrow dominated our thoughts and our conversation. We held each other and dozed, and I think both of us slept for short periods, deeply comforted to be together. What lay further between us would wait for our future, when the peril had passed. But would there even be a future? Nothing seemed certain, now.

Our lack of sleep during the night led to a deeper sleep for both of us around dawn, and as a result we overslept. Clambering reluctantly from the bed that now seemed a deliciously comfortable safe haven, we took turns to shower and dress. While I was brushing out my hair, David was checking his phone and reported that nothing major seemed to have happened overnight. But the threat still lurked, a creature lying in wait. It seemed inevitable that disaster was imminent.

We made our way downstairs and heard a car pull up

outside. Someone was paying a taxi. Then the door was flung open, rays of light appearing on the stone floor of the hall, and a tall dark-haired young woman in jeans and a cropped leather jacket burst in.

'Hi folks!'

'Henry!'

David rushed for the lovely woman who was clearly his sister. I could see how similar their colouring and build was, even their facial expressions reflected each other's. I waited, standing back against the staircase, while they hugged and held each other close.

After a few moments David released his sister and beckoned me forwards. With an appearance perhaps in her early thirties, Henry had a striking face and beautiful dark lashed eyes. Her radiant warmth enveloped me, combined with an utterly capable manner. I decided immediately that if I was ever in need of medical attention, especially for something gynaecological, this would be the person I would want to see at the other end of the scope.

Henry didn't stand on ceremony, she just pulled me into her arms and hugged me as she had David. With her lips on my cheek and her 'welcome, sister', I realised David had told her more than I had thought. I hugged her back, feeling an immediate connection with this woman.

Issa came running in from the kitchen, with Hettie not far behind and Maya bringing up the rear, Kimi desperately trying to overtake. Sylvie and Fizz galloped down the stairs from the library. It was our cue to disappear for a while and we relocated to the kitchen.

Despite neither of us claiming to have any appetite, we still managed to put away a considerable amount of toast and jam. Issa reappeared in the kitchen after a while with her arm around Henry and made her daughter toast and eggs, with Sylvie and Fizz eagerly fetching more honey and butter. Hettie and Maya provided everyone with tea and coffee. Then we sat around the kitchen table, discussing how to proceed.

We agreed that if the void around Jarn could be weakened, he might be able to break through if he was close to a weakness in the barrier and knew our intentions. His huge strength could make the difference between success and failure. The consensus was that one or two of us should return to Jarn's world this morning and attempt to suggest a time when he should be in the Undercroft. A precise time could help us to repel the filaments, if Jarn was aware when to focus his energy.

Again, it was agreed that the task was best given to David and me. As we were moving to the drawing room, a black limousine drew up outside the front door. Over my shoulder I saw Issa welcoming Sir Edward and his secretary Paul Beresford, but we walked quickly into the drawing room and almost immediately stepped.

This time I felt I had a hint of control. It seemed to me that I would now know what to do if it was left to me to do it by myself. But David controlled our stepping, and I was careful not to conflict with him. We arrived in the drawing room of the other world but found it empty.

'Father,' David called gently. A minute later, he called again, a little louder, '*Father*'.

Just as it seemed nothing would happen, the door to the hall opened and Jarn strode in, looking around him. Dressed casually in jeans and t-shirt, his presence still dominated the room.

David spoke quietly.

'Father, without going near the void, can you do your

disappearing act and join us in between worlds? But, for god's sake, don't go to the void.'

Jarn listened intently and suddenly blurred. He reappeared closer to us, still transparent but now he could clearly see us. I guessed we were also transparent to him.

He moved towards David and the difficulty he had in not reaching for his son was evident, as David made a tiny move towards Jarn. Neither dare risk it, but I could see longing and moisture in both their eyes.

'Father, now is not the time for introductions, but this is Clare. We have only recently found each other.'

Jarn's voice was deep and gruff. Either it was his normal voice or it had deepened because of the emotion he was feeling at seeing his son so close after so long.

'I know, my boy. I have seen more than you think. Clare...'

The giant of a man nodded deeply and courteously to me, and I had difficulty in stopping myself curtseying in return. Even when semi-transparent his charisma was overwhelming. He was also the most staggeringly handsome man I had ever seen.

'...I look forward to welcoming you properly into our family when this little difficulty is ended.'

'Father, we need to be quick, time is limited. There is a threat from the void, to both this world and ours. Tendrils are reaching out.'

'Yes, I have sensed something malevolent approaching. You need to summon all the forces you can, and I will try to break through. Together we may be able to amass enough power to repel it.'

An expression of love and exasperation lit David's face. 'How are you always one step ahead?'

He collected himself quickly. 'But, no matter... we are

planning for 2pm today in the Undercroft. Two hours from now, in case your time is different here. We have Mother, Clare, myself, Sylvie and Fizz. Henry has just arrived. And we may be able to persuade Maya. But we need you, Father.'

Jarn looked troubled.

'I am not sure my efforts will be enough, David, I have searched and searched for a place where I can completely break through and have failed. But I will do my best. If you can somehow target this damn barrier around me, we may have a chance.'

Footsteps could be heard in the hall. Jarn turned to us, speaking fast.

'I should warn you, there is no access to an Undercroft in this house, although I suspect the room exists here. I will try to get as close as I can.'

Jarn looked over his shoulder as the door to the hall started to open, then looked back to us. 'Tell your mother I love her.'

Jarn stepped back, reluctance in his eyes, and we stepped into our own world.

CHAPTER 29
CLARE, TERMONN HOUSE,
11TH JULY 2022

We returned to our own Termonn House, arriving back in our drawing room. Henry was standing by the fireplace, waiting for us.

'Did you see Father?'

David nodded at his sister, who grinned hugely. Her expressive face lit up, as she said, 'I really want both him and Mother to be here, when I tell them the news.'

I saw David catch his breath for a moment before gripping Henry by the arms. 'Are you saying…?'

'Yes. Finally. After so many years. He couldn't come with me, he's on duty at the hospital for another eight hours. He will take a flight later if we need to have another attempt.'

A grin and a raise of the eyebrows from David encouraged more details. Despite the seriousness of our situation, Henry was glowing with happiness.

'His name is Reth. His line…,' and I knew she meant his line of descent from an ancestor of our kind, '…descends through his father and grandfather, all from Kenya. His twin brother Raf is the same. Reth works for the same Médecins sans Frontières initiative as me, he is a surgeon.'

David hugged his sister. His happiness for her was clear, as his eyes over her shoulder were fixed on me.

As the huge grandfather clock in the hall of Termonn ticked towards 2pm, tension built but also a sense of purpose. After a light lunch in the dining room, I saw Sir Edward lower his head to Issa's with a few words exchanged, and then a respectful press of her hand. It was clear he understood the magnitude of the threat confronting us. Then he and Paul moved towards the oak front door and Paul drew out his phone, gazing at me as he started to speak into it.

With five minutes to go, we walked into the passage outside the kitchen and then down the stairs to the Undercroft, my hand warm in David's larger grip. We were followed by Henry and Issa. David led me to the chair he had shown me before, the one on the lower level nearest the gates. With a gentle kiss on my cheek and a squeeze of his hand, he moved towards his opposite chair, on the axis nearest the beacon. Our line of power completed, the channel between us was already showing a gentle glow and the vortex was rising.

Issa moved to her seat, nearest the rill and Henry took up her position on the upper level, on the chair between mine and Issa's. The emptiness of the seat opposite Issa's, Jarn's chair in line with St Michael's tower, struck me forcibly. Was it possible we could manage this without his immense strength? Only three of the lower chairs were filled.

Similarly, the chair opposite Henry was empty. But then so were Sylvie's and Fizz's. With the clock ticking towards 2pm, where were they?

The sound of steps on the stairs was followed by Sylvie and Fizz entering the Undercroft, each holding one of

Maya's hands. The aboriginal woman had a look of steely determination. I thought it hid terror, but it was very well hidden. It wasn't obvious who was giving support to who. In fact, I decided, it was mostly Maya who was supporting Sylvie and Fizz.

Maya looked towards Henry, who gave her a warm smile of encouragement. I could see her mouth 'Welcome!' And Maya took her seat opposite Henry.

With Fizz and Sylvie seating themselves on the upper level opposite each other, all the seats were filled bar one, and the lines glowed more strongly, gold and silver now spreading into all the channels. I was dimly aware of Hettie and Mordecai near the stairs, both with expressions of concern, but I had no time for them as the vortex finally rose before us with a shimmering brilliance I hadn't seen before and to a height which rose almost to the vaulted roof.

Issa moved from her chair to take up a position with both hands spread on the engraved surface of the pedestal, while still in line with her centre of power, the rill. The surface glowed with brilliant light which shone through her hands. Flames licked them and the light reflected on Issa's face, the whole room full of cold fire and flashing beams. All of our eyes were focussed on the vortex which towered above us and now reached to the roof, the spheres and lines swirling, shimmering, joining and parting.

At the centre of the vortex, the black darkness, its bulges separating it into segments, seemed to shudder and diminish slightly, the extending tendrils recoiling.

But it was only to surge again, tongues spreading out towards the worlds which were ours and Jarn's. Issa gripped the edges of the stone table and visibly gritted her teeth. The darkness diminished, but I felt it was only temporary. We were holding back something immense, defeating it was going to be difficult. The Undercroft itself seemed to shudder as eddies of shade surged out from the blackness and further tendrils developed. It was as if we had tweaked the tail of a sleeping dragon and it was flaring back at us.

I gripped the arms of my chair and saw David doing the same. The channel between us flared brilliantly and again the darkness retreated. I focussed, hard, on repelling the black, an instinctive response which I knew David was sharing and amplifying. His support surged through me, his eyes fixed on mine, and I returned it, our strengths together far stronger than we could individually have managed. Before our eyes the darting tongues of blackness shrank back. I could see Sylvie and Fizz focusing all their strength, their channel a brilliant silver. Henry and Maya's line blossomed into an explosion of silver and subtle gold rays as both gripped their seats with intense concentration.

Issa, alone on her line, had her eyes tightly closed, her knuckles white with her grip on the stone. Gold rays billowed around her, stretching towards the empty seat that was Jarn's.

We were winning. The dark centre of the void reduced to a sliver, and worlds were slowly emerging from its grip. I thought of the Shamen David had described to me and hoped their world was being released from the dark and the creatures plaguing it. As we watched, little glistening globes were gradually re-joining the vortex with a web of new and shining lines connecting them.

Perhaps we all relaxed too much. Slowly the dark re-emerged, the black hairy lines stealthily spreading again and focussing on the two worlds that mattered most to us. Issa raised her head from her focus on the brilliant engraving on the stone and looked at us all, with encouragement and determination. No words were needed to convey her message. There was no choice but to continue.

Concentration, from all seven of us. Hands gripping chair arms. Intense focus on the blackness. Outside Termonn House, I knew, without seeing it, that the four paths to the centres of power were glowing as brightly as they were in the Undercroft. The tower, the beacon, the gates and the rill were burning brilliantly. Once again, the tendrils retreated, but then slowly, slowly, they restarted their growth. Something stronger than us was feeding them.

I saw Issa start to falter, the effort requiring more strength than she had, and David's concern for his mother was clear. It was echoed on the faces of Henry and Sylvie. And we were all thinking the same thing: if our last attempt was not enough, no new one was going to work. Jarn had not been able to break through. We clung to our positions, gripping hard, but we could all see the darkness expanding, inexorably, now creeping into the Undercroft from all sides and moving down towards our seats. A chill came with it.

A movement to my right drew my focus to Maya. She had been steadfast in her position, unwaveringly projecting her channel of gleaming silvery gold towards Henry. But now her eyes were focused on Issa, with an unworldly gaze. I looked towards David, sensing that something terrible was coming, something we must avert. But his hands were clenched and his teeth gritted, in his desperate attempt to maintain our own line and to protect me. He had nothing to spare for battles elsewhere.

Issa was now clinging to the stone surface, reaching towards the centre with her arms as she tried with the last of her energy to deflect the oncoming darkness. I thought I heard a groan from deep within the vortex as the Undercroft quaked and the black centre grew steadily and remorselessly, leaving only the gold and silver channels between all of us to relieve the dark shadows now encroaching deep into the room. An icy cold was growing.

I saw Maya stand and move away from her seat, walking slowly down towards the floor and the darkness which was now shifting around the vortex, probing to find a way in. Issa suddenly saw the movement and called out.

'Maya, no! Please. No!'

But nothing could stop the woman. She walked resolutely and with no expression other than determination towards the dark surrounding the vortex, her golden path illumined around her.

At the edge of the black she turned to Issa. I saw a gentle smile light Maya's face and she bowed, deeply. Then she turned back to the stone centre. Inky blackness was spreading, engulfing the pedestal and creeping towards our chairs.

Maya walked calmly into its centre.

Instantly there was a silent explosion of white, shimmering brilliance, dazzling power conducted along the four axes but focussed on the core where Maya's body was now illumined in burning gold. In front of her, a figure emerged from the stone base, I thought a man's body. Maya moved until her shape merged with his. Then the whiteness expanded until it became blinding, shattering in its intensity over the whole Undercroft. I shut my eyes against the brilliance but could still see nothing but whiteness through my lids.

A tearing screech, as if the universe was ripping apart. Echoes reverberating between the ancient walls.

I opened my eyes as the shattering noise was followed by the sound of an impact, and a body crashed to the stone floor. A man had fallen from a height and was lying, unmoving, on the stones.

Jarn.

David gasped 'Father!' and ran from his seat, Henry and Sylvie doing likewise.

The Undercroft was lit again as normal, the darkness vanquished. Within the vortex, there was now only a sliver of black running from top to bottom. No tendrils in sight. With a sigh of relief, the vortex gently descended to the surface of the pedestal.

I was still gripping the arms of my seat. Looking round I could see Jarn being helped to his feet by David, with Sylvie on one side and Henry on the other. Fizz, immediately behind them, was grinning broadly. I heard Hettie gasp with delight.

But my attention was focused on Issa. Her hands were still on the stone surface of the pedestal. Illuminated by the fading light of the vortex she looked utterly exhausted, her face white and her eyes closed. Then they opened and she saw Jarn in front of her only a few feet away. Her face lit with radiant joy, which was immediately reflected on Jarn's face as he leapt towards her. But before he could reach her, she collapsed, her fingers losing their grip on the stone.

Her falling body was caught by Jarn. He lowered her to the ground and knelt by her side.

The family's anxiety had, for a few moments, been for the father but in an instant it transferred to the mother. We all watched, aghast. Jarn held his wife as Henry rushed to them and knelt, feeling for her mother's pulse and touching her ashen face. The rest of us watched, holding our breaths.

'She is alive, Father, but her pulse is weak and she is very cold.'

'The fight has depleted her life energy. We must warm her, and quickly.'

Jarn looked frantically around him and saw Hettie

standing by the stairs. 'Hettie, do we still have the fur cloak from Russia? Bring it, or blankets, and warming stones or bottles. Anything to heat her.'

Jarn's voice was rough and urgent. With a nod, Hettie shot back up the stairs, Mordecai following her. Now, I saw that Sir Edward had been standing behind them. He moved inside the room, observing without words, his face grim.

Jarn's attention returned to his wife, cradling her limp body in his arms and stroking her face. His bleakness and despair were hard to watch. In a few cataclysmic moments he had finally succeeded in returning home, only to find this.

I stood and moved next to David, putting an arm around him. David spoke, but his voice was only a whisper. 'Is it too late, Father?'

'She could be saved but only if we were in Dodona. And at present I do not have the energy to take her there.'

I heard Sylvie sob, Fizz's arms around her.

Sir Edward moved towards Jarn and spoke, quietly but with his usual ability to control a situation.

'Lord Dechar. Where do you need to go?'

Jarn turned to look at the newcomer, assessing him instantly. 'To Dodona. In the west of Greece.'

Sir Edward turned and moved to the stairs with a speed I would not have thought him capable of. He had pulled out his phone and now, as he mounted the stairs, he started speaking into it rapidly.

I turned my attention to Issa and watched as David knelt by his father and touched his mother's face. Was it my imagination that I saw frost touching her lips and eyelids? There was no colour left in her complexion, even her lips were pale. Henry was rubbing her mother's hands and arms, as

Fizz took off her own jacket and tenderly wrapped it round Issa.

Sylvie, on Issa's other side, choked. 'She is icy, Father.'

'That is the problem, my girl. If we could only warm her. But it is heat from inside that she really needs and there is only one place that can provide that.' Jarn's voice was distant, his attention almost entirely focused on the wife dying in his arms.

Approaching feet rushed down the stairs and then Hettie ran into the Undercroft carrying a huge fur. Mordecai was just behind her with three hot water bottles.

Jarn released his grip on his wife reluctantly, so Henry and Sylvie could wrap Issa in the fur and tuck the hot water bottles inside its folds. He then pulled her back into his arms. A little colour gradually returned to Issa's face as the warmth surrounded her.

My attention was caught by a distant beating sound. It came closer and I realised it was an approaching helicopter. I squeezed David's arm to draw his attention and he listened intently. The pulsating, whirling noise grew louder and louder until it seemed almost overhead.

Sir Edward re-entered the Undercroft.

'Lord Dechar, transport is outside, to wherever you wish to go.'

Jarn looked up, his face pale but with a glimmer of hope. 'So quick....?'

'The aircraft has been on standby at the nearest airbase for transfer to this house for the last eight hours. I ordered them to take off before 2pm and confirmed their instructions to land outside just a few minutes ago. But...', and Sir Edward spoke gently but with authority, '...*you* need to direct them, and there is, I presume, no time to lose.' He turned back to the stairs.

Jarn stood, scooping his wife up in her furry cocoon as if she was as light as a feather. He ran up the stairs behind Sir Edward, all of us on their heels. We raced through the kitchen and round the side of the house to the lawns beyond, where the noise from the helicopter engines was almost unbearable.

I looked in amazement at what was touching down on the lawn in front of us, never having seen anything remotely like it before. With a body like that of a huge helicopter, it had two long slim wings, each topped with a vertical tower on which the propellers whirled. Paul Beresford came up behind me and whispered.

'It's on loan from the US, a v-23 Osprey. Astonishing technology, newly developed. It can take off and land vertically but once in the sky it's incredibly fast, like a jet. There are very few in the world. Sir Edward thought it might be useful today.'

The central doors of the aircraft opened, and steps were lowered. A man in air force uniform leapt down the steps to the lawn and smartly saluted Sir Edward, who was just ahead of us.

'Lieutenant Martinez, sir. We are ready to depart on your orders. For full speed, our load capacity is limited to six guests.'

Sir Edward gestured to Jarn, who ran rapidly up the steps with Issa in his arms, still wrapped in fur. David and I followed them up the steps, at Sir Edward's nod, and he beckoned Paul Beresford to join us. I saw Henry put comforting arms round Sylvie and Fizz, Hettie standing close by.

In the cabin, which was clearly designed for military transport and not for comfort, a uniformed woman emerged from the cockpit. She looked to Sir Edward and then, at his nod, to Jarn.

'I am the pilot, sir. Where to?'

The aircraft might have been American but from her accent the pilot was clearly Australian. In my civil service training, I had heard of defence and military collaboration between the UK, US, Australia and others. If this loan was related to that, then I appreciated it very much.

'To Dodona, about 20 km south of Ioannina. In a narrow valley between two mountains. I will direct you once we are nearly there.'

'Not to worry, sir. My first degree was in archaeology. I know where it is.' She added, to Sir Edward, 'and as requested, sir, we have a channel of airspace cleared for us.'

We took our seats rapidly, aided by Martinez, who deftly strapped us in with double belts across our chests.

'Best to be well secured,' he said, with a wink to us all, 'this is the most powerful take-off known to man outside a trip to space.'

Within seconds we were flattened back in our seats as the aircraft launched upwards into the summer sky with immense power and then blasted off towards the south.

CHAPTER 30
CLARE, DODONA, 11TH
JULY 2022

More blankets and foil wraps were brought to Jarn and wrapped tenderly around Issa by Martinez. Issa was still in Jarn's arms, with an extended seatbelt wrapped around both her and her husband. She was by now buried in a huge cocoon of fur, blankets and foil, her blonde hair just wisps around the gap in the folds. I saw Jarn speak to her inaudibly and stroke her face.

Then his expression altered and glazed over. I looked to David, strapped into the seat next to me, with a questioning raise of my brows.

'He is speaking, inside,' David murmured. 'Father is old, and over the centuries he has become telepathic. It is something that in our kind grows with age. Mother also has the skill but hers is not so well developed, as she is younger. I think that she can transfer emotions, but not words. But she told us that Father could bore her with the complete works of Shakespeare, if he wanted to. It used to make her laugh. She would also complain that Father abused the talent to achieve his own ends.'

David looked fondly at his mother, but his deep worry was evident.

'But while Jarn was lost, they were unable to communicate like that?' I queried, confused.

'No, it is only possible when they are in the same reality. It makes sense if you think about it.'

I nodded, thoughtfully. 'Will we be able to do that, at some point?' I was keen to take David's mind off his mother's state.

'Yes, I expect so, in a few hundred years.' David smiled at me lovingly, my goal temporarily achieved, and I touched his cheek.

'Both Mother and Father, and also Henry and myself, have skills in empathy as well, something else that develops with time. And that is yet another ability Father has found very useful over the centuries. He used, and I think greatly abused, the ability without conscience for a long time. Mother has slowly taught him not to invade people's privacy, and I think he has been better behaved in the last hundred years or so.'

'So, who is he speaking to now?'

'I don't know for certain, but I am guessing he is preparing a reception committee for us.'

'In Greece?''

'Yes. We are heading to the only place on earth that can save Mother now, the temple at Dodona, and the gatekeeper there, Melite. She is ancient, far older than Father and Mother, and immensely powerful. But,' and David had a frown which worried me, 'it is not at all obvious that Melite will help.'

'Why on earth should she not?' My stomach clenched violently as the plane executed a sudden change in direction. The speed at which we were travelling meant every alteration was a physical jolt. I looked out of the window at the brilliant blue of the sky and saw an aircraft very much like ours quite close by. It appeared we had been joined by an escort.

'Why should Melite refuse if Issa can be helped?', I asked David again.

'It is complicated, and I don't understand all of it myself. But Father and Melite clashed a long time ago, and I believe it was over Mother. Melite wanted Mother to join her as a handmaid, to strengthen them against intrusions from the void, and Father refused to let her go.'

David turned to me.

'I think it relates to the mating between two of our kind. Once a *gerasi* mating bond is formed, the woman can no longer serve the gatekeeper as a handmaid. Father suspects it is because *gerasi* handmaids are in some way required to be mated to the order itself. In any case, Mother was no longer of such potential value to the temple once she had mated with Father, and Melite never fully forgave him for it. So, it is not clear now whether Melite will help him. We can only hope that her fondness for Mother will overcome her resentment of Father.'

The plane shifted in the air and began to lose altitude. I struggled not to lose my stomach, regretting this morning's breakfast toast and my lunch. This was a million times worse than turbulence on normal flights and I had never been particularly keen even on that. After a ghastly ten minutes, during which I resented my need to clutch David's hand but was too terrified to stop myself, land appeared below and the aircraft's velocity eased back. Finally, we were hovering.

Jarn released his seat belt and stood, keeping his balance without difficulty. He transferred Issa's motionless body to

David, who carefully laid her over his own and my laps, as Jarn moved to the cockpit. There, he stood behind the pilot's seat and pointed.

'You see the person in white? You need to land as close to her as you can.'

The pilot nodded and rapidly assessed the possible landing points in the patchwork of fields below. Selecting one, the aircraft made a final stomach-churning descent and touched down.

Martinez ran to open the doors and lower the steps, returning to help us unlatch our seatbelts.

Jarn scooped Issa up, and was the first out of the plane, jumping down the steps and hitting the ground running. The rest of us extricated ourselves from our seats and made our way down the steps with as much haste as we could manage, our limbs stiff from the flight.

Meanwhile, Jarn was already some distance away, rapidly approaching the white-clad figure. I followed with David at my side, Sir Edward and Paul just behind us. I could see that the figure ahead of us was that of a woman, flowing white robes and long grey hair blowing back in the wind. Her face was elderly but also elegant. A sharp nose, and the eyes of a hawk. Beyond, I could make out several other female figures dressed in white.

In the distance were the substantial remains of an amphitheatre but around us were only a few remains of a ruined temple, surrounded by cypress trees. Unlike the temple at Delphi, which I recalled from student travels around Greece, there were here just worn stones with a circular base in the centre which may at some distant time have been the base of a pedestal or a large column.

Ahead of me, Jarn was now standing only a few feet from the woman clad in white and was speaking to her in a language I recognised elements of. It was Greek, but ancient rather than modern, and my background in the Classical languages had not prepared me for Greek as it appeared it was actually spoken at the time. The woman replied to Jarn, and even at a distance and without fully understanding the language, her frosty tones were clear. David, by my side, murmured translations in my ear.

'Melite is berating Father for not taking proper care of Mother. Now, he is asking her, no, he is pleading with her to take Mother, to heal her.' David choked, emotion overwhelming him and I gripped his arm, trying to give comfort.

For moments there was an apparent stand-off. Then Melite shrugged, spoke and gestured towards the white clad young women who had approached.

'She has agreed.' With an exhalation releasing tension, the relief in David's voice was evident. 'She is instructing her maids to take Mother.'

Jarn's voice rang out clearly in English. 'Over my dead body will you take her. I will carry her, I will not leave her.' In a somewhat quieter voice he repeated the sentence, this time in old Greek.

The pair were almost nose to hawk-like nose at this point, clearly a titanic battle of wills was in progress. Finally, Melite shrugged again and gestured him impatiently towards the attendants. Then she turned to our party and I was aware that for a few seconds Melite's eyes focused acutely on me. I had the sensation of being stripped of all coverings, with scalpels applied to my innermost being. David pulled me closer to him, but I was unable to look away from the woman. What had she seen? I was certain there had been a flash of something in her eyes.

Before the sensation became too painful, the gatekeeper's eyes moved away from me. I gasped and tried to refocus, looking around at my surroundings while I recovered, David's arm pressing me to his side.

With disbelief I saw that the stony surface around us was altering. A fully intact stone floor was now spreading over the rocky ground. From the new floor, pillars grew upward, until a full temple lay before us, in shining pristine white marble. The marble glowed crisply in the afternoon sun, the shadows of cypresses crossing stones flags that were now smooth and polished. The last item to appear was the central stone base. It grew into a large, low pedestal surmounted with a huge bronze cauldron, within which burned brilliant white fire. Even at this distance, I could detect the scents of pine and juniper from the flames and could see white hot embers.

I looked at Sir Edward and Paul, standing next to us, wondering how much of this they could see. Perhaps it was only visible to *gerasi*? But from their astonished faces I realised they could see what we were seeing, the temple as visible to them as it was to us. Martinez was approaching behind them, also looking amazed.

David urged me closer to the centre, where Jarn was moving towards the pedestal and the cauldron atop it. Jarn looked from his wife's face, concealed in the blankets in his arms, and then back to David, a long piercing look. Then at a nod from Melite, and to my utter horror, Jarn lowered Issa in her furs and blankets to lie in the fiery cauldron.

The wrappings immediately caught light. They burned with a yellow fire which surged up from the cauldron, rapidly turning to charred fragments and then falling to ash, some blowing from the cauldron and drifting through the marble columns. I looked to David and gripped his arms, a silent desperate plea for him to do something to save his mother. Why was Jarn committing Issa to the flames? It went through my mind that she must already be dead and this was a horrific and public cremation. David pulled me to his side and made no attempt to intervene. His eyes were fixed on the scene before them. Slowly, I also turned back to the temple and the fire.

Issa's body lay within the cauldron, white flames surrounding her. Neither her skin nor her hair appeared affected by the fire, despite the apparently white-hot heat. Jarn stood next to her, just outside the flames and the gate-keeper stood nearby, watching. I was conscious Sir Edward and Paul had moved to our side.

Slowly, Melite turned to us and raised her arm. With a graceful gesture, she moved her hand from left to right. As she did so, I saw the scene as if a curtain was being swept across. As the edge of the invisible curtain moved, the scene changed from the complete temple back to the ruins we had first seen. I looked at David in perplexity, starting to doubt my sanity.

'The gatekeeper has drawn the veil. I am surprised she kept it open for so long.'

David's eyes continued to study the scene, now empty of life and figures. The cauldron had vanished, only the few remaining dusty stones of the pedestal still visible. There was no sign of fire. There was no Jarn, no Issa, no gatekeeper and no white-robed attendants.

Sir Edward drew closer to David.

'The files in our archives record some extraordinary things in connection with your parents, but this.... well...'. He seemed uncharacteristically lost for words, and I felt sympathy.

He swallowed and turned to David. 'Dr Dechar, what do you think? Should we stay for a while, or shall I direct the plane back to the UK?'

David replied with composure. 'I would suggest we remain for a while, Sir Edward. Perhaps we can reassess the situation when night falls.'

'Well, in that case, refreshments are in order!' Martinez said perkily as he headed back to the plane. It was clear that the air force recruitment process regarded unflappability in the most bizarre circumstances to be a most desirable attribute.

CHAPTER 31
CLARE, DODONA, 11TH JULY 2022

A few hours later, our small party had consumed snacks and drinks, and most of us had taken a wary turn around the ruined temple.

Over sandwiches, the pilot and her co-pilot, who introduced themselves as Jess Michael and Josh Lee, told us about their air force training and the fabulous aircraft which was now glowing in the evening light behind us. The posting of a lifetime was how they described it. From the aircraft windows, as they had completed their post-flight checks and logs, they had seen something of the sight we had seen, and their curiosity was evident. But I knew that neither they nor Martinez would breathe a word beyond formal debriefs. Absolute silence in perpetuity went with postings, at this level.

The sun was nearing the horizon, the shadows cast by the cypress trees now stretching long over the site. Martinez collected the remains of our meals together as Jess and Josh returned to their aircraft to start their preparations for the return flight. Sir Edward rose from the stone he had been seated on and approached us.

I suspected this was going to be the request to return to the aircraft. Should David and I leave, or should we stay here, I wondered. I was reluctant to return to Termonn without Jarn and Issa, and with no knowledge of what had become of them. And then having to tell Henry, Sylvie and Fizz that we had no idea where or how they were.

A gleam to my left refocussed my attention on the ruins.

These were now ruins no longer but were, before my eyes, reappearing as the perfect temple complex once again. I felt David stand next to me, as Sir Edward and Paul moved closer. Stone flooring spread, pillars rose, the pedestal and cauldron reappeared, but now without fire.

Jarn appeared from the depths of the temple, on the other side of the pedestal. His arm was around Issa, walking steadily next to him. Behind them were a young girl, perhaps seven or eight, and an elderly couple, who were holding the child's hands. Melite and several maids accompanied them, a little to the side and all still clad in white robes.

I studied Jarn's and Issa's appearances carefully. They looked essentially the same, but there were subtle differences. Both had hair a little longer than they had had just a few hours ago. Issa's was raised with a comb at the back of her head, long curling tendrils of golden blonde hair falling over her shoulders. Jarn's dark hair was partly secured in a small knot at the back of his neck. They were wearing clothing that was contemporary but not the clothes they had worn on the journey here. Of course, I reflected, Issa's clothes had burned off her in the fiery cauldron.

But they both looked healthy, bronzed and relaxed. I contrasted the lovely woman walking towards us with the pale lady of the manor I had first met a few short days ago.

Now there was a contentment about Issa that radiated from her.

Melite approached Jarn, who noticeably stiffened. Her words to him were inaudible but his reply was not. Fortunately, they were now speaking in English.

'The void has returned to normal and I am no longer entrapped, but there remains a battle to be fought. Winning it is more important than maintaining your complement of servants.'

'Gratitude for the life of your wife remains too much to expect, it would seem.' Melite's sniff was audible. 'You have not changed.'

'We should work together. The task needs all of us. Afterwards, we can discuss your ... staffing requirements.'

Jarn looked towards his wife and then inclined his head towards Melite. 'But if you think I am not grateful, you are wrong.' Their eyes met for long wordless moments.

Melite's gaze turned first to the young girl, standing patiently just behind Issa. Then a glance at me. Finally, her hawk-like eyes settled on David.

'And what are your intentions, son of Jarn, towards *this* young woman?' She gestured towards me.

At my side, I felt David bristling. 'My intentions are for me to know and you to guess, Melite. But Clare's wishes are in any case paramount.'

'So, history repeats. As the father, so the son. Of course, you are fully aware of her potential and are determined to withhold it from me.' Melite was clearly angered, and I found myself moving a little closer to David. 'Am I never to receive the assistance this world needs?'

After a prolonged moment of three-cornered glaring between Melite, Jarn and David, the gatekeeper stepped back with resignation. The girl moved to Issa, who smiled and placed a comforting arm around her. Melite watched the gesture but did not comment, as she turned back to Jarn.

'Jarn, you will remember our discussions. We need to act together to vanquish the threat at its true source. We must not hold back through misguided sentiment.'

Jarn looked down for a moment and then back to the gatekeeper. Moments passed. Then he responded with a nod of acknowledgement, that seemed to me to be reluctant.

Melite and all her maids retreated into the rear of the temple. Before our gaze the temple shimmered, shifted and returned to ruins.

Jarn moved to David and pulled him into his arms.

'It is good to hold you again, my son. I am sorry I had no time to spare for you when I first returned.'

'You had other things on your mind, Father.' The two drew apart but suddenly reclasped hands and arms as emotion overtook them. David briefly rested his head on his father's shoulder, and I could see his eyes were moist.

Issa approached, smiling broadly, and mother and son hugged.

'You're looking very well, Mother. You had us worried there for a while.' Issa glowed as she touched her son's face affectionately.

'But,' David said reflectively, looking closely at his mother, 'it has clearly been a little longer for you than it has been for us.' Issa nodded acknowledgement, with a smiling glance at Jarn.

Sir Edward walked to Issa and shook her hand warmly. 'I cannot say how delighted I am to see you restored to health, Lady Issa.'

Jarn, his arm again around his wife, looked down from his impressive height and took stock of my superior.

'I think, Sir Edward, we met in Whitehall in 1977. I

remember you, now, from the weapons briefing I was given at the Ministry of Defence. I apologise for not recollecting you earlier. My thoughts were elsewhere.'

Sir Edward gave his usual gentle smile.

'It is not surprising, Lord Dechar, that you failed to recognise me. I was very much younger then. In my first service position, in fact. And I have aged rather more than you have. Is it your wish to return home now?'

'Now,' said Jarn, 'we need to return home to make plans. This battle is won, but I regret to say the war lies ahead. Sir Edward, I wonder if I can prevail on you to transport three new friends?'

EPILOGUE

It was late evening, and night was falling over Termonn when Issa came in search of her husband. She spotted him seated in a reclining chair on the terrace and studied him for a few moments. It was unusual for him to be stationary for so long and she had certainly never before seen him lying back in a deckchair. Also, he was looking thoughtful, which was always something she regarded with wariness. She noticed he had what appeared to be a small booklet in one hand.

She approached and laid a hand on his shoulder. Jarn looked up directly into his wife's brilliant blue eyes and said, apologetically, 'I need to travel again.'

'Jarn, we have discussed this. No more travel until you are recovered. And you are not. You are still not at full strength.'

'This is different, my love. I owe my return to someone, and I have to repay the debt.'

'Then I will come with you. We are not going to be parted again, I will not permit it.'

His wife's face was adamant. Over the centuries, Jarn

had learnt, sometimes painfully, that it was best not to argue when she looked like that.

'So,' Issa had seen his acquiescence and stroked her husband's face gently, 'where are we going?'

'To visit a lady named Kate. She is in Australia, in the world I arrived from, one so close to ours it is practically identical. In fact, I now suspect it only differs from ours in ways that relate to Termonn somehow. She lost her husband in a freak accident. Somehow, I need to help her. I sense the window is closing, something is changing. It has to be now.'

'Melite would not be pleased if we meddle with events in another world, Jarn. It is one of her prohibitions.'

'No, I simply want us to go to Australia in this world and see how things are. Together the trip should be no problem for us. It may be that a solution will become obvious if the lines are merging.'

'Or not,' thought Issa. But this urge of Jarn's to sort things out, to have the universe running as he thought it should, was so familiar it was heart-warming, and her agreement was automatic. He had never been able to leave a debt unpaid, especially if it involved a creature in distress.

'Now?'

'Well, no time like the present,' her husband grinned.

They gripped arms and the space around them blurred and shifted as they stepped.

So, Issa thought, this was similar to where Jarn had visited on his way back to her, but it was in their own world rather than the adjacent one. She put an arm to her forehead, which was already lightly speckled with sweat. Too hot, far too hot, for an English rose. Despite this being the

Australian winter, the temperature in this particular area was punishingly hot. The land shimmered around them, endless sun-burnt savannah, sheep looking overheated in their woolly coats. They were close to a red-roofed ranch house, and its outbuildings.

Jarn moved purposefully towards the house, linking Issa's arm in his. A face all too familiar to him came out of the barn to the left.

'G'day to you but how the hell did you get here?'

Goodness, thought Jarn, some worlds were so tediously similar as to be unbelievable. Their own world's version of Mark Driffold was looking at him in surprise, doubtless astonished by Jarn's similarity in appearance to Gerald Borman.

'Good morning, sir.' It was late morning here, the relentless sun almost overhead.

'We were driving with friends and wanted to stretch our legs, so my wife and me got out and walked. I guess we will see them in the next town soon. In the meantime, I don't suppose you have a glass of water handy? My wife is rather thirsty.'

'Well, a bit foolhardy, if you don't mind me saying. Just wilderness round here. All it takes is to get off the track and...'

Driffold gave Issa a quick look, she was indeed looking a little heated, and the Australian gentleman within him came to the fore. 'Well, come on in, then.'

The man beckoned towards the barn, which overlooked the main house. Jarn noticed that the house looked tired and clearly hadn't been cared for much in the last year or so.

They were conducted through the door, and the chiller cabinet was opened.

'Here you go, two glasses. And one of my guys can give

you a lift, if you can ask your friends where they are. I'm Mark Driffold by the way. Station manager.'

'Thank you.' Jarn and Issa smiled gratefully at the man and drank the cool water, as Jarn wondered how to prolong their visit a little. Perhaps the same approach as last time?

'Do you want any help here for a few days, Mr Driffold? We can catch up with our friends later on. I'm quite handy and my wife is an excellent cook – cooked in every country in Europe, haven't you, sweetheart?'

Jarn didn't dare meet his wife's gaze at the use in public of an endearment she had never liked. He hoped she would see the point and go along; he could - he doubtless would - pay the price later.

She did, of course. 'Oh yes, from mountain chalets to Parisian hotels. Would you like some help here, Mr Driffold?'

'Well....', Driffold answered, somewhat reluctantly, 'I don't know... things have been a bit unsettled here since....' The man tailed off and looked towards the house.

'Since what?' Issa asked gently.

'Well, since the Missus's accident. He's lost his grip, and I'm doing my best but...'

'What accident was that, Mr Driffold? I'm afraid we don't know the area.' Issa gazed at Driffold with sympathy, but was already half-guessing the answer.

'Oh, it was the flooded stream. Mr Borman was in bed with flu. The stream flooded in the worst wet we'd had here for decades, and the lambs were caught in it. Mrs Borman took the Land Rover out to try to save some, and it was just one of those things. The vehicle turned over on the edge of the creek and by the time we could get there... well, it was too late, she was gone. The flying ambulance did their best, but...'

'How terrible,' Issa said, and meant it. Beside her, Jarn felt real grief. He turned his face to the window so Mark Driffold wouldn't notice the emotion.

'Yes, it was. She was a great person. And Mr Borman hasn't been the same man since. He just can't seem to get over it. We're all trying to go on but he's in pieces.'

Jarn and Issa gazed at the man, both separately wondering how they could sort out this mess, although only Jarn had both sides of the story.

Suddenly there came a rumbling from the universe, which only Jarn and Issa were aware of. Their very presence here, in this time and location, seemed to have triggered something. Both the splitting and the merging of worlds had happened to them before, sometimes good and sometimes not so good. They looked at each other and moved to grip each other's arms. As Issa had said a few minutes ago, another separation would not happen. Wherever they went, they were going to go together.

This time, worlds were not splitting but moving together, very similar realities coalescing.

They watched as the world in front of them blurred into a grey haze and then shimmered in a brief white brilliance. A few golden gleams persisted in shifting around the house and the yard as the station manager slowly settled back into a solid form.

'Gosh, that felt odd,' Mark Driffold said, sinking into a chair and putting a hand to his forehead. 'Suddenly had the strangest feeling. As if....'

He looked a bit sheepish, not being a man given to flights of fancy. '...it was like coming out of a dream when there'd been an awful accident. The mister or the missis – don't even know which, now. A daytime nightmare.'

He stood, wobbling a little, and moved to the chiller.

Taking out a can of beer, he ripped open the pull and took a huge swig. 'Thank God it was only a dream. Must be the heat today.'

'It is very hot today, Mr Driffold,' Issa nodded at him reassuringly.

A few more swigs and he braced his shoulders and moved to the door.

'Sorry, folks, I'm not normally... well, must be getting on, you two stay here and finish your drinks, and I'll get Doug to take you to wherever your friends are when they contact you.'

He left, as Jarn and Issa gazed at each other. 'Again,' said Issa with a grin. 'That was timely.'

'Yes, it was,' Jarn agreed. 'Now I just need to check on my old boss and her husband, to make sure they're both alive rather than both dead, which I guess is the other option. That would be the worst of both worlds rather than the best,' he said, knowing that in coalescing worlds there were at least two options. He just hoped the universe had made the right choice on this occasion.

Jarn made off towards the house, pulling the booklet Issa had noticed from the pocket of his jeans as he moved through the door he had painted in another world. He noticed it still needed painting in this one, the universe hadn't fixed that. He found his way to the drawing room.

Gerald - and Jarn noticed with surprise just how alike the station owner was to himself in appearance - was sitting in a chair with a bemused expression on his face, and Kate was standing next to him holding her head in her hands. They both looked as if they had woken from hibernation. A hibernation that had included nightmares.

Jarn took the passport he had been holding and quietly put it on the table, with its inclusion of 1,000 Australian dollar notes. He was about to make a tactful and discrete exit when Kate looked directly at him.

'*Jarn*?', she said. 'This was you?'

He took a step towards her and smiled. 'I may have influenced it a little bit,' he said, truthfully.

'Thank you. So much.' Kate murmured. Then she went and put her arms round her husband, who still looked pole axed.

Returning to Issa in the barn, Jarn took her in his arms and hugged her.

'All fixed. They're experiencing a severe case of *déjà vu*, but everything will be back to normal in a few minutes. The only person who will think it is anything other than a bad dream is going to be Kate, and at least she has a partial explanation.' Knowing Kate and her curiosity, Jarn reflected that it wouldn't be surprising if she arrived at Termonn at some point in the future with a truly perplexed Gerald in tow.

'Did we cause it, Jarn, or was the coalescence going to happen anyway?'

'One, or the other? I love you, wife, now let's get home, away from all these damn Australian sheep.'

'Back to our own English ones, then.'

'Wonderful.' And Jarn realised he really meant it.

Belatedly, a thought occurred to him.

'We might call in at our old house in Dublin on the way back, just to make sure that another couple of friends of mine are still doing fine in our old house.' Jarn guessed that in this newly merged world George and Laura would be in the Irish Termonn House, but it was best to check.

A mischievous expression lit her face. 'Yes.... sweetheart,' she said.

They linked arms and stepped.

NOTES

This novel is entirely fiction. However, characters and events, including possible future events, are borrowed from history and from scientific publications. Facts and characters have been amended to fit into this fictitious world. The following notes may provide a little more background.

George Villiers, the 4th Earl of Clarendon

George Villiers was born in 1800 and died in 1870. He was the British Foreign Secretary under four prime ministers at various times from 1853. In 1820, at the age of 20, he was appointed attaché to the British embassy in Saint Petersburg. There he remained for three years, gaining practical knowledge of diplomacy which would be of great use to him later in life. He was appointed British ambassador to Spain in 1833, and was appointed Lord Lieutenant (Viceroy) of Ireland (1847–52) during the disastrous Irish famine.

George Villiers married Lady Katherine in 1839. A family man, devoted to his wife and to their six children, he had great charm of manner, and was described by Gladstone as the most attractive man in the cabinet.

Arthur Wellesley, 1st Duke of Wellington – the 'Iron Duke'

Born 1769 in Dublin, Ireland, he died September 1852. Commander of the British army during the Napoleonic Wars and later prime minister of Great Britain (1828–30). Shared in the victory over Napoleon at the Battle of Waterloo (1815) and was a leading figure in the Paris meetings between the great powers later in 1815, where he met Tsar Alexander I. Wellington represented Great Britain at the funeral of Tsar Alexander I in March 1826, at which event he may have met Jarn. He may subsequently have recorded his experience for the benefit of the UK government.

The Paris World Fair, 1855

The Palais de l'Industrie (Palace of Industry) was an exhibition hall located in Paris between the Seine River and the Champs-Élysées, which was erected for the Paris World Fair in 1855. It housed the technical and industrial exhibits. Steam-powered machines ran constantly and the noise was deafening. Cockerill's steam engine was among those displayed.

The designer and architect, Barrault, worried about the stability of the structure and added enormous lead abutments, also applying a stone covering to the outside. The result was an enormous but gloomy exhibition hall.

Nuclear weapon accident

The nuclear weapon mishap involving Jarn is based on an incident which occurred during a storm on August 8th 1967, when a Vulcan bomber was struck by lightning at an RAF base in Lincolnshire. The plane was damaged, but the weapon was not. An officer was reported to have said the lightning strike was "a bit like a firework which you have lit and it has not gone bang". The event involving Jarn has been shifted forwards a decade. See https://www.theguardian.com/politics/1999/nov/15/freedomofinformation.uk

The badge of the order of St Patrick

The Most Illustrious Order of St Patrick was established in 1783, the third senior order of chivalry in the United Kingdom. The badge is a shamrock with three leaves representing the kingdoms of England, Ireland and Scotland, over the cross of St Patrick. The Order was discontinued following the secession of the Irish Republic from the United Kingdom in 1922. Only the monarch retains the order, apart from Jarn.

Termonn House

Termonn is an Irish Gaelic word meaning 'sanctuary, boundary'.

Dodona

Dodona was the oldest Hellenic oracle centre, according to the fifth-century historian Herodotus. Aristotle considered the region to have been the most ancient part of Greece and where the Hellenes originated. It was also the location of the landing place of the ark in Greek mythology.

The partition of India

Refugees began pouring into Delhi in 1947, the city ill-equipped to deal with the influx. The 1941 census listed Delhi's population as being about one third Muslim. Prime Minister Jawaharlal Nehru estimated 1,000 casualties in the city during partition. The Muslim casualties in Delhi have now been estimated to be between 20,000 and 25,000.

Meaning of names

Dechar: This unusual surname stems from the Ottoman Turkish Değer, meaning "to be of worth, to have value".

Jarn: There are many meanings of this name across the world, but Jarn's derived from the Persian names of Yaran/Yarin/Yaren – love, friendship, understanding. It is pronounced with a 'Y' not a 'J'.

Issa: Of Arabic origin, meaning strong willed. But it is also a short version of Nerissa, Shakespeare's character, and it is from this derivation that Issa acquired her name.

Reth: From African-Swahili roots, meaning 'king'.

Fizzah: Of Indian/Muslim/Arabic origin, meaning silver.

Maya: An Australian aboriginal name, meaning water.

Miray: Of Turkish origin, meaning 'glowing like the moon'.

Sylvie: Of Greek origin, meaning healing.

Reagan and Bush

The assassination attempt on the life of President Reagan in Washington on March 30th, 1981, failed in this world, although the President was seriously wounded and came close to death. It succeeded in the world Jarn visited. On hearing of the attack, Vice President George H. W. Bush returned to Washington from Fort Worth, Texas, and took charge temporary charge, in our world. In Jarn's world he became President, but died months later in a helicopter crash, leaving the presidency to another, a man of astonishingly poor judgement and education, with an inability to take advice combined with a desire for personal glory. It may be hard to imagine such a man being elected President of the USA, but of course this occurred in a different world and not our own.

'Poppy flowers' by van Gogh

Poppy Flowers is a painting by Vincent van Gogh with an estimated value of £40 million. The painting, which is of a vase of yellow and red poppies, was stolen from the Mohamed Mahmoud Khalil Museum just outside Cairo on August 21, 2010. Egyptian officials erroneously believed they had recovered the painting only hours after its theft, when two suspects attempted to board a plane at Cairo International Airport. The same painting had been stolen from the same museum on June 4, 1977 and was recovered ten years later in Kuwait. The painting measures only 65 x 54 cm. It is believed that van Gogh painted it in 1887.

Distance from Oxfordshire to Greece by plane

The distance from Oxford to Dodona is around 2200 km. A Bell-Boeing CMV-22B Osprey can carry 6,000 pounds of personnel to roughly that distance. The aircraft commandeered by Sir Edward is an improved prototype version. It can do the trip in a little over 2 hours. See https://www.naval-technology.com/projects/cmv-22b-osprey-tiltrotor-aircraft/

Dogs

Large and powerful, the **Himalayan sheepdog** is a breed of livestock guardian dog from the Himalayas. Unusually for a livestock guardian the breed is also used to assist with herding. They are friendly and sociable with family but are much more standoffish when dealing with people and animals outside of the home. Highly active, they are always looking for something to do.

Known as the Tibbie, the **Tibetan Spaniel** has been described as part monkey and part cat. They are not actually a spaniel, but the breed does come from Tibet, where they were alarm dogs at Buddhist monasteries. Tibbies retain watchdog tendencies today and have an independent spirit. They are incredibly smart and headstrong, determined to have their own way.

Earthquakes in California

A U.S. Geological Survey simulation of a magnitude 7.8 earthquake in Southern California said 50 brittle concrete buildings housing 7,500 people could completely or partially collapse and that it was plausible that five high-rise steel buildings — of a type known to be seismically vulnerable — holding 5,000 people could completely collapse. https://pubs.usgs.gov/of/2008/1150/

Deep underground stations in London

The westbound Jubilee Line platform at Westminster is very deep, at more than 25m below sea level. However, both the eastbound and westbound Jubilee platforms at Waterloo are deeper, at 26m below sea level, making them the deepest tube platforms on the network.

In 2012, services on the Central Line were suspended due to a burst water main. People were led off a train, after a Thames Water pipe burst. The burst led to water in a ventilation shaft, which subsequently flooded a track.

A 2018 report published by the Greater London Authority found that 20 stations were susceptible to severe flooding with a likelihood of once every 100 years. According to the report, ruptured water mains cause flooding on the Tube network five times a year, and even holding the water at bay is a full-time task. Most of the stations situated on the flood plain have had flood doors installed.

Ahmad Shah Massoud

The man Jarn met in Afghanistan in a different world in 1996 was Ahmad Shah Massoud, a commander resisting the Taliban and their allies in northern Afghanistan. Born in 1953, the charismatic Massoud, known as the Lion of Panjshir after his native valley, became known during the 1980's as a brilliant guerrilla commander repelling Soviet forces. A gifted linguist, he was fluent in Persian, French,

Pashtu, Hindi, and Urdu and was conversant in English and Arabic. By the late 1990s, he was fighting the Taliban and their Al-Qaeda allies. He had a library of 3,000 books at his home in Panjshir. He loved classical Persian poetry, football and chess. A fierce fighter, yet a moderate and thoughtful man, he was assassinated in 2001.

Retrocausality

Issa speculates that in two adjacent worlds very near the void, events may precede their cause. Some solutions to Einstein's field equations involve closed time-like curves, in which the world line of an object returns to its origin, and it has been speculated by some that in extreme environments of space-time, such as a region near certain cosmic strings, such closed curves may form, with a theoretical possibility of retrocausality.

Earthquake in Istanbul in 2019

It is thought very likely that an earthquake of magnitude 7 or higher will occur in the region of Istanbul before 2030, due to the potential for a break in the North Anatolian fault line under the Marmara Sea just south of Istanbul. The fault line is the meeting point of the Anatolian and the Eurasian tectonic plates. A concern for many years, the fault line was reported in 2021 to be showing new anomalies in its central segment.

It has been suggested that the ancient buildings in Istanbul, including the Hagia Sophia and the Blue Mosque, would be likely to survive a major earthquake as they were soundly built many centuries ago by architects and engineers familiar with earthquakes. They have already withstood earthquakes over more than a millennia without irreparable damage. Unfortunately, few modern buildings were constructed with earthquake survivability in mind.

In our world a 5.8 magnitude earthquake shook the south-west of Istanbul at 13.59 local time on 26 September 2019. One person died due to a heart attack and there were tens of casualties.

In Miray's world, adjacent to this one, the earthquake on the same date but one year later, was much, much larger.

Henry VIII's wine cellar under the Ministry of Defence in Whitehall

The last remaining part of the Palace of Westminster from the time of Henry VIII, the cellar was preserved after the Second World War when the Ministry of Defence building was reconstructed. Shifted slightly and lowered from its original location in an impressive feat of engineering, the cellar is now far below street level.

See, for example, http://www.londonmylondon.co.uk/a-real-hidden-gem-henry-viiis-wine-cellar/

AUTHOR BIOGRAPHY

Stephanie Izzard lives on the edge of the Cotswolds with her family and two dogs. She has been writing in her head since she was a child but took time off for a career in science, a doctorate, a husband and a child (not quite in that order). Now she writes in a variety of genres, including contemporary fantasy, history and paranormal romance. She is inspired by the magic of her area, the honey stone villages and the tales their stones want to tell. Her books revisit world shaping events from the perspective of the magical Termonn family.

To find out more about Termonn, and the adventures of Jarn, Issa and their family, visit https://stephanieizzard.com/